MUTANTS

MUTANTS

Eleven Stories of Science Fiction

Edited by
Robert Silverberg

THOMAS NELSON INC., PUBLISHERS
Nashville, Tennessee / New York, New York

Acknowledgments

Tomorrow's Children, by Poul Anderson and F. N. Waldrop, copyright 1947 by Street & Smith Publications, Inc. (now Condé Nast Publications, Inc.) Reprinted by permission of the authors' agents, Scott Meredith Literary Agency, Inc.

It's a Good *Life*, by Jerome Bixby, copyright 1953 by Ballantine Books, Inc. Reprinted by permission of the author.

The Mute Question, by Forrest J Ackerman, copyright 1950 by Clark Publishing Company. Reprinted by permission of the author.

Let the Ants Try, by Frederik Pohl, copyright 1949 by Love Romances Publishing Co. Reprinted by permission of the author.

The Conqueror, by Mark Clifton, copyright 1952 by Street & Smith Publications, Inc. (now Condé Nast Publications, Inc.). Reprinted by permission of Forrest J Ackerman.

Liquid Life, by Ralph Milne Farley, copyright 1936 by Beacon Magazines, Inc. Reprinted by permission of Forrest J Ackerman.

Hothouse, by Brian W. Aldiss, copyright © 1960 by Mercury Press, Inc. Reprinted by permission of the author and his agents, A. P. Watt & Son.

Ozymandias, by Terry Carr, copyright © 1972 by Harlan Ellison. Reprinted by permission of the author.

The Man Who Never Forgot, by Robert Silverberg, copyright © 1957 by Fantasy House, Inc. Reprinted by permission of the author and his agents, Scott Meredith Literary Agency, Inc.

Ginny Wrapped in the Sun, by R. A. Lafferty, copyright © 1967 by Galaxy Publishing Corp. Reprinted by permission of the author and his agent, Virginia Kidd.

Watershed, by James Blish, copyright 1955 by Quinn Publishing Co., Inc. Reprinted by permission of the author and his agent, Robert P. Mills, Ltd.

Contents

Introduction

The Latin word *mutare* means "to change," and from it, late in the nineteenth century, the Dutch botanist-geneticist Hugo de Vries coined the terms "mutation" and "mutant." De Vries, experimenting with breeding evening primroses, had observed sudden striking changes in his flowers as he crossed and recrossed different strains. His research led him to the conclusion that all living things are subject to such changes or mutations, and that mutant forms frequently pass their altered traits on to later generations; thus the evolutionary process itself can be viewed as a succession of mutations.

De Vries's theories have long since been confirmed by modern genetic research. We know now that the physical appearance of living organisms is determined by bodies known as genes, within the nuclei of cells; the genes themselves are composed of complex molecules arranged in elaborate patterns, and any change in the pattern (or "code") of the genetic material that substitutes one molecule for another will produce a mutation. Mutations arise spontaneously in nature, induced by chemical processes in the nucleus or by temperature conditions or by cosmic rays striking a gene; they can also be produced artificially by subjecting the nucleus to X rays, ultraviolet light, or other hard radiation.

Mutations seldom are spectacular. Those mutants that are startlingly different from their parents tend not to survive long, either because the mutation renders them unable to function normally or because they are rejected by those who sired them. The mutants that succeed in passing their mutations along to their descendants are generally only slightly altered forms, and large evolutionary changes result from an accumulation of small mutations rather than from any one startling genetic leap.

Of course, writers of science fiction take certain liberties with prosaic scientific truth, or else there would be no science fiction. The mutant theme has long been one of science fiction's favorites—especially since the development of the atomic bomb turned a productive source of new mutations loose in everyday life. Though some of the mutants of science fiction differ from their parents only in one relatively inconspicuous (but startling) trait, others show immense and fantastic degrees of variation, and both sorts are represented in this book. Thus we have some stories in which the mutant *looks* normal but has extraordinary mental powers, and others populated by two-headed people, giant insects, plants with teeth, and other wonders. They all demonstrate science fiction's marvelous diversity. Science fiction is primarily a literature of change, a literature of infinite possibility—and, I think, the mutant theme shows those infinite possibilities to particularly good advantage.

ROBERT SILVERBERG

Tomorrow's Children

Poul Anderson and F. N. Waldrop

*The atomic bombs that brought World War II to a sudden and fright-
ful close had, as might be expected, a powerful impact on the imagina-
tions of science-fiction writers. For years after Hiroshima and
Nagasaki, the pages of science-fiction magazines were filled with
stories describing in grim detail the horrifying human mutations that
would come into the world after the atomic devastation of World
War III. There were so many of these stories that readers wearied of
them and editors stopped buying them; most of them are altogether
forgotten today.*

*But in all that glut of mutant-horror stories one stood out above
the others: taut, dramatic, vivid, human, it said everything that
needed to be said about the genetic damage an atomic war might
wreak. Its authors were a pair of unknown young men, barely old
enough to vote, making their debuts as professional authors. So far
as we know, no further stories have come from the pen of F. N.
Waldrop; but Poul Anderson has gone on to become one of the grand
masters of science fiction, and his long and productive career has
more than fulfilled the promise of this, his first story.*

On the world's loom
Weave the Norns doom,
Nor may they guide it nor change.
—WAGNER, SIEGFRIED

Ten miles up, it hardly showed. Earth was a cloudy green and brown
blur, the vast vault of the stratosphere reaching changelessly out to
spatial infinities, and beyond the pulsing engine there was silence and
serenity no man could ever touch. Looking down, Hugh Drummond
could see the Mississippi gleaming like a drawn sword, and its slow
curve matched the contours shown on his map. The hills, the sea, the
sun and wind and rain, they didn't change. Not in less than a million
slow-striding years, and human efforts flickered too briefly in the unending night for that.

Farther down, though, and especially where cities had been. . . .
The lone man in the solitary stratojet swore softly, bitterly, and his
knuckles whitened on the controls. He was a big man, his gaunt rangy
form sprawling awkwardly in the tiny pressure cabin, and he wasn't
quite forty. But his dark hair was streaked with gray, in the shabby
flying suit his shoulders stooped, and his long, homely face was
drawn into haggard lines. His eyes were black-rimmed and sunken
with weariness, dark and dreadful in their intensity. He'd seen too
much, survived too much, until he began to look like most other people of the world. *Heir of the ages,* he thought dully.

Mechanically, he went through the motions of following his course.
Natural landmarks were still there, and he had powerful binoculars
to help him. But he didn't use them much. They showed too many
broad shallow craters, their vitreous smoothness throwing back sunlight in the flat blank glitter of a snake's eye, the ground about them a
churned and blasted desolation. And there were the worse regions of
—deadness. Twisted dead trees, blowing sand, tumbled skeletons,
perhaps at night a baleful blue glow of fluorescence. The bombs had
been nightmares, riding in on wings of fire and horror to shake the
planet with the death blows of cities. But the radioactive dust was
worse than any nightmare.

He passed over villages, even small towns. Some of them were
deserted, the blowing colloidal dust, or plague, or economic break-
down making them untenable. Others still seemed to be living a feeble

half-life. Especially in the Midwest, there was a pathetic struggle to return to an agricultural system, but the insects and blights—

Drummond shrugged. After nearly two years of this, over the scarred and maimed planet, he should be used to it. The United States had been lucky. Europe, now—

Der Untergang des Abendlandes, he thought grayly. *Spengler fore-saw the collapse of a top-heavy civilization. He didn't foresee atomic bombs, radioactive-dust bombs, bacteria bombs, blight bombs—the bombs, the senseless inanimate bombs flying like monster insects over the shivering world. So he didn't guess the extent of the collapse.*

Deliberately he pushed the thoughts out of his conscious mind. He didn't want to dwell on them. He'd lived with them two years, and that was two eternities too long. And anyway, he was nearly home now.

The capital of the United States was below him, and he sent the stratojet slanting down in a long thunderous dive toward the mountains. Not much of a capital, the little town huddled in a valley of the Cascades, but the waters of the Potomac had filled the grave of Washington. Strictly speaking, there was no capital. The officers of the government were scattered over the country, keeping in precarious touch by plane and radio, but Taylor, Oregon, came as close to being the nerve center as any other place.

He gave the signal again on his transmitter, knowing with a faint spine-crawling sensation of the rocket batteries trained on him from the green of those mountains. When one plane could carry the end of a city, all planes were under suspicion. Not that anyone outside was supposed to know that that innocuous little town was important. But you never could tell. The war wasn't officially over. It might never be, with sheer personal survival overriding the urgency of treaties.

A light-beam transmitter gave him a cautious: "O.K. Can you land in the street?"

It was a narrow, dusty track between two wooden rows of houses, but Drummond was a good pilot and this was a good jet. "Yeah," he said. His voice had grown unused to speech.

He cut speed in a spiral descent until he was gliding with only the faintest whisper of wind across his ship. Touching wheels to the street, he slammed on the brake and bounced to a halt.

Silence struck at him like a physical blow. The engine stilled, the sun beating down from a brassy blue sky on the drabness of rude "temporary" houses, the total-seeming desertion beneath the impassive mountains—home! Hugh Drummond laughed, a short harsh bark with nothing of humor in it, and swung open the cockpit canopy.

There were actually quite a few people, he saw, peering from doorways and side streets. They looked fairly well fed and dressed, many in uniform; they seemed to have purpose and hope. But this, of course, was the capital of the United States of America, the world's most fortunate country.

"Get out—quick!"

The peremptory voice roused Drummond from the introspection into which those lonely months had driven him. He looked down at a gang of men in mechanics' outfits, led by a harassed-looking man in captain's uniform. "Oh—of course," he said slowly. "You want to hide the plane. And, naturally, a regular landing field would give you away."

"Hurry, get out, you infernal idiot! Anyone, *anyone* might come over and see—"

"They wouldn't go unnoticed by an efficient detection system, and you still have that," said Drummond, sliding his booted legs over the cockpit edge. "And anyway, there won't be any more raids. The war's over."

"Wish I could believe that, but who are you to say? Get a move on!"

The grease monkeys hustled the plane down the street. With an odd feeling of loneliness, Drummond watched it go. After all, it had been his home for—how long?

The machine was stopped before a false house whose whole front was swung aside. A concrete ramp led downward, and Drummond could see a cavernous immensity below. Light within it gleamed off silvery rows of aircraft.

"Pretty neat," he admitted. "Not that it matters any more. Probably it never did. Most of the hell came over on robot rockets. Oh, well." He fished his pipe from his jacket. Colonel's insignia glittered briefly as the garment flipped back.

"Oh . . . sorry, sir!" exclaimed the captain. "I didn't know—"

" 'S O.K. I've gotten out of the habit of wearing a regular uniform. A lot of places I've been, an American wouldn't be very popular."

Drummond stuffed tobacco into his briar, scowling. He hated to think how often he'd had to use the Colt at his hip, or even the machine guns in his plane, to save himself. He inhaled smoke gratefully. It seemed to drown out some of the bitter taste.

"General Robinson said to bring you to him when you arrived, sir," said the captain. "This way, please."

They went down the street, their boots scuffing up little acrid clouds of dust. Drummond looked sharply about him. He'd left very shortly after the two-month Ragnarok which had tapered off when the organization of both sides broke down too far to keep on making and sending the bombs, and maintaining order with famine and disease starting their ghastly ride over the homeland. At that time, the United States was a cityless, anarchic chaos, and he'd had only the briefest of radio exchanges since then, whenever he could get at a long-range set still in working order. They'd made remarkable progress meanwhile. How much, he didn't know, but the mere existence of something like a capital was sufficient proof.

Robinson— His lined face twisted into a frown. He didn't know the man. He'd been expecting to be received by the President, who had sent him and some others out. Unless the others had— No, he was the only one who had been in eastern Europe and western Asia. He was sure of that.

Two sentries guarded the entrance to what was obviously a converted general store. But there were no more stores. There was nothing to put in them. Drummond entered the cool dimness of an antechamber. The clatter of a typewriter, the Wac operating it . . . He gaped and blinked. That was—impossible! Typewriters, secretaries —hadn't they gone out with the whole world, two years ago? If the Dark Ages had returned to Earth, it didn't seem—*right*—that there should still be typewriters. It didn't fit, didn't—

He grew aware that the captain had opened the inner door for him. As he stepped in, he grew aware how tired he was. His arm weighed a ton as he saluted the man behind the desk.

"At ease, at ease." Robinson's voice was genial. Despite the five stars on his shoulders, he wore no tie or coat, and his round face was smiling. Still, he looked tough and competent underneath. To run things nowadays, he'd have to be.

"Sit down, Colonel Drummond." Robinson gestured to a chair near his and the aviator collapsed into it, shivering. His haunted eyes traversed the office. It was almost well-enough outfitted to be a prewar place.

Prewar! A word like a sword, cutting across history with a brutality of murder, hazing everything in the past until it was a vague golden glow through drifting, red-shot black clouds. And—only two years.

Only two years! Surely sanity was meaningless in a world of such nightmare inversions. Why, he could barely remember Barbara and the kids. Their faces were blotted out in a tide of other visages—starved faces, dead faces, human faces become beast-formed with want and pain and eating throttled hate. His grief was lost in the agony of a world, and in some ways he had become a machine himself.

"You look plenty tired," said Robinson.

"Yeah . . . yes, sir—"

"Skip the formality. I don't go for it. We'll be working pretty close together, can't take time to be diplomatic."

"Uh-huh. I came over the North Pole, you know. Haven't slept since . . . Rough time. But, if I may ask, you—" Drummond hesitated.

"I? I suppose I'm President. Ex officio, pro tem, or something. Here, you need a drink." Robinson got bottle and glasses from a drawer. The liquor gurgled out in a pungent stream. "Prewar Scotch. Till it gives out I'm laying off this modern hooch. *Gambai.*"

The fiery, smoky brew jolted Drummond to wakefulness. Its glow was pleasant in his empty stomach. He heard Robinson's voice with a surrealistic sharpness:

"Yes, I'm at the head now. My predecessors made the mistake of sticking together, and of traveling a good deal in trying to pull the country back into shape. So I think the sickness got the President, and I know it got several others. Of course, there was no means of holding an election. The armed forces had almost the only organization left, so we had to run things. Berger was in charge, but he shot himself when he learned he'd breathed radiodust. Then the command fell to me. I've been lucky."

"I see." It didn't make much difference. A few dozen more deaths weren't much, when over half the world was gone. "Do you expect to—continue lucky?" A brutally blunt question, maybe, but words weren't bombs.

"I do." Robinson was firm about that. "We've learned by experience, learned a lot. We've scattered the army, broken it into small outposts at key points throughout the country. For quite a while, we stopped travel altogether except for absolute emergencies, and then with elaborate precautions. That smothered the epidemics. The microorganisms were bred to work in crowded areas, you know. They were almost immune to known medical techniques, but without hosts and carriers they died. I guess natural bacteria ate up most of them. We still take care in traveling, but we're fairly safe now."

"Did any of the others come back? There were a lot like me, sent out to see what really had happened to the world."

"One did, from South America. Their situation is similar to ours, though they lacked our tight organization and have gone further toward anarchy. Nobody else returned but you."

It wasn't surprising. In fact, it was a cause for astonishment that anyone had come back. Drummond had volunteered after the bomb erasing St. Louis had taken his family, not expecting to survive and not caring much whether he did. Maybe that was why he had.

"You can take your time in writing a detailed report," said Robinson, "but in general, how are things over there?"

Drummond shrugged. "The war's over. Burned out. Europe has gone back to savagery. They were caught between America and Asia, and the bombs came both ways. Not many survivors, and they're starving animals. Russia, from what I saw, has managed something like you've done here, though they're worse off than we. Naturally, I couldn't find out much there. I didn't get to India or China, but in Russia I heard rumors— No, the world's gone too far into disintegration to carry on war."

"Then we can come out in the open," said Robinson softly. "We can really start rebuilding. I don't think there'll ever be another war, Drummond. I think the memory of this one will be carved too deeply on the race for us ever to forget."

"Can you shrug it off that easily?"

"No, no, of course not. Our culture hasn't lost its continuity, but it's had a terrific setback. We'll never wholly get over it. But—we're on our way up again."

The general rose, glancing at his watch. "Six o'clock. Come on, Drummond, let's get home."

"Home?"

"Yes, you'll stay with me. Man, you look like the original zombie. You'll need a month or more of sleeping between clean sheets, of home cooking and home atmosphere. My wife will be glad to have you; we see almost no new faces. And as long as we'll work together, I'd like to keep you handy. The shortage of competent men is terrific."

They went down the street, an aide following. Drummond was again conscious of the weariness aching in every bone and fiber of him. A home—after two years of ghost towns, of shattered chimneys above blood-dappled snow, of flimsy lean-tos housing starvation and death.

"Your plane will be mighty useful, too," said Robinson. "Those atomic-powered craft are scarcer than hens' teeth used to be." He chuckled hollowly, as at a rather grim joke. "Got you through close to two years of flying without needing fuel. Any other trouble?"

"Some, but there were enough spare parts." No need to tell of those frantic hours and days of slaving, of desperate improvisation with hunger and plague stalking him who stayed overlong. He'd had his troubles getting food, too, despite the plentiful supplies he'd started out with. He'd fought for scraps in the winter, beaten off howling maniacs who would have killed him for a bird he'd shot or a dead horse he'd scavenged. He hated that plundering, and would not have cared personally if they'd managed to destroy him. But he had a mission, and the mission was all he'd had left as a focal point for his life, so he'd clung to it with fanatic intensity.

And now the job was over, and he realized he couldn't rest. He didn't dare. Rest would give him time to remember. Maybe he could find surcease in the gigantic work of reconstruction. Maybe.

"Here we are," said Robinson.

Drummond blinked in new amazement. There was a car, camouflaged under brush, with a military chauffeur—*a car!* And in pretty fair shape, too.

"We've got a few oil wells going again, and a small patched-up refinery," explained the general. "It furnishes enough gas and oil for what traffic we have."

They got in the rear seat. The aide sat in front, a rifle ready. The car started down a mountain road.

"Where to?" asked Drummond a little dazedly.

Robinson smiled. "Personally," he said, "I'm almost the only lucky man on Earth. We had a summer cottage on Lake Taylor, a few miles from here. My wife was there when the war came, and stayed, and nobody came along till I brought the head offices here with me. Now I've got a home all to myself."

"Yeah. Yeah, you're lucky," said Drummond. He looked out the window, not seeing the sun-spattered woods. Presently he asked, his voice a little harsh: "How is the country really doing now?"

"For a while it was rough. Damn rough. When the cities went, our transportation, communication, and distribution systems broke down.

In fact, our whole economy disintegrated, though not all at once. Then there was the dust and the plagues. People fled, and there was open fighting when overcrowded safe places refused to take in any more refugees. Police went with the cities, and the army couldn't do much patrolling. We were busy fighting the enemy troops that'd flown over the Pole to invade. We still haven't gotten them all. Bands are roaming the country, hungry and desperate outlaws, and there are plenty of Americans who turned to banditry when everything else failed. That's why we have this guard, though so far none have come this way.

"The insect and blight weapons just about wiped out our crops, and that winter everybody starved. We checked the pests with modern methods, though it was touch and go for a while, and next year got some food. Of course, with no distribution as yet, we failed to save a lot of people. And farming is still a tough proposition. We won't really have the bugs licked for a long time. If we had a research center as well equipped as those which produced the things . . . But we're gaining. We're gaining."

"Distribution . . ." Drummond rubbed his chin. "How about railroads? Horse-drawn vehicles?"

"We have some railroads going, but the enemy was as careful to dust most of ours as we were to dust theirs. As for horses, they were nearly all eaten that first winter. I know personally of only a dozen. They're on my place; I'm trying to breed enough to be of use, but"— Robinson smiled wryly—"by the time we've raised that many, the factories should have been going quite a spell."

"And so now . . . ?"

"We're over the worst. Except for outlaws, we have the population fairly well controlled. The civilized people are fairly well fed, with some kind of housing. We have machine shops, small factories, and the like going, enough to keep our transportation and other mechanism 'level.' Presently we'll be able to expand these, begin actually increasing what we have. In another five years or so, I guess, we'll be integrated enough to drop martial law and hold a general election. A big job ahead, but a good one."

The car halted to let a cow lumber over the road, a calf trotting at her heels. She was gaunt and shaggy, and skittered nervously from the vehicle into the brush.

"Wild," explained Robinson. "Most of the real wildlife was killed off for food in the last two years, but a lot of farm animals escaped

when their owners died or fled, and have run free ever since. They—"
He noticed Drummond's fixed gaze. The pilot was looking at the calf.
Its legs were half the normal length.

"Mutant," said the general. "You find a lot such animals. Radiation
from bombed or dusted areas. There are even a lot of human abnormal births." He scowled, worry clouding his eyes. "In fact, that's
just about our worst problem. It—"

The car came out of the woods onto the shore of a small lake. It
was a peaceful scene, the quiet waters like molten gold in the slanting
sunlight, trees ringing the circumference and all about them the mountains. Under one huge pine stood a cottage, a woman on the porch.

It was like one summer with Barbara— Drummond cursed under
his breath and followed Robinson toward the little building. It wasn't,
it wasn't, it could never be. Not ever again. There were soldiers
guarding this place from chance marauders, and— There was an odd-
looking flower at his foot. A daisy, but huge and red and irregularly
formed.

A squirrel chittered from a tree. Drummond saw that its face was
so blunt as to be almost human.

Then he was on the porch, and Robinson was introducing him to
"my wife Elaine." She was a nice-looking young woman with eyes
that were sympathetic on Drummond's exhausted face. The aviator
tried not to notice that she was pregnant.

He was led inside, and reveled in a hot bath. Afterward there was
supper, but he was numb with sleep by then and hardly noticed it
when Robinson put him to bed.

Reaction set in, and for a week or so Drummond went about in a
haze, not much good to himself or anyone else. But it was surprising
what plenty of food and sleep could do, and one evening Robinson
came home to find him scribbling on sheets of paper.

"Arranging my notes and so on," he explained. "I'll write out the
complete report in a month, I guess."

"Good. But no hurry." Robinson settled tiredly into an armchair.
"The rest of the world will keep. I'd rather you'd just work at this off
and on, and join my staff for your main job."

"O.K. Only what'll I do?"

"Everything. Specialization is gone; too few surviving specialists
and equipment. I think your chief task will be to head the census
bureau."

"Eh?"

Robinson grinned lopsidedly. "You'll *be* the census bureau, except for what few assistants I can spare you." He leaned forward, said earnestly: "And it's one of the most important jobs there is. You'll do for this country what you did for central Eurasia, only in much greater detail. Drummond, we have to *know*."

He took a map from a desk drawer and spread it out. "Look, here's the United States. I've marked regions known to be uninhabitable in red." His fingers traced out the ugly splotches. "Too many of 'em, and doubtless there are others we haven't found yet. Now, the blue X's are army posts." They were sparsely scattered over the land, near the centers of population groupings. "Not enough of those. It's all we can do to control the more or less well-off, orderly people. Bandits, enemy troops, homeless refugees—they're still running wild, skulking in the backwoods and barrens, and raiding whenever they can. And they spread the plague. We won't really have it licked till everybody's settled down, and that'd be hard to enforce. Drummond, we don't even have enough soldiers to start a feudal system for protection. The plague spread like a prairie fire in those concentrations of men.

"We have to *know*. We have to know how many people survived —half the population, a third, a quarter, whatever it is. We have to know where they are, and how they're fixed for supplies, so we can start up an equitable distribution system. We have to find all the small-town shops and labs and libraries still standing, and rescue their priceless contents before looters or the weather beat us to it. We have to locate doctors and engineers and other professional men, and put them to work rebuilding. We have to find the outlaws and round them up. We—I could go on forever. Once we have all that information, we can set up a master plan for redistributing population, agriculture, industry, and the rest most efficiently, for getting the country back under civil authority and police, for opening regular transportation and communication channels—for getting the nation back on its feet."

"I see," nodded Drummond. "Hitherto, just surviving and hanging on to what was left has taken precedence. Now you're in a position to start expanding, *if* you know where and how much to expand."

"Exactly." Robinson rolled a cigarette, grimacing. "Not much tobacco left. What I have is perfectly foul. Lord, that war was crazy!"

"All wars are," said Drummond dispassionately, "but technology advanced to the point of giving us a knife to cut our throats with. Before that, we were just beating our heads against the wall. Robinson,

we can't go back to the old ways. We've *got* to start on a new track—
a track of sanity."

"Yes. And that brings up—" The other man looked toward the
kitchen door. They could hear the cheerful rattle of dishes there, and
smell mouth-watering cooking odors. He lowered his voice. "I might
as well tell you this now, but don't let Elaine know. She . . . she
shouldn't be worried. Drummond, did you see our horses?"

"The other day, yes. The colts—"

"Uh-huh. There've been five colts born of eleven mares in the last
year. Two of them were so deformed they died in a week, another in
a few months. One of the two left has cloven hooves and almost no
teeth. The last one looks normal—so far. One out of eleven, Drummond."

"Were those horses near a radioactive area?"

"They must have been. They were rounded up wherever found
and brought here. The stallion was caught near the site of Portland, I
know. But if he were the only one with mutated genes, it would hardly
show in the first generation, would it? I understand nearly all mutations are Mendelian recessives. Even if there were one dominant, it
would show in all the colts, but none of these looked alike."

"Hm-m-m—I don't know much about genetics, but I do know hard
radiation, or rather the secondary charged particles it produces, will
cause mutations. Only mutants are rare, and tend to fall into certain
patterns—"

"*Were* rare!" Suddenly Robinson was grim, something coldly frightened in his eyes. "Haven't you noticed the animals and plants?
They're fewer than formerly, and . . . well, I've not kept count, but
at least half those seen or killed have something wrong, internally or
externally."

Drummond drew heavily on his pipe. He needed something to
hang on to, in a new storm of insanity. Very quietly, he said:

"In my college biology course, they told me the vast majority of
mutations are unfavorable. More ways of not doing something than
of doing it. Radiation might sterilize an animal, or might produce
several degrees of genetic change. You could have a mutation
so violently lethal the possessor never gets born, or soon dies. You
could have all kinds of more or less handicapping factors, or just
random changes not making much difference one way or the other.
Or in a few rare cases you might get something actually favorable,
but you couldn't really say the possessor is a true member of the

species. And favorable mutations themselves usually involve a price in the partial or total loss of some other function."

"Right." Robinson nodded heavily. "One of your jobs on the census will be to try and locate any and all who know genetics, and send them here. But your real task, which only you and I and a couple of others must know about, the job overriding all other considerations, will be to find the human mutants."

Drummond's throat was dry. "There've been a lot of them?" he whispered.

"Yes. But we don't know how many or where. We only know about those people who live near an army post, or have some other fairly regular intercourse with us, and they're only a few thousand, all told. Among them, the birth rate has gone down to about half the prewar ratio. And over half the births they do have are abnormal."

"Over half—"

"Yeah. Of course, the violently different ones soon die, or are put in an institution we've set up in the Alleghenies. But what can we do with viable forms, if their parents still love them? A kid with deformed or missing or abortive organs, twisted internal structure, a tail, or something even worse . . . well, it'll have a tough time in life, but it can generally survive. And perpetuate itself—"

"And a normal-looking one might have some unnoticeable quirk, or a characteristic that won't show up for years. Or even a normal one might be carrying recessives, and pass them on—God!" The exclamation was half blasphemy, half prayer. "But how'd it happen? People weren't all near atom-hit areas."

"Maybe not, though a lot of survivors escaped from the outskirts. But there was that first year, with everybody on the move. One could pass near enough to a blasted region to be affected, without knowing it. And that damnable radiodust, blowing on the wind. It's got a long half-life. It'll be active for decades. Then, as in any collapsing culture, promiscuity was common. Still is. Oh, it'd spread itself, all right."

"I still don't see why it spread itself so much. Even here—"

"Well, I don't know why it shows up here. I suppose a lot of the local flora and fauna came in from elsewhere. This place is safe. The nearest dusted region is three hundred miles off, with mountains between. There must be many such islands of comparatively normal conditions. We have to find them too. But elsewhere—"

"Soup's on," announced Elaine, and went from the kitchen to the dining room with a loaded tray.

The men rose. Grayly, Drummond looked at Robinson and said tonelessly: "O.K. I'll get your information for you. We'll map mutation areas and safe areas, we'll check on our population and resources, we'll eventually get all the facts you want. But—what are you going to do then?"

"I wish I knew," said Robinson haggardly. "I wish I knew."

Winter lay heavily on the north, a vast gray sky seeming frozen solid over the rolling white plains. The last three winters had come early and stayed long. Dust, colloidal dust of the bombs, suspended in the atmosphere and cutting down the solar constant by a deadly percent or two. There had even been a few earthquakes, set off in geologically unstable parts of the world by bombs planted right. Half California had been ruined when a sabotage bomb started the San Andreas Fault on a major slip. And that kicked up still more dust.

Fimbulwinter, thought Drummond bleakly. *The doom of the prophecy. But no, we're surviving. Though maybe not as men—*

Most people had gone south, and there overcrowding had made starvation and disease and internecine struggle the normal aspects of life. Those who'd stuck it out up here, and had luck with their pest-ridden crops, were better off.

Drummond's jet slid above the cratered black ruin of the Twin Cities. There was still enough radioactivity to melt the snow, and the pit was like a skull's empty eye socket. The man sighed, but he was becoming calloused to the sight of death. There was so much of it. Only the struggling agony of life mattered any more.

He strained through the sinister twilight, swooping low over the unending fields. Burned-out hulks of farmhouses, bones of ghost towns, sere deadness of dusted land—but he'd heard travelers speak of a fairly powerful community up near the Canadian border, and it was up to him to find it.

A lot of things had been up to him in the last six months. He'd had to work out a means of search, and organize his few, overworked assistants into an efficient staff, and go out on the long hunt.

They hadn't covered the country. That was impossible. Their few planes had gone to areas chosen more or less at random, trying to get a cross-section of conditions. They'd penetrated wildernesses of hill and plain and forest, establishing contact with scattered, still demoralized out-dwellers. On the whole, it was more laborious than anything else. Most were pathetically glad to see any symbol of law and order and the paradisical-seeming "old days." Now and then there was danger and trouble, when they encountered wary or sullen or outright hostile groups suspicious of a government they associated with disaster, and once there had even been a pitched battle with roving outlaws. But the work had gone ahead, and now the preliminaries were about over.

Preliminaries— It was a bigger job to find out exactly how matters stood than the entire country was capable of undertaking right now. But Drummond had enough facts for reliable extrapolation. He and his staff had collected most of the essential data and begun correlating it. By questioning, by observation, by seeking and finding, by any means that came to hand, they'd filled their notebooks. And in the sketchy outlines of a Chinese drawing, and with the same stark realism, the truth was there.

Just this one more place, and I'll go home, thought Drummond for the—thousandth?—time. His brain was getting into a rut, treading the same terrible circle and finding no way out. *Robinson won't like what I tell him, but there it is.* And darkly, slowly: *Barbara, maybe it was best you and the kids went as you did. Quickly, cleanly, not even knowing it. This isn't much of a world. It'll never be our world again.*

He saw the place he sought, a huddle of buildings near the frozen shores of the Lake of the Woods, and his jet murmured toward the white ground. The stories he'd heard of this town weren't overly encouraging, but he supposed he'd get out all right. The others had his data anyway, so it didn't matter.

By the time he'd landed in the clearing just outside the village, using the jet's skis, most of the inhabitants were there waiting. In the gathering dusk they were a ragged and wild-looking bunch, clumsily dressed in whatever scraps of cloth and leather they had. The bearded, hard-eyed men were armed with clubs and knives and a few guns. As Drummond got out, he was careful to keep his hands away from his own automatics.

"Hello," he said. "I'm friendly."

"Y' better be," growled the big leader. "Who are you, where from, an' why?"

"First," lied Drummond smoothly, "I want to tell you I have another man with a plane who knows where I am. If I'm not back in a certain time, he'll come with bombs. But we don't intend any harm or interference. This is just a sort of social call. I'm Hugh Drummond of the United States Army."

They digested that slowly. Clearly, they weren't friendly to the government, but they stood in too much awe of aircraft and armament to be openly hostile. The leader spat. "How long you staying?"

"Just overnight, if you'll put me up. I'll pay for it." He held up a small pouch. "Tobacco."

Their eyes gleamed, and the leader said, "You'll stay with me. Come on."

Drummond gave him the bribe and went with the group. He didn't like to spend such priceless luxuries this freely, but the job was more important. And the boss seemed thawed a little by the fragrant brown flakes. He was sniffing them greedily.

"Been smoking bark an' grass," he confided. "Terrible."

"Worse than that," agreed Drummond. He turned up his jacket collar and shivered. The wind starting to blow was bitterly cold.

"Just what y' here for?" demanded someone else.

"Well, just to see how things stand. We've got the government started again, and are patching things up. But we have to know where folks are, what they need, and so on."

"Don't want nothing t' do with the gov'ment," muttered a woman. "They brung all this on us."

"Oh, come now. We didn't ask to be attacked." Mentally, Drummond crossed his fingers. He neither knew nor cared who was to blame. Both sides, letting mutual fear and friction mount to hysteria— In fact, he wasn't sure the United States hadn't sent out the first rockets, on orders of some panicky or aggressive officials. Nobody was alive who admitted knowing.

"It's the jedgment o' God, for the sins of our leaders," persisted the woman. "The plague, the fire-death, all that, ain't it foretold in the Bible? Ain't we living in the last days of the world?"

"Maybe." Drummond was glad to stop before a long, low cabin. Religious argument was touchy at best, and with a lot of people nowadays it was dynamite.

They entered the rudely furnished but fairly comfortable structure. A good many crowded in with them. For all their suspicion, they were curious, and an outsider in an aircraft was a blue-moon event these days.

Drummond's eyes flickered unobtrusively about the room, noticing details. Three women—that meant a return to concubinage. Only to be expected in a day of few men and strong-arm rule. Ornaments and utensils, tools and weapons of good quality—yes, that confirmed the stories. This wasn't exactly a bandit town, but it had waylaid travelers and raided other places when times were hard, and built up a sort of dominance of the surrounding country. That, too, was common.

There was a dog on the floor nursing a litter. Only three pups, and one of those was bald, one lacked ears, and one had more toes than it should. Among the wide-eyed children present, there were several two years old or less, and with almost no obvious exceptions, they were also different.

Drummond sighed heavily and sat down. In a way, this clinched it. He'd known for a long time, and finding mutation here, as far as any place from atomic destruction, was about the last evidence he needed.

He had to get on friendly terms, or he wouldn't find out much about things like population, food production, and whatever else there was to know. Forcing a smile to stiff lips, he took a flask from his jacket. "Prewar rye," he said. "Who wants a nip?"

"Do we!" The answer barked out in a dozen voices and words. The flask circulated, men pawing and cursing and grabbing to get at it. *Their homebrew must be pretty bad,* thought Drummond wryly.

The chief shouted an order, and one of his women got busy at the primitive stove. "Rustle you a mess o' chow," he said heartily. "An' my name's Sam Buckman."

"Pleased to meet you, Sam." Drummond squeezed the hairy paw hard. He had to show he wasn't a weakling, a conniving city slicker.

"What's it like, outside?" asked someone presently. "We ain't heard for so long . . ."

"You haven't missed much," said Drummond between bites. The food was pretty good. Briefly, he sketched conditions. "You're better off than most," he finished.

"Yeah. Mebbe so." Sam Buckman scratched his tangled beard. "What I'd give f'r a razor blade—! It ain't easy, though. The first year we weren't no better off 'n anyone else. Me, I'm a farmer, I kept some ears o' corn an' a little wheat an' barley in my pockets all that winter, even though I was starving. A bunch o' hungry refugees plundered my place, but I got away an' drifted up here. Next year I took an empty farm here an' started over."

Drummond doubted that it had been abandoned, but said nothing. Sheer survival outweighed a lot of considerations.

"Others came an' settled here," said the leader reminiscently. "We farm together. We have to; one man couldn't live by hisself, not with the bugs an' blight, an' the crops sproutin' into all new kinds, an' the outlaws aroun'. Not many up here, though we did beat off some enemy troops last winter." He glowed with pride at that, but Drummond wasn't particularly impressed. A handful of freezing starveling conscripts, lost and bewildered in a foreign enemy's land, with no hope of ever getting home, weren't formidable.

"Things getting better, though," said Buckman. "We're heading up." He scowled blackly, and a palpable chill crept into the room. "If 'twern't for the births—"

"Yes—the births. The new babies. Even the stock an' plants." It was an old man speaking, his eyes glazed with near madness. "It's the mark o' the beast. Satan is loose in the world—"

"Shut up!" Huge and bristling with wrath, Buckman launched himself out of his seat and grabbed the oldster by his scrawny throat. "Shut up 'r I'll bash y'r lying head in. Ain't no son o' mine being marked by the devil."

"Or mine—" "Or mine—" The rumble of voices ran about the cabin, sullen and afraid.

"It's God's jedgment, I tell you!" The woman was shrilling again. "The end o' the world is near. Prepare f'r the Second Coming—"

"An' you shut up too, Mag Schmidt," snarled Buckman. He stood bent over, gnarled arms swinging loose, hands flexing, little eyes darting red and wild about the room. "Shut y'r trap an' keep it shut. I'm still boss here, an' if you don't like it you can get out. I still don't think that funny-looking brat o' y'rs fell in the lake by accident."

The woman shrank back, lips tight. The room filled with a crackling silence. One of the babies began to cry. It had two heads.

Slowly and heavily, Buckman turned to Drummond, who sat immobile against the wall. "You see?" he asked dully. "You see how it is? Maybe it is the curse o' God. Maybe the world is ending. I dunno. I just know there's few enough babies, an' most o' them *de*formed. Will it go on? Will all our kids be monsters? Should we . . . kill these an' hope we get some human babies? What is it? What to do?"

Drummond rose. He felt a weight as of centuries on his shoulders, the weariness, blank and absolute, of having seen that smoldering panic and heard that desperate appeal too often, too often.

"Don't kill them," he said. "That's the worst kind of murder, and anyway it'd do no good at all. It comes from the bombs, and you can't stop it. You'll go right on having such children, so you might as well get used to it."

By atomic-powered stratojet it wasn't far from Minnesota to Oregon, and Drummond landed in Taylor about noon the next day. This time there was no hurry to get his machine under cover, and up on the mountain was a raw scar of earth where a new airfield was slowly being built. Men were getting over their terror of the sky. They had another fear to face now, and it was one from which there was no hiding.

Drummond walked slowly down the icy main street to the central office. It was numbingly cold, a still, relentless intensity of frost eating through clothes and flesh and bone. It wasn't much better inside. Heating systems were still poor improvisations.

"You're back!" Robinson met him in the antechamber, suddenly galvanized with eagerness. He had grown thin and nervous, looking ten years older, but impatience blazed from him. "How is it? How is it?"

Drummond held up a bulky notebook. "All here," he said grimly. "All the facts we'll need. Not formally correlated yet, but the picture is simple enough."

Robinson laid an arm on his shoulder and steered him into the office. He felt the general's hand shaking, but he'd sat down and had a drink before business came up again.

"You've done a good job," said the leader warmly. "When the country's organized again, I'll see you get a medal for this. Your men in the other planes aren't in yet."

"No, they'll be gathering data for a long time. The job won't be finished for years. I've only got a general outline here, but it's enough. It's enough." Drummond's eyes were haunted again.

Robinson felt cold at meeting that too-steady gaze. He whispered shakily: "Is it—bad?"

"The worst. Physically, the country's recovering. But biologically we've reached a crossroads and taken the wrong fork."

"What do you mean? *What do you mean?*"

Drummond let him have it then, straight and hard as a bayonet thrust. "The birth rate's a little over half the prewar," he said, "and about seventy-five per cent of all births are mutant, of which possibly two-thirds are viable and presumably fertile. Of course, that doesn't include late-maturing characteristics, or those undetectable by naked-eye observation, or the mutated recessive genes that must be carried by a lot of otherwise normal zygotes. And it's everywhere. There are no safe places."

"I see," said Robinson after a long time. He nodded, like a man struck a stunning blow and not yet fully aware of it. "I see. The reason—"

"Is obvious."

"Yes. People going through radioactive areas—"

"Why, no. That would only account for a few. But—"

"No matter. The fact's there, and that's enough. We have to decide what to do about it."

"And soon." Drummond's jaw set. "It's wrecking our culture. We at least preserved our historical continuity, but even that's going now. People are going crazy as birth after birth is monstrous. Fear of the unknown, striking at minds still stunned by the war and its immediate aftermath. Frustration of parenthood, perhaps the most basic instinct there is. It's leading to infanticide, desertion, despair, a cancer at the root of society. We've got to act."

"How? How?" Robinson stared numbly at his hands.

"I don't know. You're the leader. Maybe an educational campaign, though that hardly seems practicable. Maybe an acceleration of your program for reintegrating the country. Maybe—I don't know."

Drummond stuffed tobacco into his pipe. He was near the end of what he had, but would rather take a few good smokes than a lot of niggling puffs. "Of course," he said thoughtfully, "it's probably not the end of things. We won't know for a generation or more, but I rather imagine the mutants can grow into society. They'd better, for they'll outnumber the humans. The thing is, if we just let matters drift there's no telling where they'll go. The situation is unprecedented. We may end up in a culture of specialized variations, which would be very bad from an evolutionary standpoint. There may be fighting between mutant types, or with humans. Interbreeding may produce worse freaks, particularly when accumulated recessives start showing up. Robinson, if we want any say at all in what's going to happen in the next few centuries, we have to act quickly. Otherwise it'll snowball out of all control."

"Yes. Yes, we'll have to act fast. And hard." Robinson straightened in his chair. Decision firmed his countenance, but his eyes were staring. "We're mobilized," he said. "We have the men and the weapons and the organization. They won't be able to resist."

The ashy cold of Drummond's emotions stirred, but it was with a horrible wrenching of fear. "What are you getting at?" he snapped.

"Racial death. All mutants and their parents to be sterilized whenever and wherever detected."

"You're crazy!" Drummond sprang from his chair, grabbed Robinson's shoulders across the desk, and shook him. "You . . . why, it's impossible! You'll bring revolt, civil war, final collapse!"

"Not if we go about it right." There were little beads of sweat studding the general's forehead. "I don't like it any better than you, but it's got to be done or the human race is finished. Normal births a minority—" He surged to his feet, gasping. "I've thought a long time about this. Your facts only confirmed my suspicions. This tears it. Can't you see? Evolution has to proceed slowly. Life wasn't meant for such a storm of change. Unless we can save the true human stock, it'll be absorbed and differentiation will continue till humanity is a collection of freaks, probably intersterile. Or . . . there must be a lot of lethal recessives. In a large population, they can accumulate unnoticed till nearly everybody has them, and then start emerging all at once. That'd wipe us out. It's happened before, in rats and other species. If we eliminate mutant stock now, we can still save the race. It won't be cruel. We have sterilization techniques which are quick and painless, not upsetting the endocrine balance. But it's got to be done." His voice rose to a raw scream, broke. "It's got to be done!"

Drummond slapped him, hard. He drew a shuddering breath, sat down, and began to cry, and somehow that was the most horrible sight of all.

"You're crazy," said the aviator. "You've gone nuts with brooding alone on this the last six months, without knowing or being able to act. You've lost all perspective.

"We can't use violence. In the first place, it would break our tottering cracked culture irreparably, into a mad-dog finish fight. We'd not even win it. We're outnumbered, and we couldn't hold down a continent, eventually a planet. And remember what we said once, about abandoning the old savage way of settling things, that never brings a real settlement at all? We'd throw away a lesson our noses were rubbed in not three years ago. We'd return to the beast—to ultimate extinction.

"And anyway," he went on very quietly, "it wouldn't do a bit of good. Mutants would still be born. The poison is everywhere. Normal parents will give birth to mutants, somewhere along the line. We

just have to accept that fact, and live with it. The *new* human race
will have to."

"I'm sorry." Robinson raised his face from his hands. It was a
ghastly visage, gone white and old, but there was calm on it. "I—blew
my top. You're right. I've been thinking of this, worrying and wondering, living and breathing it, lying awake nights, and when I finally
sleep I dream of it. I . . . yes, I see your point. And you're right."

"It's O.K. You've been under a terrific strain. Three years with
never a rest, and the responsibility for a nation, and now this— Sure,
everybody's entitled to be a little crazy. We'll work out a solution,
somehow."

"Yes, of course." Robinson poured out two stiff drinks and gulped
his. He paced restlessly, and his tremendous ability came back in
waves of strength and confidence. "Let me see—Eugenics, of course.
If we work hard, we'll have the nation tightly organized inside of ten
years. Then . . . well, I don't suppose we can keep the mutants from
interbreeding, but certainly we can pass laws to protect humans and
encourage their propagation. Since radical mutations would probably
be intersterile anyway, and most mutants handicapped one way or
another, a few generations should see humans completely dominant
again."

Drummond scowled. He was worried. It wasn't like Robinson to
be unreasonable. Somehow, the man had acquired a mental blind
spot where this most ultimate of human problems was concerned. He
said slowly, "That won't work either. First, it'd be hard to impose and
enforce. Second, we'd be repeating the old *Herrenvolk* notion. Mutants are inferior, mutants must be kept in their place—to enforce
that, especially on a majority, you'd need a full-fledged totalitarian
state. Third, that wouldn't work either, for the rest of the world, with
almost no exceptions, is under no such control and we'll be in no
position to take over that control for a long time—generations. Before
then, mutants will dominate everywhere over there, and if they resent
the way we treat their kind here, we'd better run for cover."

"You assume a lot. How do you know those hundreds or thousands
of diverse types will work together? They're less like each other than
like humans, even. They could be played off against each other."

"Maybe. But *that* would be going back onto the old road of treach-
ery and violence, the road to Hell. Conversely, if every not-quite-
human is called a 'mutant,' like a separate class, he'll think he is, and
act accordingly against the lumped-together 'humans.' No, the only

way to sanity—to *survival*—is to abandon class prejudice and race hate altogether, and work as individuals. We're all . . . well, Earthlings, and subclassification is deadly. We all have to live together, and might as well make the best of it."

"Yeah . . . yeah, that's right too."

"Anyway, I repeat that all such attempts would be useless. All Earth is infected with mutation. It will be for a long time. The purest human stock will still produce mutants."

"Y-yes, that's true. Our best bet seems to be to find all such stock and withdraw it into the few safe areas left. It'll mean a small human population, but a *human* one."

"I tell you, that's impossible," clipped Drummond. "There is no safe place. Not one."

Robinson stopped pacing and looked at him as at a physical antagonist. "That so?" he almost growled. "Why?"

Drummond told him, adding incredulously, "Surely you knew that. Your physicists must have measured the amount of it. Your doctors, your engineers, that geneticist I dug up for you. You obviously got a lot of this biological information you've been slinging at me from him. They *must* all have told you the same thing."

Robinson shook his head stubbornly. "It can't be. It's not reasonable. The concentration wouldn't be great enough."

"Why, you poor fool, you need only look around you. The plants, the animals— Haven't there been any births in Taylor?"

"No. This is still a man's town, though women are trickling in and several babies are on the way—" Robinson's face was suddenly twisted with desperation. "Elaine's is due any time now. She's in the hospital here. Don't you see, our other kid died of the plague. This one's all we have. We want him to grow up in a world free of want and fear, a world of peace and sanity where he can play and laugh and become a man, not a beast starving in a cave. You and I are on our way out. We're the old generation, the one that wrecked the world. It's up to us to build it again, and then retire from it to let our children have it. The future's theirs. We've got to make it ready for them."

Sudden insight held Drummond motionless for long seconds. Understanding came, and pity, and an odd gentleness that changed his sunken, bony face. "Yes," he murmured, "yes, I see. That's why you're working with all that's in you to build a normal, healthy world. That's why you nearly went crazy when this threat appeared. That . . . that's why you can't, just can't comprehend—"

He took the other man's arm and guided him toward the door. "Come on," he said. "Let's go see how your wife's making out. Maybe we can get her some flowers on the way."

The silent cold bit at them as they went down the street. Snow crackled underfoot. It was already grimy with town smoke and dust, but overhead the sky was incredibly clean and blue. Breath smoked whitely from their mouths and nostrils. The sound of men at work rebuilding drifted faintly between the bulking mountains.

"We couldn't emigrate to another planet, could we?" asked Robinson, and answered himself: "No, we lack the organization and resources to settle them right now. We'll have to make out on Earth. A few safe spots—there *must* be others besides this one—to house the true humans till the mutation period is over. Yes, we can do it."

"There are no safe places," insisted Drummond. "Even if there were, the mutants would still outnumber us. Does your geneticist have any idea how this'll come out, biologically speaking?"

"He doesn't know. His specialty is still largely unknown. He can make an intelligent guess, and that's all."

"Yeah. Anyway, our problem is to learn to live with the mutants, to accept anyone as—Earthling—no matter how he looks, to quit thinking anything was ever settled by violence or connivance, to build a culture of individual sanity. Funny," mused Drummond, "how the impractical virtues, tolerance and sympathy and generosity, have become the fundamental necessities of simple survival. I guess it was always true, but it took the death of half the world and the end of a biological era to make us see that simple little fact. The job's terrific. We've got half a million years of brutality and greed, superstition and prejudice, to lick in a few generations. If we fail, mankind is done. But we've got to try."

They found some flowers, potted in a house, and Robinson bought them with the last of his tobacco. By the time he reached the hospital, he was sweating. The sweat froze on his face as he walked.

The hospital was the town's biggest building, and fairly well equipped. A nurse met them as they entered.

"I was just going to send for you, General Robinson," she said. "The baby's on the way."

"How . . . is she?"

"Fine, so far. Just wait here, please."

Drummond sank into a chair and with haggard eyes watched Robinson's jerky pacing. *The poor guy. Why is it expectant fathers are supposed to be so funny? It's like laughing at a man on the rack. I know, Barbara, I know.*

"They have some anesthetics," muttered the general. "They . . . Elaine never was very strong."

"She'll be all right." *It's afterward that worries me.*

"Yeah— Yeah— How long, though, how long?"

"Depends. Take it easy." With a wrench, Drummond made a sacrifice to a man he liked. He filled his pipe and handed it over. "Here, you need a smoke."

"Thanks." Robinson puffed raggedly.

The slow minutes passed, and Drummond wondered vaguely what he'd do when—it—happened. It didn't have to happen. But the chances were all against such an easy solution. He was no psychologist. Best just to let things happen as they would.

The waiting broke at last. A doctor came out, seeming an inscrutable high priest in his white garments. Robinson stood before him, motionless.

"You're a brave man," said the doctor. His face, as he removed the mask, was stern and set. "You'll need your courage."

"She—" It was hardly a human sound, the croak.

"Your wife is doing well. But the baby—"

A nurse brought out the little wailing form. It was a boy. But his limbs were rubbery tentacles terminating in boneless digits.

Robinson looked, and something went out of him as he stood there. When he turned, his face was dead.

"You're lucky," said Drummond, and meant it. He'd seen too many other mutants. "After all, if he can use those hands he'll get along all right. He'll even have an advantage in certain types of work. It isn't a deformity, really. If there's nothing else, you've got a good kid."

"*If!* You can't tell with mutants."

"I know. But you've got guts, you and Elaine. You'll see this through, together." Briefly, Drummond felt an utter personal desolation. He went on, perhaps to cover that emptiness:

"I see why you didn't understand the problem. You *wouldn't*. It was a psychological block, suppressing a fact you didn't dare face. That boy is really the center of your life. You couldn't think the truth about him, so your subconscious just refused to let you think rationally on that subject at all.

"Now you know. Now you realize there's no safe place, not on all the planet. The tremendous incidence of mutant births in the first generation could have told you that alone. Most such new characteristics are recessive, which means both parents have to have it for it to show in the zygote. But genetic changes are random, except for a tendency to fall into roughly similar patterns. Four-leaved clovers, for instance. Think how vast the total number of such changes must be, to produce so many corresponding changes in a couple of years. Think how many, *many* recessives there must be, existing only in gene patterns till their mates show up. We'll just have to take our chances of something really deadly accumulating. We'd never know till too late."

"The dust—"

"Yeah. The radiodust. It's colloidal, and uncountable other radiocolloids were formed when the bombs went off, and ordinary dirt gets into unstable isotopic forms near the craters. And there are radiogases too, probably. The poison is all over the world by now, spread by wind and air currents. Colloids can be suspended indefinitely in the atmosphere.

"The concentration isn't too high for life, though a physicist told me he's measured it as being very near the safe limit and there'll probably be a lot of cancer. But it's everywhere. Every breath we draw, every crumb we eat and drop we drink, every clod we walk on, the dust is there. It's in the stratosphere, clear on down to the surface, probably a good distance below. We could only escape by sealing ourselves in air-conditioned vaults and wearing spacesuits whenever we got out, and under present conditions that's impossible.

"Mutations were rare before, because a charged particle has to get pretty close to a gene and be moving fast before its electromagnetic effect causes physico-chemical changes, and then that particular chromosome has to enter into reproduction. Now the charged particles, and the gamma rays producing still more, are everywhere. Even at the comparatively low concentration, the odds favor a given organism having so many cells changed that at least one will give rise to a mutant. There's even a good chance of like recessives meeting the first generation, as we've seen. Nobody's safe, no place is free."

"The geneticist thinks some true humans will continue."

"A few, probably. After all, the radioactivity isn't too concentrated, and it's burning itself out. But it'll take fifty or a hundred years for the process to drop to insignificance, and by then the pure stock will be way in the minority. And there'll still be all those unmatched recessives, waiting to show up."

"You were right. We should never have created science. It brought the twilight of the race."

"I never said that. The race brought its own destruction, through misuse of science. Our culture was scientific anyway, in all except its psychological basis. It's up to us to take that last and hardest step. If we do, the race may yet survive."

Drummond gave Robinson a push toward the inner door. "You're exhausted, beat up, ready to quit. Go on in and see Elaine. Give her my regards. Then take a long rest before going back to work. I still think you've got a good kid."

Mechanically, the *de facto* President of the United States left the room. Hugh Drummond stared after him a moment, then went out into the street.

It's a Good Life

Jerome Bixby

*Jerome Bixby is a slender, youthful-looking man who at various peri-
ods in his life has earned his living as a professional pianist, a maga-
zine illustrator, an editor, and a Hollywood scriptwriter, among other
things. However wide his range of talents, he seems destined to be
remembered best for a single short story, the dark and sinister tale
you are about to read, which depicts one of the most terrifying super-
children any writer has ever created. In 1969 the Science Fiction
Writers of America chose* It's a Good Life *for the Science Fiction
Hall of Fame, a volume intended to collect the greatest science-fiction
stories of all time.*

*At last report Bixby and his family were living in the San Bernar-
dino Mountains of Southern California and planning to emigrate to
Central America, where he hopes, he says, "to get a small business
going, maybe import/export, and just relax."*

Aunt Amy was out on the front porch, rocking back and forth in the
highbacked chair and fanning herself, when Bill Soames rode his
bicycle up the road and stopped in front of the house.

Perspiring under the afternoon "sun," Bill lifted the box of groceries out of the big basket over the front wheel of the bike, and came
up the front walk.

Little Anthony was sitting on the lawn, playing with a rat. He had caught the rat down in the basement—he had made it think that it smelled cheese, the most rich-smelling and crumbly-delicious cheese a rat had ever thought it smelled, and it had come out of its hole, and now Anthony had hold of it with his mind and was making it do tricks.

When the rat saw Bill Soames coming, it tried to run, but Anthony thought at it, and it turned a flip-flop on the grass, and lay trembling, its eyes gleaming in small black terror.

Bill Soames hurried past Anthony and reached the front steps, mumbling. He always mumbled when he came to the Fremont house, or passed by it, or even thought of it. Everybody did. They thought about silly things, things that didn't mean very much, like two-and-two-is-four-and-twice-is-eight and so on; they tried to jumble up their thoughts and keep them skipping back and forth, so Anthony couldn't read their minds. The mumbling helped. Because if Anthony got anything strong out of your thoughts, he might take a notion to do something about it—like curing your wife's sick headaches or your kid's mumps, or getting your old milk cow back on schedule, or fixing the privy. And while Anthony mightn't actually mean any harm, he couldn't be expected to have much notion of what was the right thing to do in such cases.

That was if he liked you. He might try to help you, in his way. And that could be pretty horrible.

If he didn't like you . . . well, that could be worse.

Bill Soames set the box of groceries on the porch railing, and stopped his mumbling long enough to say, "Everythin' you wanted, Miss Amy."

"Oh, fine, William," Amy Fremont said lightly. "My, ain't it terrible hot today?"

Bill Soames almost cringed. His eyes pleaded with her. He shook his head violently *no,* and then interrupted his mumbling again, though obviously he didn't want to: "Oh, don't say that, Miss Amy . . . it's fine, just fine. A real *good* day!"

Amy Fremont got up from the rocking chair, and came across the porch. She was a tall woman, thin, a smiling vacancy in her eyes. About a year ago, Anthony had gotten mad at her, because she'd told him he shouldn't have turned the cat into a cat-rug, and although he had always obeyed her more than anyone else, which was hardly at all, this time he'd snapped at her. With his mind. And that had been the end of Amy Fremont's bright eyes, and the end of Amy Fremont as everyone had known her. And that was when word got around in Peaksville (population: 46) that even the members of Anthony's own family weren't safe. After that, everyone was twice as careful.

Someday Anthony might undo what he'd done to Aunt Amy. Anthony's Mom and Pop hoped he would. When he was older, and maybe sorry. If it was possible, that is. Because Aunt Amy had changed a lot, and besides, now Anthony wouldn't obey anyone.

"Land alive, William," Aunt Amy said, "you don't have to mumble like that. Anthony wouldn't hurt you. My goodness, Anthony likes you!" She raised her voice and called to Anthony, who had tired of the rat and was making it eat itself. "Don't you, dear? Don't you like Mr. Soames?"

Anthony looked across the lawn at the grocery man—a bright, wet, purple gaze. He didn't say anything. Bill Soames tried to smile at him. After a second Anthony returned his attention to the rat. It had already devoured its tail, or at least chewed it off—for Anthony had made it bite faster than it could swallow, and little pink and red furry pieces lay around it on the green grass. Now the rat was having trouble reaching its hindquarters.

Mumbling silently, thinking of nothing in particular as hard as he could, Bill Soames went stiff legged down the walk, mounted his bicycle and pedaled off.

"We'll see you tonight, William," Aunt Amy called after him.

As Bill Soames pumped the pedals, he was wishing deep down that he could pump twice as fast, to get away from Anthony all the faster, and away from Aunt Amy, who sometimes just forgot how *careful* you had to be. And he shouldn't have thought that. Because Anthony caught it. He caught the desire to get away from the Fremont house as if it was something *bad,* and his purple gaze blinked, and he snapped a small, sulky thought after Bill Soames—just a small one, because he was in a good mood today, and besides, he liked Bill Soames, or at least didn't dislike him, at least today. Bill Soames wanted to go away—so, petulantly, Anthony helped him.

Pedaling with superhuman speed—or rather, appearing to, because in reality the bicycle was pedaling *him*—Bill Soames vanished down the road in a cloud of dust, his thin, terrified wail drifting back across the summerlike heat.

Anthony looked at the rat. It had devoured half its belly, and had died from pain. He thought it into a grave out deep in the cornfield—his father had once said, smiling, that he might as well do that with the things he killed—and went around the house, casting his odd shadow in the hot, brassy light from above.

In the kitchen, Aunt Amy was unpacking the groceries. She put the Mason-jarred goods on the shelves, and the meat and milk in the icebox, and the beet sugar and coarse flour in big cans under the sink. She put the cardboard box in the corner, by the door, for Mr. Soames to pick up next time he came. It was stained and battered and torn and worn fuzzy, but it was one of the few left in Peaksville. In faded red letters it said *Campbell's Soup*. The last cans of soup, or of anything else, had been eaten long ago, except for a small communal hoard which the villagers dipped into for special occasions—but the box lingered on, like a coffin, and when it and the other boxes were gone, the men would have to make some out of wood.

Aunt Amy went out in back, where Anthony's Mom—Aunt Amy's sister—sat in the shade of the house, shelling peas. The peas, every time Mom ran a finger along a pod, went *lollop-lollop-lollop* into the pan on her lap.

"William brought the groceries," Aunt Amy said. She sat down wearily in the straightbacked chair beside Mom, and began fanning herself again. She wasn't really old; but ever since Anthony had snapped at her with his mind, something had seemed to be wrong with her body as well as her mind, and she was tired all the time.

"Oh, good," said Mom. *Lollop* went the fat peas into the pan.

Everybody in Peaksville always said "Oh, fine," or "Good," or "Say, that's swell!" when almost anything happened or was mentioned—even unhappy things like accidents or even deaths. They'd always say "Good," because if they didn't try to cover up how they really felt, Anthony might overhear with his mind, and then nobody knew what might happen. Like the time Mrs. Kent's husband, Sam, had come walking back from the graveyard, because Anthony liked Mrs. Kent and had heard her mourning.

Lollop.

"Tonight's television night," said Aunt Amy. "I'm glad. I look forward to it so much every week. I wonder what we'll see tonight."

"Did Bill bring the meat?" asked Mom.

"Yes." Aunt Amy fanned herself, looking up at the featureless brassy glare of the sky. "Goodness, it's so hot! I wish Anthony would make it just a little cooler—"

"*Amy!*"

"Oh!" Mom's sharp tone had penetrated, where Bill Soames' agonized expression had failed. Aunt Amy put one thin hand to her mouth in exaggerated alarm. "Oh . . . I'm sorry, dear." Her pale blue eyes shuttled around, right and left, to see if Anthony was in sight. Not that it would make any difference if he was or wasn't—he didn't have to be near you to know what you were thinking. Usually, though, unless he had his attention on somebody, he would be occupied with thoughts of his own.

But some things attracted his attention—you could never be sure just what.

"This weather's just *fine*," Mom said.

Lollop.

"Oh, yes," Aunt Amy said. "It's a wonderful day. I wouldn't want it changed for the world!"

Lollop.

Lollop.

"What time is it?" Mom asked.

Aunt Amy was sitting where she could see through the kitchen window to the alarm clock on the shelf above the stove. "Four-thirty," she said.

Lollop.

"I want tonight to be something special," Mom said. "Did Bill bring a good lean roast?"

"Good and lean, dear. They butchered just today, you know, and sent us over the best piece."

"Dan Hollis will be *so* surprised when he finds out that tonight's television party is a birthday party for him too!"

"Oh, *I* think he will! Are you sure nobody's told him?"

"Everybody swore they wouldn't."

"That'll be real nice." Aunt Amy nodded, looking off across the cornfield. "A birthday party."

"Well—" Mom put the pan of peas down beside her, stood up and brushed her apron. "I'd better get the roast on. Then we can set the table." She picked up the peas.

Anthony came around the corner of the house. He didn't look at them, but continued on down through the carefully kept garden—*all* the gardens in Peaksville were carefully kept, very carefully kept—and went past the rustling, useless hulk that had been the Fremont family car, and went smoothly over the fence and out into the cornfield.

"Isn't this a lovely day!" said Mom, a little loudly, as they went toward the back door.

Aunt Amy fanned herself. "A beautiful day, dear. Just *fine!*"

Out in the cornfield, Anthony walked between the tall, rustling rows of green stalks. He liked to smell the corn. The alive corn overhead, and the dead corn underfoot. Rich Ohio earth, thick with weeds and brown, dry-rotting ears of corn, pressed between his bare toes with every step—he had made it rain last night so everything would smell and feel nice today.

He walked clear to the edge of the cornfield, and over to where a grove of shadowy green trees covered cool, moist, dark ground, and lots of leafy undergrowth, and jumbled moss-covered rocks, and a small spring that made a clear, clean pool. Here Anthony liked to rest and watch the birds and insects and small animals that rustled and scampered and chirped about. He liked to lie on the cool ground and look up through the moving greenness overhead, and watch the insects flit in the hazy soft sunbeams that stood like slanting, glowing bars between ground and treetops. Somehow, he liked the thoughts of the little creatures in this place better than the thoughts outside; and while the thoughts he picked up here weren't very strong or very clear, he could get enough out of them to know what the little creatures liked and wanted, and he spent a lot of time making the grove more like what they wanted it to be. The spring hadn't always been here; but one time he had found thirst in one small furry mind, and had brought subterranean water to the surface in a clear, cold flow, and had watched blinking as the creature drank, feeling its pleasure. Later he had made the pool, when he found a small urge to swim.

He had made rocks and trees and bushes and caves, and sunlight here and shadows there, because he had felt in all the tiny minds around him the desire—or the instinctive want—for this kind of resting place, and that kind of mating place, and this kind of place to play, and that kind of home.

And somehow the creatures from all the fields and pastures around the grove had seemed to know that this was a good place, for there were always more of them coming in—every time Anthony came out here there were more creatures than the last time, and more desires and needs to be tended to. Every time there would be some kind of creature he had never seen before, and he would find its mind, and see what it wanted, and then give it to it.

He liked to help them. He liked to feel their simple gratification.

Today, he rested beneath a thick elm, and lifted his purple gaze to a red and black bird that had just come to the grove. It twittered on a branch over his head, and hopped back and forth, and thought its tiny thoughts, and Anthony made a big, soft nest for it, and pretty soon it hopped in.

A long, brown, sleek-furred animal was drinking at the pool. Anthony found its mind next. The animal was thinking about a smaller creature that was scurrying along the ground on the other side of the pool, grubbing for insects. The little creature didn't know that it was in danger. The long, brown animal finished drinking and tensed its legs to leap, and Anthony thought it into a grave in the cornfield.

He didn't like those kinds of thoughts. They reminded him of the thoughts outside the grove. A long time ago some of the people outside had thought that way about *him,* and one night they'd hidden and waited for him to come back from the grove—and he'd just thought them all into the cornfield. Since then, the rest of the people hadn't thought that way—at least, very clearly. Now their thoughts were all mixed up and confusing whenever they thought about him or near him. So he didn't pay much attention.

He liked to help them too, sometimes—but it wasn't simple, or very gratifying either. They never thought happy thoughts when he did— just the jumble. So he spent more time out here.

He watched all the birds and insects and furry creatures for a while, and played with a bird, making it soar and dip and streak madly around tree trunks until, accidentally, when another bird caught his attention for a moment, he ran it into a rock. Petulantly, he thought the rock into a grave in the cornfield; but he couldn't do anything more with the bird. Not because it was dead, though it was; but because it had a broken wing. So he went back to the house. He didn't feel like walking back through the cornfield, so he just *went* to the house, right down into the basement.

It was nice down here. Nice and dark and damp and sort of fragrant, because once Mom had been making preserves in a rack along the far wall, and then she'd stopped coming down ever since Anthony had started spending time here, and the preserves had spoiled and leaked down and spread over the dirt floor, and Anthony liked the smell.

He caught another rat, making it smell cheese, and after he played with it, he thought it into a grave right beside the long animal he'd killed in the grove. Aunt Amy hated rats, and so he killed a lot of them, because he liked Aunt Amy most of all and sometimes did things that Aunt Amy wanted. Her mind was more like the little furry minds out in the grove. She hadn't thought anything bad at all about him for a long time.

After the rat, he played with a big black spider in the corner under the stairs, making it run back and forth until its web shook and shimmered in the light from the cellar window like a reflection in silvery water. Then he drove fruit flies into the web until the spider was frantic trying to wind them all up. The spider liked flies, and its thoughts were stronger than theirs, so he did it. There was something bad in the way it liked flies, but it wasn't clear—and besides, Aunt Amy hated flies too.

He heard footsteps overhead—Mom moving around in the kitchen. He blinked his purple gaze, and almost decided to make her hold still—but instead he *went* up to the attic, and, after looking out the circular window at the front end of the long V-roofed room for a while at the front lawn and the dusty road and Henderson's tip-waving wheat field beyond, he curled into an unlikely shape and went partly to sleep.

Soon people would be coming for television, he heard Mom think.

He went more to sleep. He liked television night. Aunt Amy had always liked television a lot, so one time he had thought some for her, and a few other people had been there at the time, and Aunt Amy had felt disappointed when they wanted to leave. He'd done something to them for that—and now everybody came to television.

He liked all the attention he got when they did.

Anthony's father came home around six thirty, looking tired and dirty and bloody. He'd been over in Dunn's pasture with the other men, helping pick out the cow to be slaughtered this month and doing the job, and then butchering the meat and salting it away in Soames' icehouse. Not a job he cared for, but every man had his turn. Yesterday, he had helped scythe down old McIntyre's wheat. Tomorrow, they would start threshing. By hand. Everything in Peaksville had to be done by hand.

He kissed his wife on the cheek and sat down at the kitchen table. He smiled and said, "Where's Anthony?"

"Around someplace," Mom said.

Aunt Amy was over at the wood-burning stove, stirring the big pot

of peas. Mom went back to the oven and opened it and basted the
roast.

"Well, it's been a *good* day," Dad said. By rote. Then he looked
at the mixing bowl and breadboard on the table. He sniffed at the
dough. "M'm," he said. "I could eat a loaf all by myself, I'm so
hungry."

"No one told Dan Hollis about its being a birthday party, did
they?" his wife asked.

"Nope. We kept as quiet as mummies."

"We've fixed up such a lovely surprise!"

"Um? What?"

"Well . . . you know how much Dan likes music. Well, last week
Thelma Dunn found a *record* in her attic!"

"No!"

"Yes! And we had Ethel sort of ask—you know, without really
asking—if he had that one. And he said no. Isn't that a wonderful
surprise?"

"Well, now, it sure is. A record, imagine! That's a real nice thing
to find! What record is it?"

"Perry Como, singing 'You Are My Sunshine.' "

"Well, I'll be darned. I always liked that tune." Some raw carrots
were lying on the table. Dad picked up a small one, scrubbed it on
his chest, and took a bite. "How did Thelma happen to find it?"

"Oh, you know—just looking around for new things."

"M'm." Dad chewed the carrot. "Say, who has that picture we found
a while back? I kind of liked it—that old clipper sailing along—"

"The Smiths. Next week the Sipichs get it, and they give the Smiths
old McIntyre's music-box, and we give the Sipichs—" And she went
down the tentative order of things that would exchange hands among
the women at church this Sunday.

He nodded. "Looks like we can't have the picture for a while, I
guess. Look, honey, you might try to get that detective book back from
the Reillys. I was so busy the week we had it, I never got to finish all
the stories—"

"I'll try," his wife said doubtfully. "But I hear the van Husens have
a stereoscope they found in the cellar." Her voice was just a little ac-
cusing. "They had it two whole months before they told anybody
about it—"

"Say," Dad said, looking interested. "That'd be nice, too. Lots of
pictures?"

"I suppose so. I'll see on Sunday. I'd like to have it—but we still owe the van Husens for their canary. I don't know why that bird had to pick *our* house to die . . . it must have been sick when we got it. Now there's just no satisfying Betty van Husen—she even hinted she'd like our *piano* for a while!"

"Well, honey, you try for the stereoscope—or just anything you think we'll like." At last he swallowed the carrot. It had been a little young and tough. Anthony's whims about the weather made it so that people never knew what crops would come up, or what shape they'd be in if they did. All they could do was plant a lot; and always enough of something came up any one season to live on. Just once there had been a grain surplus; tons of it had been hauled to the edge of Peaksville and dumped off into the nothingness. Otherwise, nobody could have breathed, when it started to spoil.

"You know," Dad went on. "It's nice to have the new things around. It's nice to think that there's probably still a lot of stuff nobody's found yet, in cellars and attics and barns and down behind things. They help, somehow. As much as anything can help—"

"Sh-h!" Mom glanced nervously around.

"Oh," Dad said, smiling hastily. "It's all right! The new things are *good!* It's *nice* to be able to have something around you've never seen before, and know that something you've given somebody else is making them happy . . . that's a real *good* thing."

"A good thing," his wife echoed.

"Pretty soon," Aunt Amy said, from the stove, "there won't be any more new things. We'll have found everything there is to find. Goodness, that'll be too bad—"

"*Amy!*"

"Well—" Her pale eyes were shallow and fixed, a sign of her recurrent vagueness. "It will be kind of a shame—no new things—"

"Don't *talk* like that," Mom said, trembling. "Amy, be *quiet!*"

"It's *good,*" said Dad, in the loud, familiar, wanting-to-be-overheard tone of voice. "Such talk is *good.* It's okay, honey—don't you see? It's good for Amy to talk any way she wants. It's good for her to feel bad. Everything's good. Everything has to be good . . ."

Anthony's mother was pale. And so was Aunt Amy—the peril of the moment had suddenly penetrated the clouds surrounding her mind. Sometimes it was difficult to handle words so that they might not prove disastrous. You just never *knew.* There were so many things it was wise not to say, or even think—but remonstration for

saying or thinking them might be just as bad, if Anthony heard and
decided to do anything about it. You could just never tell what Anthony was liable to do.

Everything had to be good. Had to be fine just as it was, even if
it wasn't. Always. Because any change might be worse. So terribly
much worse.

"Oh, my goodness, yes, of course it's good," Mom said. "You
talk any way you want to, Amy, and it's just fine. Of course, you want
to remember that some ways are *better* than others . . ."

Aunt Amy stirred the peas, fright in her pale eyes.

"Oh, yes," she said. "But I don't feel like talking right now. It . . .
it's *good* that I don't feel like talking."

Dad said tiredly, smiling, "I'm going out and wash up."

They started arriving around eight o'clock. By that time, Mom and
Aunt Amy had the big table in the dining room set, and two more
tables off to the side. The candles were burning, and the chairs situ-
ated, and Dad had a big fire going in the fireplace.

The first to arrive were the Sipichs, John and Mary. John wore his
best suit, and was well scrubbed and pinkfaced after his day in
McIntyre's pasture. The suit was neatly pressed, but getting thread-
bare at elbow and cuffs. Old McIntyre was working on a loom, de-
signing it out of schoolbooks, but so far it was slow going. McIntyre
was a capable man with wood and tools, but a loom was a big order
when you couldn't get metal parts. McIntyre had been one of the ones
who, at first, had wanted to try to get Anthony to make things the villagers needed, like clothes and canned goods and medical supplies
and gasoline. Since then, he felt that what had happened to the whole
Terrance family and Joe Kinney was his fault, and he worked hard
trying to make it up to the rest of them. And since then, no one
had tried to get Anthony to do anything.

Mary Sipich was a small, cheerful woman in a simple dress. She
immediately set about helping Mom and Aunt Amy put the finishing
touches on the dinner.

The next arrivals were the Smiths and the Dunns, who lived right
next to each other down the road, only a few yards from the nothingness. They drove up in the Smiths' wagon, drawn by their old horse.

Then the Reillys showed up, from across the darkened wheat field,
and the evening really began. Pat Reilly sat down at the big upright
in the front room, and began to play from the popular sheet music

on the rack. He played softly, as expressively as he could—and no-body sang. Anthony liked piano playing a whole lot, but not singing; often he would come up from the basement, or down from the attic, or just *come,* and sit on top of the piano, nodding his head as Pat played "Lover" or "Boulevard of Broken Dreams" or "Night and Day." He seemed to prefer ballads, sweet-sounding songs—but the one time somebody had started to sing, Anthony had looked over from the top of the piano and done something that made everybody afraid of singing from then on. Later, they'd decided that the piano was what Anthony had heard first, before anybody had ever tried to sing, and now anything else added to it didn't sound right and dis-tracted him from his pleasure.

So, every television night, Pat would play the piano, and that was the beginning of the evening. Wherever Anthony was, the music would make him happy, and put him in a good mood, and he would know that they were gathering for television and waiting for him.

By eight-thirty everybody had shown up, except for the seventeen children and Mrs. Soames, who was off watching them in the school-house at the far end of town. The children of Peaksville were never, never allowed near the Fremont house—not since little Fred Smith had tried to play with Anthony on a dare. The younger children weren't even told about Anthony. The others had mostly forgotten about him, or were told that he was a nice, nice goblin but they must never go near him.

Dan and Ethel Hollis came late, and Dan walked in not suspecting a thing. Pat Reilly had played the piano until his hands ached—he'd worked pretty hard with them today—and now he got up, and every-body gathered around to wish Dan Hollis a happy birthday.

"Well, I'll be darned," Dan grinned. "This is swell. I wasn't ex-pecting this at all . . . gosh, this is *swell!*"

They gave him his presents—mostly things they had made by hand, though some were things that people had possessed as their own and now gave him as his. John Sipich gave him a watch charm, hand-carved out of a piece of hickory wood. Dan's watch had broken down a year or so ago, and there was nobody in the village who knew how to fix it, but he still carried it around because it had been his grand-father's and was a fine old heavy thing of gold and silver. He attached the charm to the chain, while everybody laughed and said John had done a nice job of carving. Then Mary Sipich gave him a knitted neck-tie, which he put on, removing the one he'd worn.

The Reillys gave him a little box they had made, to keep things in. They didn't say what things, but Dan said he'd keep his personal jewelry in it. The Reillys had made it out of a cigar box, carefully peeled of its paper and lined on the inside with velvet. The outside had been polished, and carefully if not expertly carved by Pat—but his carving got complimented too. Dan Hollis received many other gifts —a pipe, a pair of shoelaces, a tie pin, a knit pair of socks, some fudge, a pair of garters made from old suspenders.

He unwrapped each gift with vast pleasure, and wore as many of them as he could right there, even the garters. He lit up the pipe, and said he'd never had a better smoke; which wasn't quite true, because the pipe wasn't broken in yet. Pete Manners had had it lying around ever since he'd received it as a gift four years ago from an out-of-town relative who hadn't known he'd stopped smoking.

Dan put the tobacco into the bowl very carefully. Tobacco was precious. It was only pure luck that Pat Reilly had decided to try to grow some in his backyard just before what had happened to Peaksville had happened. It didn't grow very well, and then they had to cure it and shred it and all, and it was just precious stuff. Everybody in town used wooden holders old McIntyre had made, to save on butts.

Last of all, Thelma Dunn gave Dan Hollis the record she had found.

Dan's eyes misted even before he opened the package. He knew it was a record.

"Gosh," he said softly. "What one is it? I'm almost afraid to look . . ."

"You haven't got it, darling," Ethel Hollis smiled. "Don't you remember, I asked about 'You Are My Sunshine'?"

"Oh, gosh," Dan said again. Carefully he removed the wrapping and stood there fondling the record, running his big hands over the worn grooves with their tiny, dulling crosswise scratches. He looked around the room, eyes shining, and they all smiled back, knowing how delighted he was.

"Happy birthday, darling!" Ethel said, throwing her arms around him and kissing him.

He clutched the record in both hands, holding it off to one side as she pressed against him. "Hey," he laughed, pulling back his head. "Be careful . . . I'm holding a priceless object! He looked around again, over his wife's arms, which were still around his neck. His eyes were hungry. "Look . . . do you think we could play it? Lord, what

I'd give to hear some new music . . . just the first part, the orchestra part, before Como sings?"

Faces sobered. After a minute, John Sipich said, "I don't think we'd better, Dan. After all, we don't know just where the singer comes in—it'd be taking too much of a chance. Better wait till you get home."

Dan Hollis reluctantly put the record on the buffet with all his other presents. "It's *good*," he said automatically, but disappointedly, "that I can't play it here."

"Oh, yes," said Sipich. "It's good." To compensate for Dan's disappointed tone, he repeated, "It's *good*."

They ate dinner, the candles lighting their smiling faces, and ate it all right down to the last delicious drop of gravy. They complimented Mom and Aunt Amy on the roast beef, and the peas and carrots, and the tender corn on the cob. The corn hadn't come from the Fremonts' cornfield, naturally—everybody knew what was out there; and the field was going to weeds.

Then they polished off the dessert—homemade ice cream and cookies. And then they sat back, in the flickering light of the candles, and chatted, waiting for television.

There never was a lot of mumbling on television night—everybody came and had a good dinner at the Fremonts', and that was nice, and afterward there was television, and nobody really thought much about that—it just had to be put up with. So it was a pleasant enough get-together, aside from your having to watch what you said just as carefully as you always did everyplace. If a dangerous thought came into your mind, you just started mumbling, even right in the middle of a sentence. When you did that, the others just ignored you until you felt happier again and stopped.

Anthony liked television night. He had done only two or three awful things on television night in the whole past year.

Mom had put a bottle of brandy on the table, and they each had a tiny glass of it. Liquor was even more precious than tobacco. The villagers could make wine, but the grapes weren't right, and certainly the techniques weren't, and it wasn't very good wine. There were only a few bottles of real liquor left in the village—four rye, three Scotch, three brandy, nine real wine and half a bottle of Drambuie belonging to old McIntyre (only for marriages)—and when those were gone, that was it.

Afterward, everybody wished that the brandy hadn't been brought out. Because Dan Hollis drank more of it than he should have, and mixed it with a lot of the homemade wine. Nobody thought anything about it at first, because he didn't show it much outside, and it was his birthday party and a happy party, and Anthony liked these get-togethers and shouldn't see any reason to do anything even if he was listening.

But Dan Hollis got high, and did a fool thing. If they'd seen it coming, they'd have taken him outside and walked him around.

The first thing they knew, Dan stopped laughing right in the middle of the story about how Thelma Dunn had found the Perry Como record and dropped it and it hadn't broken because she'd moved faster than she ever had before in her life and caught it. He was fondling the record again, and looking longingly at the Fremonts' gramophone over in the corner, and suddenly he stopped laughing and his face got slack, and then it got ugly, and he said, "Oh, *Christ!*"

Immediately the room was still. So still they could hear the whir-ring movement of the grandfather's clock out in the hall. Pat Reilly had been playing the piano, softly. He stopped, his hands poised over the yellowed keys.

The candles on the dining-room table flickered in a cool breeze that blew through the lace curtains over the bay window.

"Keep playing, Pat," Anthony's father said softly.

Pat started again. He played "Night and Day," but his eyes were sidewise on Dan Hollis, and he missed notes.

Dan stood in the middle of the room, holding the record. In his other hand he held a glass of brandy so hard his hand shook.

They were all looking at him.

"*Christ,*" he said again, and he made it sound like a dirty word.

Reverend Younger, who had been talking with Mom and Aunt Amy by the dining-room door, said "Christ" too—but he was using it in a prayer. His hands were clasped, and his eyes were closed.

John Sipich moved forward. "Now, Dan . . . it's *good* for you to talk that way. But you don't want to talk too much, you know."

Dan shook off the hand Sipich put on his arm.

"Can't even play my record," he said loudly. He looked down at the record, and then around at their faces. "Oh, my *God* . . ."

He threw the glassful of brandy against the wall. It splattered and ran down the wallpaper in streaks.

Some of the women gasped.

"Dan," Sipich said in a whisper. "Dan, cut it out—"

Pat Reilly was playing "Night and Day" louder, to cover up the sounds of the talk. It wouldn't do any good, though, if Anthony was listening.

Dan Hollis went over to the piano and stood by Pat's shoulder, swaying a little.

"Pat," he said. "Don't play *that*. Play *this*." And he began to sing. Softly, hoarsely, miserably: "Happy birthday to me . . . Happy birthday to me . . ."

"*Dan!*" Ethel Hollis screamed. She tried to run across the room to him. Mary Sipich grabbed her arm and held her back. "Dan," Ethel screamed again. "Stop—"

"My God, be quiet!" hissed Mary Sipich, and pushed her toward one of the men, who put his hand over her mouth and held her still.

". . . Happy birthday, dear Danny," Dan sang. "Happy birthday to me!" He stopped and looked down at Pat Reilly. "Play it, Pat. Play it, so I can sing right . . . you know I can't carry a tune unless somebody plays it!"

Pat Reilly put his hands on the keys and began "Lover"—in a slow waltz tempo, the way Anthony liked it. Pat's face was white. His hands fumbled.

Dan Hollis stared over at the dining-room door. At Anthony's mother, and at Anthony's father, who had gone to join her.

"*You* had him," he said. Tears gleamed on his cheeks as the candlelight caught them. "*You* had to go and *have* him. . . ."

He closed his eyes, and the tears squeezed out. He sang loudly, "You are my sunshine . . . my only sunshine . . . you make me happy . . . when I am blue. . . ."

Anthony *came* into the room.

Pat stopped playing. He froze. Everybody froze. The breeze rippled the curtains. Ethel Hollis couldn't even try to scream—she had fainted.

"Please don't take my sunshine . . . away. . . ." Dan's voice faltered into silence. His eyes widened. He put both hands out in front of him, the empty glass in one, the record in the other. He hiccupped, and said, "*No—*"

"Bad man," Anthony said, and thought Dan Hollis into something like nothing anyone would have believed possible, and then he thought the thing into a grave deep, deep in the cornfield.

The glass and record thumped on the rug. Neither broke.

Anthony's purple gaze went around the room.

Some of the people began mumbling. They all tried to smile. The sound of mumbling filled the room like a far-off approval. Out of the murmuring came one or two clear voices:

"Oh, it's a very *good* thing," said John Sipich.

"A good thing," said Anthony's father, smiling. He'd had more practice in smiling than most of them. "A wonderful thing."

"It's swell . . . just swell," said Pat Reilly, tears leaking from eyes and nose, and he began to play the piano again, softly, his trembling hands feeling for "Night and Day."

Anthony climbed up on top of the piano, and Pat played for two hours.

Afterward, they watched television. They all went into the front room, and lit just a few candles, and pulled up chairs around the set. It was a small-screen set, and they couldn't all sit close enough to it to see, but that didn't matter. They didn't even turn the set on. It wouldn't have worked anyway, there being no electricity in Peaksville.

They just sat silently, and watched the twisting, writhing shapes on the screen, and listened to the sounds that came out of the speaker, and none of them had any idea of what it was all about. They never did. It was always the same.

"It's real nice," Aunt Amy said once, her pale eyes on the meaningless flickers and shadows. "But I liked it a little better when there were cities outside and we could get real—"

"Why, Amy!" said Mom. "It's good for you to say such a thing. Very good. But how can you mean it? Why, this television is *much* better than anything we ever used to get!"

"Yes," chimed John Sipich. "It's fine. It's the best show we've ever seen!"

He sat on the couch, with two other men, holding Ethel Hollis flat against the cushions, holding her arms and legs and putting their hands over her mouth, so she couldn't start screaming again.

"It's really *good!*" he said again.

Mom looked out of the front window, across the darkened road, across Henderson's darkened wheat field to the vast, endless, gray nothingness in which the little village of Peaksville floated like a soul

—the huge nothingness that was most evident at night, when Anthony's brassy day had gone.

It did no good to wonder where they were . . . no good at all. Peaksville was just someplace. Someplace away from the world. It was wherever it had been since that day three years ago when Anthony had crept from her womb and old Doc Bates—God rest him —had screamed and dropped him and tried to kill him, and Anthony had whined and done the thing. Had taken the village someplace. Or had destroyed the world and left only the village, nobody knew which.

It did no good to wonder about it. Nothing at all did any good— except to live as they must live. Must always, always live, if Anthony would let them.

These thoughts were dangerous, she thought.

She began to mumble. The others started mumbling too. They had all been thinking, evidently.

The men on the couch whispered and whispered to Ethel Hollis, and when they took their hands away, she mumbled too.

While Anthony sat on top of the set and made television, they sat around and mumbled and watched the meaningless, flickering shapes far into the night.

Next day it snowed, and killed off half the crops—but it was a *good* day.

The Mute Question

Forrest J Ackerman

Forrest J Ackerman didn't invent science fiction, but sometimes it seems that way. He was one of the first ardent science-fiction fans, back in the late 1920's; his Hollywood home is a veritable museum of science-fiction artifacts; most of the great West Coast science-fiction writers have been close friends of his; he has been a literary agent representing such figures as A. E. van Vogt, L. Ron Hubbard, and Ed Earl Repp; he has served as a consultant to the movie industry on a number of science-fiction films. He has also written, over the past thirty-odd years, a number of short, whimsical science-fiction stories, much infested by puns and double entendres, such as the neat little item that follows.

Twinhead was puzzling over the old problem. "Do you think," he reflected, in the queer lisp that was the heritage of his cleft tongue, "that Man could have made mutant in His own image?"

His acquaintance of the twilight hour vouchsafed no opinion.

The mutant's second head arched its neck forward from the cave wall against which it rested. With its twang, characteristic of its double tongue, it argued, "But if Man's son, Adam, created us all with the Adam bomb—?"

"I don't hold with that Bomb birth story," his opposite head lisped in negation. "Do you, stranger?"

Still the stranger did not respond; why, it could not be directly discerned, for it was very dark in the cave.

Twang-tongue declared: "But for Man to have made mutie in His own image, He would have had to have been a polymorph! Part of Him would have had to have been two-headed, like us, and part like our Siamese sisters and part like little Roll Ball and part like the Octo-Arms we met last week and part like the Centi-Feets and part like our cousin Snaky. Why, He would have been a monster! Don't you agree, stranger?"

In the dark recess of the cave the stranger stirred, but still no sound issued from his direction. And so this philosophical discussion of the late 1990's stalemated itself.

Then the moon's clouded rays, slowly, as though fearful of what they might reveal, crept into the cave. The wavering shaft moved hesitantly up the misshapen body of Twinhead, and at last reluctantly illumined the entire mutie. Was it an illusion, or did the face of the Man in the Moon pale? There was no man left on Earth to tell.

The beam's slow progress continued, until the second mutie too was visible. Then it became evident why this stranger did not speak.

Rather, it must be put this way: It would have become evident, had there been a man there with eyes to see. It remained a mystery to Twinhead for, though he had more than his share of eyes—six, to be exact—they were all albino white, pupilless ovals of jellyfish flesh that failed to function. Twinhead, since birth, was blind.

And the stranger—well, he was silent because . . .

The muties have a proverb: Two heads are better than none.

Let the Ants Try

Frederik Pohl

In the bad old days of science fiction, when melodramatic plots were the rule and only a few writers worried much about scientific plausibility, the giant-ant story was one of the standard themes. Again and again the terrifying six-legged invaders, antennae waving and mandibles clicking, pillaged countryside and city in cheerful defiance of the square-cube law—a principle that states that if an insect's size were to be doubled, its strength and the area of its breathing passages would increase fourfold, but its mass would increase eightfold. Alas for those who wrote of ants the size of men, any insect so huge would collapse under its own weight if it didn't suffocate first.

Because Frederik Pohl has always been one of science-fiction's most capable craftsmen, this somber and intricate little story makes an attempt to find a way around the square-cube law. It does not altogether succeed—no story could—but nevertheless the attempt is an honorable one, and "Let the Ants Try" is a long way from the wild giant-ant melodramas of yesterday. Besides, no science-fiction anthology dealing with mutations would be truly complete if the giant-ant myth went unrepresented.

Gordy survived the Three-Hour War, even though Detroit didn't; he was on his way to Washington, with his blueprints and models in his bag, when the bombs struck.

He had left his wife behind in the city, and not even a trace of her body was ever found. The children, of course, weren't as lucky as that. Their summer camp was less than twenty miles away, and unfortunately in the direction of the prevailing wind. But they were not in any pain until the last few days of the month they had left to live. Gordy managed to fight his way back through the snarled, frantic airline controls to them. Even though he knew they would certainly die of radiation sickness, and they suspected it, there was still a whole blessed week of companionship before the pain got too bad.

That was about all the companionship Gordy had for the whole year of 1960.

He came back to Detroit as soon as the radioactivity had died down; he had nowhere else to go. He found a house on the outskirts of the city and tried to locate someone to buy it from. But the Emergency Administration laughed at him. "Move in, if you're crazy enough to stay."

When Gordy thought about it all, it occurred to him that he was in a sort of state of shock. His fine, trained mind almost stopped functioning. He ate and slept, and when it grew cold he shivered and built fires, and that was all. The War Department wrote him two or three times, and finally a government man came around to ask what had happened to the things that Gordy had promised to bring to Washington. But he looked queerly at the pink, hairless mice that fed unmolested in the filthy kitchen, and he stood a careful distance away from Gordy's hairy face and torn clothes.

He said, "The Secretary sent me here, Mr. Gordy. He takes a personal interest in your discovery."

Gordy shook his head. "The Secretary is dead," he said. "They were all killed when Washington went."

"There's a new Secretary," the man explained. He puffed on his cigarette and tossed it into the patch Gordy was scrabbling into a truck garden. "Arnold Cavanagh. He knows a great deal about you, and he told me, 'If Salva Gordy has a weapon, we must have it. Our strength has been shattered. Tell Gordy we need his help.'"

Gordy crossed his hands like a lean Buddha.

"I haven't got a weapon," he said.

"You have something that can be used as a weapon. You wrote to Washington, before the war came, and said—"

"The war is over," said Salva Gordy.

The government man sighed and tried again, but in the end he went away. He never came back. The thing, Gordy thought, was undoubtedly written off as a crackpot idea after the man made his report; it was exactly that kind of a discovery, anyhow.

It was May when John de Terry appeared. Gordy was spading his garden. "Give me something to eat," said the voice behind Gordy's back.

Salva Gordy turned around and saw the small, dirty man who spoke. He rubbed his mouth with the back of his hand. "You'll have to work for it," he said.

"All right." The newcomer set down his pack. "My name is John de Terry. I used to live here in Detroit."

Salva Gordy said, "So did I."

Gordy fed the man, and accepted a cigarette from him after they had eaten. The first puffs made him light-headed—it had been that long since he'd smoked—and through the smoke he looked at John de Terry amiably enough. Company would be all right, he thought. The pink mice had been company, of a sort; but it turned out that the mutation that made them hairless had also given them an appetite for meat. And after the morning when he had awakened to find tiny toothmarks in his leg, he'd had to destroy them. And there had been no other animal since, nothing but the ants.

"Are you going to stay?" Gordy asked.

De Terry said, "If I can. What's your name?" When Gordy told him, some of the animal look went out of his eyes, and wonder took its place. "*Doctor* Salva Gordy?" he asked. "Mathematics and physics in Pasadena?"

"Yes, I used to teach at Pasadena."

"And I studied there." John de Terry rubbed absently at his ruined clothes. "That was a long time ago. You didn't know me; I majored in biology. But I knew you."

Gordy stood up and carefully put out the stub of his cigarette. "It was too long ago," he said. "I hardly remember. Shall we work in the garden now?"

Together they sweated in the spring sunlight that afternoon, and Gordy discovered that what had been hard work for one man went quickly enough for two. They worked clear to the edge of the plot before the sun reached the horizon. John de Terry stopped and leaned on his spade, panting.

He gestured to the rank growth beyond Gordy's patch. "We can make a bigger garden," he said. "Clear out that truck, and plant more food. We might even—" He stopped. Gordy was shaking his head.

"You can't clear it out," said Gordy. "It's rank stuff, a sort of crabgrass with a particularly tough root. I can't even cut it. It's all around here, and it's spreading."

De Terry grimaced. "Mutation?"

"I think so. And look." Gordy beckoned to the other man and led him to the very edge of the cleared area. He bent down, picked up something red and wriggling between his thumb and forefinger.

De Terry took it from his hand. "Another mutation?" He brought the thing close to his eyes. "It's almost like an ant," he said. "Except —well, the thorax is all wrong. And it's soft-bodied." He fell silent, examining the thing.

He said something under his breath, and threw the insect from him. "You wouldn't have a microscope, I suppose? No—and yet, that thing is hard to believe. It's an ant, but it doesn't seem to have a tracheal breathing system at all. It's something different."

"Everything's different," Gordy said. He pointed to a couple of abandoned rows. "I had carrots there. At least, I thought they were carrots; when I tried to eat them they made me sick." He sighed heavily. "Humanity has had its chance, John," he said. "The atomic bomb wasn't enough; we had to turn everything into a weapon. Even I, I made a weapon out of something that had nothing to do with war. And our weapons have blown up in our faces."

De Terry grinned. "Maybe the ants will do better. It's their turn now."

"I wish it were." Gordy stirred earth over the boiling entrance to an anthole and watched the insects in their consternation. "They're too small, I'm afraid."

"Why, no. These ants are different, Dr. Gordy. Insects have always been small because their breathing system is so poor. But these are mutated. I think—I think they actually have lungs. They could grow, Dr. Gordy. And if ants were the size of men . . . they'd rule the world."

"Lunged ants!" Gordy's eyes gleamed. "Perhaps they will rule the world, John. Perhaps when the human race finally blows itself up once and for all . . ."

De Terry shook his head, and looked down again at his tattered, filthy clothes. "The next blow-up is the last blow-up," he said. "The ants come too late, by millions and millions of years."

He picked up his spade. "I'm hungry again, Dr. Gordy," he said.

They went back to the house and, without conversation, they ate. Gordy was preoccupied, and de Terry was too new in the household to force him to talk.

It was sundown when they had finished, and Gordy moved slowly to light a lamp. Then he stopped.

"It's your first night, John," he said. "Come down cellar. We'll start the generator and have real electric lights in your honor."

De Terry followed the older man down a flight of stairs, groping in the dark. By candlelight they worked over a gasoline generator; it was stiff from disuse, but once it started it ran cleanly. "I salvaged it from my own," Gordy explained. "The generator—and that."

He swept an arm toward a corner of the basement. "I told you I invented a weapon," he added. "That's it."

De Terry looked. It was as much like a cage as anything, he thought—the height of a man and almost cubical. "What does it do?" he asked.

For the first time in months, Salva Gordy smiled. "I can't tell you in English," he said. "And I doubt that you speak mathematics. The closest I can come is to say that it displaces temporal co-ordinates. Is that gibberish?"

"It is," said de Terry. "What does it do?"

"Well, the War Department had a name for it—a name they borrowed from H. G. Wells. They called it a time machine." He met de Terry's shocked, bewildered stare calmly. "A time machine," he repeated. "You see, John, we can give the ants a chance after all, if you like."

Fourteen hours later they stepped into the cage, its batteries charged again and its strange motor whining . . .

And, forty million years earlier, they stepped out onto quaking, humid soil.

Gordy felt himself trembling, and with an effort managed to stop. "No dinosaurs or saber-toothed tigers in sight," he reported.

"Not for a long time yet," de Terry agreed. Then, "My Lord!"

He looked around him with his mouth open wide. There was no wind, and the air was warm and wet. Large trees were clustered quite thickly around them—or what looked like trees; de Terry decided they were rather some sort of soft-stemmed ferns or fungi. Overhead was deep cloud.

Gordy shivered. "Give me the ants," he ordered.

Silently de Terry handed them over. Gordy poked a hole in the soft earth with his finger and carefully tilted the flask, dropped one of the ant queens he had unearthed in the back yard. From her belly hung a slimy mass of eggs. A few yards away—it should have been farther, he thought, but he was afraid to get too far from de Terry and the machine—he made another hole and repeated the process.

There were eight queens. When the eighth was buried he flung the bottle away and came back to de Terry.

"That's it," he said.

De Terry exhaled. His solemn face cracked in a sudden embarrassed smile. "I—I guess I feel like God," he said. "Good Lord, Dr. Gordy! Talk about your great moments in history—this is all of them! I've been thinking about it, and the only event I can remember that measures up is the Flood. Not even that. We've created a race!"

"If they survive, we have." Gordy wiped a drop of condensed moisture off the side of his time machine and puffed. "I wonder how they'll get along with mankind," he said.

They were silent for a moment, considering. From somewhere in the fern jungle came a raucous animal cry. Both men looked up in quick apprehension, but moments passed and the animal did not appear.

Finally de Terry said, "Maybe we'd better go back."

"All right." Stiffly they climbed into the closet-sized interior of the time machine.

Gordy stood with his hand on the control wheel, thinking about the ants. Assuming that they survived—assuming that in forty million years they grew larger and developed brains—what would happen? Would men be able to live in peace with them? Would it—might it not make men brothers, joined against an alien race?

Might this thing prevent human war, and—his thoughts took an insane leap—could it have prevented the war that destroyed Gordy's family?

Beside him, de Terry stirred restlessly. Gordy jumped, and turned the wheel, and was in the dark mathematical vortex that might have been a fourth dimension.

They stopped the machine in the middle of a city, but the city was not Detroit. It was not a human city at all.

The machine was at rest in a narrow street, half blocking it. Around them towered conical metal structures, some of them a hundred feet high. There were vehicles moving in the street, one coming toward them and stopping.

"Dr. Gordy!" de Terry whispered. "Do you see them?"

Salva Gordy swallowed. "I see them," he said.

He stepped out of the time machine and stood waiting to greet the race to which he had given life.

For these were the children of ants in the three-wheeled vehicle. Behind a transparent windshield he could see them clearly.

De Terry was standing close behind him now, and Gordy could feel the younger man's body shaking. "They're ugly things," Gordy said mildly.

"Ugly! They're filthy!"

The antlike creatures were as big as a man, but hard-looking and as obnoxious as black beetles. Their eyes, Gordy saw with surprise, had mutated more than their bodies. For, instead of faceted insect eyes, they possessed iris, cornea, and pupil—not round, or vertical like a cat's eyes, or horizontal like a horse's eyes, but irregular and blotchy. But they seemed like a vertebrate's eyes, and they were strange and unnatural in the parchment blackness of an ant's bulged head.

Gordy stepped forward, and simultaneously the ants came out of their vehicle. For a moment they faced each other, the humans and the ants, silently.

"What do I do now?" Gordy asked de Terry over his shoulder.

De Terry laughed—or gasped. Gordy wasn't sure. "Talk to them," he said. "What else is there to do?"

Gordy swallowed. He resolutely did not attempt to speak in English to these creatures, knowing as surely as he knew his name that English—and probably any other language involving sound—would be incomprehensible to them. But he found himself smiling pacifically to them, and that was of course as bad . . . the things had no expressions of their own that he could see, and certainly they would have no precedent to help interpret a human smile.

Gordy raised his hand in the semantically sound gesture of peace, and waited to see what the insects would do.

They did nothing.

Gordy bit his lip and, feeling idiotic, bowed stiffly to the ants.

The ants did nothing. De Terry said from behind, "Try talking to them, Dr. Gordy."

"That's silly," Gordy said. "They can't hear." But it was no sillier than anything else. Irritably, but making the words very clear, he said, "We . . . are . . . friends."

The ants did nothing. They just stood there, with the unwinking pupiled eyes fixed on Gordy. They didn't shift from foot to foot as a human might, or scratch themselves, or even show the small movement of human breathing. They just stood there.

"Oh, for heaven's sake," said de Terry. "Here, let me try."

He stepped in front of Gordy and faced the ant-things. He pointed to himself. "I am human," he said. "Mammalian." He pointed to the ants. "You are insects. That—" he pointed to the time machine—"took us to the past, where we made it possible for you to exist." He waited for reaction, but there wasn't any. De Terry clicked his tongue and began again. He pointed to the tapering metal structures. "This is your city," he said.

Gordy, listening to him, felt the hopelessness of the effort. Something disturbed the thin hairs at the back of his skull, and he reached absently to smooth them down. His hand encountered something hard and inanimate—not cold, but, like spongy wood, without temperature at all. He turned around. Behind them were half a dozen larger ants. Drones, he thought—or did ants have drones? "John," he said softly . . . and the inefficient, fragile-looking pincer that had touched him clamped his shoulder. There was no strength to it, he thought at once. Until he moved, instinctively, to get away, and then a thousand sharp serrations slipped through the cloth of his coat and into the skin. It was like catching oneself on a cluster of tiny fishhooks. He shouted, "John! Watch out!"

De Terry, bending low for the purpose of pointing at the caterpillar treads of the ant vehicle, straightened up, startled. He turned to run, and was caught in a step. Gordy heard him yell, but Gordy had troubles of his own and could spare no further attention for de Terry.

When two of the ants had him, Gordy stopped struggling. He felt warm blood roll down his arm, and the pain was like being flayed.

From where he hung between the ants, he could see the first two, still standing before their vehicle, still motionless.

There was a sour reek in his nostrils, and he traced it to the ants that held him, and wondered if he smelled as bad to them. The two smaller ants abruptly stirred and moved forward rapidly on eight thin legs to the time machine. Gordy's captors turned and followed them, and for the first time since the scuffle he saw de Terry. The younger man was hanging limp from the lifted forelegs of a single ant, with two more standing guard beside. There was pulsing blood from a wound on de Terry's neck. Unconscious, Gordy thought mechanically, and turned his head to watch the ants at the machine.

It was a disappointing sight. They merely stood there, and no one moved. Then Gordy heard de Terry grunt and swear weakly. "How are you, John?" he called.

De Terry grimaced. "Not very good. What happened?"

Gordy shook his head, and sought for words to answer. But the two ants turned in unison from the time machine and glided toward de Terry, and Gordy's words died in his throat. Delicately one of them extended a foreleg to touch de Terry's chest.

Gordy saw it coming. "John!" he shrieked—and then it was all over, and de Terry's scream was harsh in his ear and he turned his head away. Dimly from the corner of his eye he could see the sawlike claws moving up and down, but there was no life left in de Terry to protest.

Salva Gordy sat against a wall and looked at the ants who were looking at him. If it hadn't been for what had been done to de Terry, he thought, there would really be nothing to complain about.

It was true that the ants had given him none of the comforts that humanity lavishes on even its criminals . . . but they had fed him, and allowed him to sleep—when it suited their convenience, of course —and there were small signs that they were interested in his comfort, in their fashion. When the pulpy mush they first offered him came up thirty minutes later, his multi-legged hosts brought him a variety of foods, of which he was able to swallow some fairly palatable fruits. He was housed in a warm room. And, if it had neither chairs nor windows, Gordy thought, that was only because ants had no use for these themselves. And he couldn't ask for them.

That was the big drawback, he thought. That . . . and the memory of John de Terry.

He squirmed on the hard floor until his shoulder blades found a new spot to prop themselves against, and stared again at the committee of ants who had come to see him.

They were working an angular thing that looked like a camera—at least, it had a glittering something that might be a lens. Gordy stared into it sullenly. The sour reek was in his nostrils again. . . .

Gordy admitted to himself that things hadn't worked out just as he had planned. Deep under the surface of his mind—just now beginning to come out where he could see it—there had been a furtive hope. He had hoped that the rise of the ants, with the help he had given them, would aid and speed the rise of mankind. For hatred, Gordy knew, started in the recoil from things that were different. A man's first enemy is his family—for he sees them first—but he sides with them against the families across the way. And still his neighbors are allies against the ghettos and Harlems of his town—and his town to him is the heart of the nation—and his nation commands life and death in war.

For Gordy, there had been a buried hope that a separate race would make a whipping boy for the passions of humanity. And that, if there was struggle, it would not be between man and man, but between the humans . . . and the ants.

There had been this buried hope, but the hope was denied. For the ants simply had not allowed man to rise.

The ants put up their cameralike machine, and Gordy looked up in expectation. Half a dozen of them left, and two stayed on. One was the smallish creature with a bangle on the foreleg, who seemed to be his personal jailer; the other was a stranger to Gordy, as far as he could tell.

The two ants stood motionless for a period of time that Gordy found tedious. He changed his position, and lay on the floor, and thought of sleeping. But sleep would not come. There was no evading the knowledge that he had wiped out his own race—annihilated them by preventing them from birth, forty million years before his own time. He was like no other murderer since Cain, Gordy thought, and wondered that he felt no blood on his hands.

There was a signal that he could not perceive, and his guardian ant came forward to him, nudged him outward from the wall. He moved as he was directed—out the low exit-hole (he had to navigate it on hands and knees) and down a corridor to the bright day outside.

The light set Gordy blinking. Half blind, he followed the bangled ant across a square to a conical shed. More ants were waiting there, circled around a litter of metal parts. Gordy recognized them at once. It was his time machine, stripped piece by piece.

After a moment the ant nudged him again, impatiently, and Gordy understood what they wanted. They had taken the machine apart for study, and they wanted it put together again.

Pleased with the prospect of something to do with his fingers and his brain, Gordy grinned and reached for the curious ant-made tools. . . .

He ate four times, and slept once, never moving from the neighborhood of the cone-shaped shed. And then he was finished.

Gordy stepped back. "It's all yours," he said proudly. "It'll take you anywhere. A present from humanity to you."

The ants were very silent. Gordy looked at them and saw drone-ants in the group, all still as statues.

"Hey!" he said in startlement, unthinking. And then the needle-jawed ant claw took him from behind.

Gordy had a moment of nausea—and then terror and hatred swept it away.

Heedless of the needles that laced his skin, he struggled and kicked against the creatures that held him. One arm came free, leaving gobbets of flesh behind, and his heavy-shod foot plunged into a pulpy eye. The ant made a whistling, gasping sound and stood erect on four hairy legs.

Gordy felt himself jerked a dozen feet into the air, then flung free in the wild, silent agony of the ant. He crashed into the ground, cowering away from the staggering monster. Sobbing, he pushed himself to his feet; the machine was behind him; he turned and blundered into it a step ahead of the other ants, and spun the wheel.

A hollow insect leg, detached from the ant that had been closest to him, was flopping about on the floor of the machine; it had been that close.

Gordy stopped the machine where it had started, on the same quivering, primordial bog, and lay crouched over the controls for a long time before he moved.

He had made a mistake, he and de Terry; there weren't any doubts left at all. And there was . . . there *might* be a way to right it.

He looked out at the Coal Measure forest. The fern trees were not the fern trees he had seen before; the machine had been moved in space. But the time, he knew, was identically the same; trust the machine for that. He thought: I gave the world to the ants, right here. I can take it back. I can find the ants I buried and crush them underfoot . . . or intercept myself before I bury them. . . .

He got out of the machine, suddenly panicky. Urgency squinted his eyes as he peered around him.

Death had been very close in the ant city; the reaction still left Gordy limp. And was he safe here? He remembered the violent animal scream he had heard before and shuddered at the thought of furnishing a casual meal to some dinosaur . . . while the ant queens lived safely to produce their horrid young.

A gleam of metal through the fern trees made his heart leap. Burnished metal here could mean but one thing—the machine!

Around a clump of fern trees, their bases covered with thick club mosses, he ran, and saw the machine ahead. He raced toward it— then came to a sudden stop, slipping on the damp ground. For there were *two* machines in sight.

The farther machine was his own, and through the screening mosses he could see two figures standing in it, his own and de Terry's.

But the nearer was a larger machine, and a strange design.

And from it came a hastening mob—not a mob of men, but of black insect shapes racing toward him.

Of course, thought Gordy, as he turned hopelessly to run—of course, the ants had had infinite time to work in. Time enough to build a machine after the pattern of his own—and time to realize what they had to do to him, to ensure their own race safety.

Gordy stumbled, and the first of the black things was upon him.

As his panicky lungs filled with air for the last time, Gordy knew what animal had screamed in the depths of the Coal Measure forest.

The Conqueror

Mark Clifton

Not all mutants are two-headed monsters or beady-eyed super-ants. Mutations occur in the plant kingdom as well . . . and, as this crisp little story deftly shows, a trifling shift in the genetic structure of the innocent dahlia could have extraordinary consequences for mankind.

The late Mark Clifton was a California-based industrial engineer and management consultant. His novel They'd Rather Be Right, *written in collaboration with Frank Riley, won the Hugo award in 1955.*

FACTS ON THE CULTURE OF DAHLIAS

1. The dahlia does not breed true from seed. Every seedling is a mutant.
2. A favorable mutant is propagated by tuber division, and as such remains reasonably fast.
3. It is possible to average ten plants from one each year. In twelve years one could have a hundred billion plants from one mutation.
4. Every gardener who grows dahlias throws away bushels of unwanted tubers. He has speculated numerous times on what a bountiful food supply they would make if they were only edible.
5. The dahlia is not too fussy about its soil, and with proper selection and care it may be matured from the equator to the arctic.

6. The dahlia grows wild in Guatemala, and through the centuries has self-seeded into endless mutations. It is reasonable to assume that one of these mutations might have peculiar properties —most peculiar indeed.

Padre Tomás christened him Juan Rafael de la Medina Torres, and so of naturally he was called Pepe. By the time he was of five years his body had begun to lose its infant roundness and his Indian cheekbones already showed their promise. Under his tangled black hair and behind his snapping black eyes there were dreams.

For one who knew only the path leading down the side of the volcano to the village at its foot, where also stood the mission, or the path leading up the side of the mountain to his papa's precarious corn and bean patches, or the path leading around the side of the volcano and down to the coffee finca, these were dreams indeed.

His papa would shake his head in slow bewilderment and remind Pepe, without too much affection or harshness, either, that instead of conquering the world he would better think more about gathering the grass to dry his mama's weaving, or to thatch the roof, or sleep upon the dirt floor of their hut.

Sometimes Pepe was to be a powerful brujo, even more respected than the wizard of the village—yes, much more than such a one who was old and without teeth and did not use his magic powers to make people do things. When he became so powerful, then would he torture and shame his sister for her taunts and jibes. Of naturally, he would not hurt her too much, for that would make Padre Tomás angry with him. So, after he had caused her enough suffering then would he forgive her and dress her as rich as the señora norteamericana he saw one day in the village market place.

But most of the time he dreamed much grander dreams than that. He dreamed of being even as el Presidente de Guatemala. Pepe had never seen el Presidente who lived in a fine palace in Guatemala City, but he suspected that such a one might be almost as grand as Padre Tomás himself.

Then there would be plenty of tortillas and beans always. Everyone could pack his belly so tight it would glisten like a shining gourd in the sun. No, that was not too much for such a powerful politico as he would be. To all the world he would become even as a father. It would be necessary for him first to conquer the world, and perhaps he would have to punish people a little to make them respect him, but then he would give it of all these things.

Such were the dreams of Pepe, christened Juan Rafael de la Medina Torres.

So it was until one day.

Of naturally, Pepe knew the wild dahlia roots were not fit to eat. All the world knows that much, even that ignorant señora norteameri-cana who knew nothing else, no nothing never at all. The silly ques-tions she asked about every little thing. Still, the dahlia tubers were so succulent to look upon, almost like the yam, each time he dug them up he would taste them a little, just perhaps.

One day while he was supposed to be gathering grass he acciden-tally tugged and strained and finally pulled up one dahlia. It was a fine one with a big stalk and many tubers. Tentatively, he broke one of the tubers and tasted of it. A look of bliss came over his face, for it was indeed good to eat.

His sister, ever loud in the mouth, was hiding in a grevile tree, spying on him. She scrambled to the ground and ran tattling to her mama that Pepe was eating of the dirt again. Mama wearily lay down her weaving of the grass mats and stood to her feet. Ordinarily Pepe would have run away to hide when he saw her coming, shouting im-precations at him, but this time he sat and handed his mamacita a piece of the tuber when she came up to him.

His unusual conduct so startled her that instead of cuffing at him, she stopped and sniffed at the root suspiciously. The same rapture spread over her face when she tasted. She carefully gathered up the tightly packed bunch of tubers containing the crown where the next year's plant buds lay dormant and waiting.

Marguerita, the sister, watched them both with wide eyes and with her buck-toothed mouth closed for once. Wiping her nose with her finger, she came closer, but not so close that Pepe could strike out and hit her. She stretched out her hand for a taste. Her slanting eyes stretched wider still and her mouth hung open in surprise when Pepe as well as her mama freely offered her bits of the tuber. The little wild one tasted also of the root.

No one looked on in surprise when she threw her arms about her little brother and called him "Pepito." Even this unheard-of action did not ruffle his serenity.

Now with care the three of them uprooted all the other dahlias in the glade beside the path, but these were harsh and bitter. Only this one plant was good of the taste.

Mama handled her machete as skillfully as a surgeon's scalpel when she split the crown again and again, so that each bud had one tuber hanging below it for stored food to grow upon. While Pepe and his sister stood by and watched, she planted the ten tubers in the rich volcanic earth close by the doorway of their hut. There she could watch and care for them tenderly.

Papa would think she had gone sick in the head if he knew she was growing the dahlia, so she cut a small bit from the end of one of the tubers and saved it for him.

All through the rest of the day, she and her children worked peacefully and industriously together. So long as he could return frequently to look upon the place where the tubers had been planted, Pepe was happy. He gathered more grass to weave than ever before.

Marguerita, too, for the first time, bent herself willingly to the task of learning to weave of the petates. She stopped her work only to get up occasionally and look upon the moist soft earth where the dahlias had been planted. Mama did not scold her for this, for mama also found that she must look upon the spot a little time more or less.

The sun was down and the cold wet clouds were swirling around the mountain when papa came back from his day of work in the coffee finca. His black eyes glittered with sudden anger and his face became as the thunder of Fuego when he saw no smoke filtering through the grass thatch of their roof, and smelled no odor of beans cooking for his supper. But the unusual sight of his wife and children weaving industriously in the dusk stopped his outburst.

When mama saw his shadow darken the doorway, she sprang to her feet like a light and active girl again. She held out a piece of the tuber as he came through the doorway. He took it, looked at it, and back at her.

"Eat of it," she said.

With bewilderment and perhaps a little fear replacing his anger, he bit tentatively at the edge of the fragment. With the one taste his face took on the same rapture which his family had known all through the afternoon.

It was the middle of the next day before any of them knew hunger again.

In several more days the bliss faded from their faces as the narcotic value of the tuber wore away. Pepe and his sister fought like wild animals again, while mama cuffed and shouted at them as ever. Papa was alternately harsh and silent as usual.

Still, all the family carefully watched the patch where the dahlias had been planted. Even in their most angry scuffling, Pepe and Marquerita never failed to keep clear of the dahlia bed.

The pale and succulent shoots came to the surface of the ground and grew with great rapidity. Daily, and almost hourly, the family watched the ten plants to see that no worm or bug damaged the shoots, to see that the bony wild chickens did not pick off the tender buds, to see that the yellow dog did not make a bed among them where it could ease its rickety bones.

In two months the dahlias began to bloom, and the Torres family knew that under the cover of the soil new clusters of tubers were forming. The leaves, the petals of the flower, these were not good of the taste, but when the blossoms opened there was a delicate perfume which wafted through the doorway of the hut and around the yard.

Again, in the fragrance, the Torres family became peaceful and good. Now there was no harsh word spoken. Now papa was no longer to be found lying in the perfume of the suquinay tree drinking of his chica where one minute he would threaten his friends with the machete and the next he would weep with remorse. Marguerita no longer teased Pepe but spent her days crooning monotonously at her weaving. No longer did Pepe fashion of the traps to catch and torture the parrots.

No longer were there the many and many sins to confess to Padre Tomás.

Finally Padre Tomás could bear it no longer. Well he knew his Indians, and he knew there must be something most wrong at the house of Torres. No Indians could possibly be as good as these pretended in the confessional. He began to fear for their very souls.

So it was in his rounds he came upon the Torres hut one day when they were digging the plants of the dahlia. He looked with great surprise upon their careful handling of this wild plant, and even greater surprise upon the serenity and rapture of their faces.

When Mama Torres saw him coming, she broke off a bit of tuber and handed it to the good Padre, indicating that he should eat it. For the sake of his work and his success among his children, the Padre Tomás had endured many things. He showed no hesitancy of eating this acrid and bitter root if that was needed to regain their confidence.

Standing there with the black earth torn up about his feet, at the doorway of the hut, suddenly Padre Tomás felt as though the choir of Heaven itself burst into rapture in his head.

This time there were more than a hundred plants. Padre Tomás stayed and helped until the last was safely back in the good earth.

When he found that he also wished no more food until the following day, he came back to the house of Torres and instructed them, "Guard them with care, my children."

They had saved a few loose tubers and they gave him a share. He took them back to the mission and planted them.

When Pepe was of the years eight, there were a thousand plants. By the time he was nine there were ten thousand plants spread over all the village. Now there was peace and prosperity in the village. No man's hand was raised against his brother. Even the chickens, the pigs, and the dogs received good care.

Long since, Padre Tomás had sent tubers of the plant to other villages and missions. Before very long all of Guatemala was eating regularly of the dahlia.

It had been well known to everyone that the military was carefully plotting the overthrow of el Presidente, *mañana,* and some day they might even be moved to do so. So well along was the plot that another plot back of that was formed to overthrow that dictatorship in its turn.

Now one by one the leaders of the revolution, and the second revolution, found they preferred to cultivate their gardens of the dahlia. They found they preferred to spend long hours and many successful conferences with one another in determining new ways by which they could save money for the taxed, even to send the soldiers to help the citizens in peaceful pursuits.

The politicos stopped robbing the treasury and sending monies to banks in foreign lands to live in luxury after the revolutions they engineered to give them excuse to leave the country had succeeded. They began to build of the schools and roads for the people instead.

In all Guatemala there was no unhappiness, no laziness, no evil. Every day was a fiesta, for fiesta was most of all the time for enjoyment. What greater enjoyment could there be than that of growing the dahlia? Each day the market place must be piled high with the tubers so that every city dweller might receive his share of the miracle food.

And the market place was constantly filled with tourists as from all the world who bought of the plant to send to their homes and friends for the growing there.

As everywhere, at the embassies at Guatemala City there had been the endless game of spying and counter-spying. No norteamericano businessman made a move but what a countermove was made by the English counterpart. Every Hindu watched a Moslem, and every Moslem watched a Hindu. Even Wun Sing Low, laundryman for twenty years, was now known to be a Red spy, sending out his messages by marks upon the shirts of businessmen. All were enemies to the Soviet, and that embassy chose to see a world threat in the blink of every peon's eyes.

The governments of the world were accustomed to these voluminous reports, and they sifted through them with yawns of boredom. A man's diplomatic worth was judged by the poundage of his reports and the frequency of the crises he might uncover. Even so, it took some time before the governments became aware of the cessation of such reports from Guatemala.

Peace and prosperity and goodwill permeated all the reports from all the spy headquarters. No man could believe ill of his neighbor, for no man could partake of evil, or evil thought, where the dahlia was to be eaten.

Moscow, ever wary in its inferiority complex, and never ceasing to jockey for position, was the first of the capitals to summon its embassy's return. It demanded an account of these un-Marxian reports of serenity and peace in a capitalistic country. It wished to know why if there was no indigenous trouble some had not been manufactured.

The embassy took with it a plentiful supply of the tubers of the dahlia and ate heavily of them. It had been learned that the human body could store the food value of the dahlia for months and they were taking no chances. Throughout the routine of their torture, they maintained their rapture. Finally their inquisitors had no course left but to taste of the dahlia itself to check these fantastic tales and so give the lie to the diplomats.

Then the inquisitors in turn must endure the torture, for they no longer wished to carry forth their duties, and in turn their questioners ate. It became that there were none left but the Politbureau itself to carry on the torture since there were none others to be trusted to carry out the true democratic blessings upon their fellow men.

So it came about that one by one the members of the Politbureau tasted of the dahlia, even to the leader himself.

All of this took much time, and meanwhile the heads of other nations who were not so suspicious of every shadow, and not so inaccessible, were eating regularly of the dahlia.

When finally the sincere word of peace and goodwill came ringing from Moscow to all the world, it was echoed back with all sincerity.

By the end of twelve years, over all the world the dahlia grew and thrived and was eaten. The Bering Strait Eskimo, the Congo Pigmy, the Australian Bushman, the Tibetan yak herder, each had his carefully bred offshoot of the dahlia. For the first time within written history the wretched masses of India and the famine-accustomed Chinese knew the full belly and peace and progress.

So it became in the world. There was but goodwill and happiness for all.

Pepe was now seventeen, and well beyond the age to marry. But there was not the economic urgency there once had been and children were permitted to remain without so much responsibility a little longer.

But today he was seventeen and today was his wedding day. Today was a most important day and he would not be called Pepe. He would be called for this one day by his true name of Juan Rafael de la Medina Torres. Now he was a grown man and his village was prosperous and everyone was happy.

Dimly he was aware that there was a world beyond his own village. But like all his forebears it had no reality for him. In truth he still knew only the path leading down the side of the volcano to the village; or the path up the mountain to where they once had brown corn and beans and now grew dahlias; or the path around the volcano and down to the coffee finca.

Barefoot still, but with his finest knee breeches striped like peppermint candy, with his red cummerbund wrapped around his slender waist, he trotted down the path toward the mission where Maria waited and where the good Padre Tomás would make them as one person. This was his world.

Half walking, half running in eagerness, the sight of the particular glade where he had first found the dahlia recalled his memory of himself as a little boy.

He laughed joyously and threw his shoulders back and breathed the mountain air of the morning in ecstasy. "What a one I was," he called aloud and shouted again with laughter. "I remember I was so fierce in those days. Why, I was going to conquer all the world!"

Liquid Life

Ralph Milne Farley

"Ralph Milne Farley" was the pseudonym of the late Roger Sherman Hoar, a man of many careers. Under his rightful name he acquired three degrees at Harvard and distinguished himself as an engineer, a physicist, and a patent attorney. He was an expert on ballistics who served as a technical officer in World War I and was responsible for many inventions, including a device for aiming large guns. Late in life he held high political office in Wisconsin. Meanwhile, as "Farley," he was one of the most prolific and popular writers of imaginative fiction of the 1920's and 1930's, delighting the readers of Argosy, Top Notch, *and many other magazines with such novels as* The Radio Man, The Golden City, *and* The Radio Planet.*

Farley's "Liquid Life," a lighthearted account of a mutated virus that attains intelligent consciousness, was first published in 1936. Most science-fiction stories of that era are unreadable today, but the charm and good humor of Farley's storytelling have kept his work alive.

Millionaire Metcalf drew his Inverness cape more tightly about his tall, spare frame and shivered slightly, although it was a warm June day.

"That's Salt Pond, Dee!" he announced, with a wave of his hand.

His companion, a broad-shouldered blond young man, stared with interest at the little body of water flanked by pine-clad slopes.

Its dark and turbid surface seemed to absorb, rather than cast back, the reflection of the fleecy clouds floating lazily overhead. The water heaved and rolled slightly, though there was no perceptible breeze. Dee remembered having once seen just this sort of sluggish, undulant motion in a maggoty cistern full of liquid swill. He, too, shivered.

A grim smile spread across the lean face of his millionaire patron.

"So you feel it too, eh?" asked Metcalf. "Well, you haven't yet seen the half of it. Not a lily pad nor a reed, you will note. The fish are all gone. There are not even any bugs on the surface." Then, as Dee approached the water's edge, "Careful there! Don't let any of the spray get on you—it burns like an acid."

Dee knelt on the beach and gingerly filled several glass-stoppered bottles with water from the pond. Then he and Metcalf walked slowly and thoughtfully down the road until they came to a pasture at the end of the pond.

"Here is the latest victim," Metcalf announced. "It has not been disturbed."

Lying on the grass, about fifty feet from the water, was a dead, half-eaten cow. Dee stooped down to examine it.

"See how the legs and tail taper off to a point at their upper ends, as though they had been dipped in acid," he said. "I pulled a half-dead frog out of a snake's mouth once, and the whole rear end of the poor frog had been dissolved to a point, just like that. You don't suppose—"

"No," Metcalf replied. "There is nothing in that pond large enough to eat a cow. I have had it dredged with dragnets from end to end. The nets were eaten away, and several of the men got badly burned by drops of water, but not a thing did they bring to the surface."

"Well," Dee said, "I've seen enough to start on. Let's get me back to Boston, so that I can analyze these samples."

Dee entered the laboratory of John Dee Service, Inc., and placed his glass-stoppered bottles on the long central table strewn with chemical paraphernalia.

Along the right-hand wall ran a table containing a radio set and some partially dissected cats. A white-coated young man, dark and with a pointed black moustache, laid down the scalpel with which he had been working on one of the cats and strolled over to the central table.

Along the left-hand wall ran a table, littered like the central one with beakers, test tubes, and such. Here a stocky, bearded young man in a gray smock was working. He too got up and joined the group about the new arrival.

"Well, fellows," Dee announced, "old man Metcalf has given us a chance to repay him for the money he advanced to us."

"I hope," the tall cat-dissector stated seriously, "that the assignment is something which will be of some real use to the world."

"Bah!" spat the stocky bullet-headed one. "You two fellows make me tired. All that Jack thinks about is playing square with an old friend. All that Ivan thinks about is the welfare of the so-called human race. Me, I'm practical. I hope that this job will get the load of debt off our heads. Go on and tell us about it, Jack."

Dee rapidly sketched the lethal effect of the waters of Salt Pond and the strange fate of the partially devoured cows. "It looks to me altogether too pat," he insisted. "The acid effect of the water, for the chemist Jack Dee to investigate; its lethal effect, for the biochemist Hans Schmidt; and the cow-eating entity, for the biologist Ivan Zenoff. Just a kindly invention of Metcalf's so as to free us of our debt without insulting us by merely canceling it."

"Salt Pond?" asked Zenoff interestedly. "Is it really salt, Jack? Way up in the White Mountains?"

"Yes, Ivan," Dee replied. "Almost like seawater. Metcalf transplanted a lot of flounders, eels, crabs, and mussels there about ten years ago; and they all did very nicely until this year."

"Salt water, eh?" Zenoff said thoughtfully. "The elixir of life. Life originated in the sea, and when it had evolved enough so that it could crawl out onto dry land, it carried the sea with it in its bloodstream. Every living cell of our bodies is lapped by the waves of the sea, or it could not survive."

"But from what you say, Jack," Schmidt interposed, "I don't believe that you will find that it analyzes like ordinary seawater now. Your description of the remains of the dead cows sounds to me as though they had been dissolved in some very powerful, burning acid."

"We'll soon see." Dee pulled a laboratory smock over his head. "Ivan, you get back to your cats' brains; and Hans, you get back to your filterable virus. Let me tackle this. This seems to be a question in inorganic chemistry."

He sat down at his work bench, poured some of one of his samples of pond water into a test tube, and set to work. His two partners returned to their own benches. For about an hour there was silence in the laboratory.

Then suddenly Dee cried out in pain. "Burned myself!" he shouted, and looked frantically around for an antidote.

Then Schmidt rushed over and poured something from a small brown bottle onto Dee's hand.

"Dilute carbolic," he announced, in response to a questioning look.

"What! An acid to counteract an acid? How absurd!" Dee declared.

"Well, it worked!"

"But what on earth made you think of using carbolic, Hans?"

"I merely acted instinctively," Schmidt rather sheepishly replied. "When anything goes wrong, a bacteriologist instinctively reaches for his carbolic acid. That's all."

Ivan Zenoff joined them.

"Let me see the hand. Um! Pretty badly burned. I'll dress it for you." He returned to his own bench, got some gauze bandage and salve, and neatly wrapped up the injured member.

"How far had you got, Jack?" Schmidt inquired.

"Nowhere," Dee admitted. "It is nothing but seawater, with—well—perhaps a slight excess of organic residue. But no acid; nothing to account for its burning effect."

"How does it react to litmus?"

"Why, I never tried. Took it for granted that it was acid." He dipped a small piece of lavender paper in the sample. If anything, it turned even bluer. "Hm! Certainly not acid. Perhaps it's some caustic alkali, and that's why the carbolic acid neutralized it."

"Too quick-acting for a caustic alkali, if you'd ask me," Schmidt commented. "Give me a sample with which to experiment. I have an idea."

For several days Dee and Schmidt worked on their analyses, while Zenoff busied himself with his cats.

Finally Dee admitted himself licked.

"It's nothing but seawater," he maintained.

"So?" asked Schmidt, his pale-blue eyes twinkling. "Chemically, perhaps yes. But *bio*chemically, no."

"What do you mean?"

"I mean that Salt Pond is infected with some new sort of very deadly filterable virus."

"And just what is a filterable virus?"

"Up until recently it was supposed that a filterable virus was merely a culture of germs so minute that even the finest porcelain filter could not remove them from the liquid. But early in 1936 it was discovered that the reason why these germs wouldn't filter out was that there were no germs there. The liquid itself was alive—a sort of living colloidal crystalline solution."

"Living?" exclaimed Zenoff, looking up from his dissection. "How can a liquid live?"

"What *is* life?" Schmidt countered. "Life is the ability to grow, to assimilate food, and to reproduce. Filterable viruses do all of that. A filterable virus is a living liquid."

"And you think that Salt Pond is infected with such a virus?" Dee asked.

"Yes. In fact, I've been able to grow some of the Salt Pond virus in a culture. That would account for the fact that a germicide saved your hand the other day."

"Say, look here," interposed Zenoff, getting up from his dissected cats, and joining them. "Here's a chance to try my experiment on a new form of life."

"You mean your proof that anesthesia does not dull the brain?" asked Dee.

"Exactly! By sinking two electrical contacts in the auditory center of the brain of an anesthetized cat, and by amplifying their impulse by means of radio tubes, I have reproduced in the loudspeaker whatever sounds enter the cat's ear. Unconsciousness doesn't affect the brain at all—it merely disconnects the mind. The cat's physical body keeps right on thinking, but she doesn't know it!"

"Well?" Dee encouraged.

"Well, it occurred to me that perhaps the living tissues of the brain merely served as a sort of aerial to pick up the sounds; and so I tried every other sort of living tissue I could obtain. But no go. My apparatus can pick up a sound only from the auditory center of a living brain. Now I shall make one final try with the—"

A crash on the table beside them caused the three men to look hastily around. One of Ivan Zenoff's cats, not yet operated upon, had jumped onto the bench, knocked over one of the bottles of Salt Pond water, and was now busily engaged in lapping it up, evidently relishing its saline taste.

"Why, the poor beast! She'll be horribly burned!" cried Dee. "Quick, Hans, the antiseptic!"

But too late! For with a shriek of pain the cat began turning somersaults on the bench.

To save his apparatus from destruction, Dee cuffed the cat into the sink, where it twitched convulsively for a moment, and then lay still.

"Quick-working poison!" Zenoff dryly observed, twirling his moustache. "Now, as I was saying when I was interrupted, I'm going to take my apparatus, and see if a filterable virus can pick up sounds. If not, and as I have already tried about everything else, then we are pretty safe in assuming that my phenomenon is one of brain activity."

"Look!" exclaimed Dee, pointing to the dead cat lying in the sink. For the cat's belly had opened up, and a slimy colorless liquid was oozing out.

Hastily he placed a glass stopper in the drain hole of the sink. Then, as the three men stood and watched, the cat slowly dissolved, until presently the sink was filled with nothing but a sluggish opalescent liquid, the surface of which throbbed and heaved.

"Liquid life!" Dee exclaimed. "This explains the dead cows."

"But," Schmidt objected, "the cow's head and legs and tail remained!"

"And so would the cat's have done," said Zenoff, "if the liquid had run down the drain. When it oozed out of the cow's belly, it undoubtedly sank into the ground before it had time to dissolve any more than the upper ends of the legs and tail."

"Let's dish this out," Dee suggested.

Schmidt brought over a two-gallon cylindrical glass jar and very carefully bailed up all the liquid with a granite-ware dipper.

"Now for my experiment," Zenoff announced, carrying the jar with its slimy, heaving contents over to his own bench and setting it down beside his radio. Switching on the current, he picked up a slender black rubber rod with two sharp metal points at its end connected to the radio set by two wires, and carefully dipped the contacts into the liquid.

"Hello there!" he shouted. But no sound came out of the loudspeaker.

"Well," said Hans Schmidt, shrugging his shoulders, "I guess this is the last proof necessary—"

"Hello there!" boomed the loudspeaker.

Zenoff jumped, and nearly dropped his contact points into the seething liquid.

"Well," remarked the loudspeaker, with exactly Schmidt's accent, "I guess this is the last proof necessary."

"Delayed rebroadcasting!" Zenoff exclaimed, his dark eyes flashing. "Say! This *is* something! A new phenomenon!"

"Let's dish this out," spoke the loudspeaker, this time in Dee's tones.

Dee's jaw dropped.

"Why, it repeats things in a different order than we said them!" he exclaimed.

"Fellows," Zenoff solemnly announced, "this isn't mere repeating! It's something more!"

"Huh! Perhaps the cat's brain is still active," scornfully sniffed Hans Schmidt.

. For about an hour the three friends sat around the dissolved dead cat, discussing what had happened, and advancing theory after theory, only to discard each one of them in turn.

Finally Zenoff reinserted his contacts in the jar and announced, "Well, fellows, I believe that this liquid, whether on account of the cat part of it, or the filterable virus part of it, has some sort of low-order intelligence. Now I'm going to holler something at it again."

"Fellows," interrupted the loudspeaker, "it is *you* who have the low order of intelligence. You—not I."

"Now the thing is improvising!" Zenoff exclaimed jubilantly.

But, although he held the electrical contacts in place, and talked and shouted, and finally read aloud from a book for several hours, not another sound came out of the loudspeaker.

The next morning, however, when he repeated the experiment, he got an immediate response.

"Read to me some more," boomed the loudspeaker. "Your thesis on the souls of cats was very interesting. Read me something about filterable viruses."

"Hey, Hans, do you hear that!" Zenoff shouted across the laboratory. "Bring us your thesis. This tub of suds wants to hear your thesis now."

"Don't call *me* a tub of suds!" sternly admonished the loudspeaker.

Schmidt and Dee both hastened over to Zenoff's bench.

"Well, of all the cockeyed performances!" Dee exclaimed. "Here are we, three supposedly sane individuals, carrying on a serious conversation with a radio set hooked up to a dead cat dissolved in some extremely caustic salt water!"

"The cat has nothing whatever to do with the matter," the loudspeaker interpolated. "I merely ate the cat. Do you imagine, Jack, that that apple which you were just eating when you entered the laboratory is what is talking to me through you?"

"Now, I know this is a frame-up," said Dee, and there was sadness in his tones. "Ivan, you're playing a trick on us."

"Indeed I'm not!" Zenoff indignantly exclaimed.

"Indeed he's not!" echoed the loudspeaker.

"No," said Zenoff. "We've stumbled onto something big! Those savants who evolved the theory that a filterable virus is liquid fire merely discovered a new order of being. We have discovered a new type of mind!"

"Or perhaps a mere mechanical thinking machine," Schmidt suggested.

"You, and your mechanistic philosophy," sneered Zenoff.

"Read me that thesis about filterable viruses!" boomed the loudspeaker imperatively.

"Yes, sir," Zenoff meekly replied, picking up the bound manuscript.

"That's better," said the loudspeaker, in a satisfied tone.

The rest of the day was spent by the three partners taking turns reading to the jar of colorless liquid.

When at five o'clock Zenoff reached out to remove the electrical contacts, the loudspeaker peremptorily commanded, "Stop! Don't cut me off! Keep on reading!"

"But we have to rest," Zenoff politely explained.

" 'Rest'? What is 'rest'?" the thing asked, and was not satisfied until Zenoff produced and read to it the *Encyclopaedia Britannica* article on "Sleep," and several of the cross-references. Then Zenoff was permitted to remove the contacts, and the three friends went home.

In the days that followed, they read aloud book after book, and thesis after thesis, to the insatiable liquid in the glass jar. They even read it the daily papers, and were astounded at the intelligent interest which it soon developed about current events.

But daily the liquid became more and more irritable and rude in its attitude toward them until finally Zenoff, exasperated, threatened to remove the contacts.

"Am I irritable?" asked the loudspeaker conciliatingly. "I am sorry. Let me think a moment." A long pause; then, "I believe that my trouble is due to insufficient saline content. Please add a little more salt to me."

Schmidt brought the salt, and put in a pinch at a time, stirring the liquid with a glass rod, until the liquid announced, "Okay. I feel fine now. Go on with the reading."

Dee sighed. "I believe we've got ourselves an 'old man of the sea,'" he said. Then, of course, he had to explain that allusion to the liquid.

When he had finished the explanation, the liquid spoke. "Not at all. You know, I believe that by putting my superior mind to work on your problems, I can help you solve them. All that I ask in return is food, salt, and water."

"What are you, anyway?" Zenoff blurted out. The three had never put this question to the thing—had never even discussed it in its presence.

"I've been thinking about that myself," came haltingly from the loudspeaker. "I am somewhat like the filterable viruses, of which you have read to me, and yet I am different. I am liquid life. I was once a part of the life of Salt Pond. How long that life persisted there, I cannot say; because back in those days we knew nothing of what you human beings call 'time.' I have enjoyed learning how the world seems to you. We, the virus of the pond, never knew anything except pure thought, until you brought me here."

"Hold on!" Dee interrupted. "You speak of 'I,' 'we,' 'the virus in pond,' 'the rest of me'; it's quite confusing. Just what is your relationship to the virus that is left in the pond?"

"Your mere human mentality," the virus patronizingly replied, "is not able to grasp the significance of that relationship. I am a distinct individual.

"Yet, if you were to divide me into two jars, each would be I, and the other would be someone else. If you were to feed me, let me grow, subdivide me until there were enough of us to overwhelm the earth, nevertheless we, they, I, whatever you choose to call it, would all still be me, capable of recombining and redividing indefinitely. The human language has no personal pronouns applicable to a filterable virus."

That night, on their way home from the laboratory, Zenoff remarked to the others, "You know, that crack of the virus' about overwhelming the earth threw rather a chill into me. We must be careful not to feed him, it, them, too much."

The next morning, when Schmidt was salting the virus, his hand slipped and dumped in about half a cupful of salt. Instantly the liquid in the jar commenced to boil. Tongues of foam, like the tentacles of a small octopus, leaped from its surface, only to fall back again. And from the loudspeaker there came a harsh croaking, "Gimme more salt! Hooray! Feed me! Feed me more dead cats! I want to grow—and divide—and grow and divide. Conquer the earth. Eat everything—everybody!"

Zenoff leaped to the radio set and snapped it off.

"My God!" he exclaimed. "The thing's drunk!"

Dee got up thoughtfully from his own bench, and squared his broad shoulders. "We've a problem on our hands," he asserted. "It'll be weeks and weeks before the effect of that salt wears off."

"And," Schmidt added, "if we try to precipitate it out with silver nitrate, so as to get a silver chloride precipitate, the residual sodium nitrate, being mildly germicidal, may kill the poor thing."

"All that I can suggest is to dilute it," said Dee. He did some figuring on a piece of paper. "About ten gallons of water should do the trick."

They dumped the drunken liquid into a large tub, and added water until its pulsating boiling subsided.

"And now what?" asked Zenoff. "We have too much of it now."

"Pour most of it down the sink," Schmidt suggested. "The small remaining part would still have the mentality of the whole, according to its own theories of individuality."

"And," Dee grimly added, "the large quantity that went down the drain would eventually reach the ocean, and would feed and multiply there until it destroyed all marine life, and made the sea as burningly dangerous as Salt Pond now is. No!"

"My God!" Zenoff exclaimed. "That is what would happen, too, if Salt Pond ever got loose!"

"We've got to kill all but the small part which we save," Schmidt asserted callously.

"It would be like killing an old friend," Dee objected.

"But any part is equal to the whole," said Zenoff. "Come on!"

They dished back into the glass jar just the quantity which they had had before the unfortunate overdose of salt; and poured carbolic acid into what was left in the tub.

Then they inserted the electrodes in the jar, and listened.

"Food! Give me food!" came a faint voice from the loudspeaker.

"He's still alive!" Dee joyously exclaimed.

"And sober," Zenoff added, tossing in a piece of dead cat.

The voice came louder now.

"Thank you, my friends. There seems to be a gap in my memory. Tell me what happened."

They told him. They explained the analogy of human drunkenness. But they omitted all mention of the killing of the virus which had remained in the big tub.

"What became of the rest of me, of my brothers or my children? Oh, your language is so inexpressive!" the virus complained.

"We—poured it down the sink," Dee lied.

The liquid in the jar foamed fiercely for a moment. "You had no right to do that!" stormed its voice out of the radio set. "I—it—the rest of me—is dead now. Too much dilution with fresh water will kill us. I am dead now."

The three men exchanged significant glances, but said nothing. Finally the virus calmed down.

"You individuals cannot appreciate my loss. Although there is as much of me as there was originally, most of me is now dead and gone. It's too late to remedy that now, but don't let it happen again!"

Millionaire Metcalf's increasing insistency on a report on the mystery of Salt Pond presented a problem. The three young scientists did not dare tell their patron that a virus was responsible for the trouble, for he would have insisted on killing it off; and that would have infuriated the portion of the virus in the jar in their laboratory. To explain to Mr. Metcalf that their pet virus was an intelligent talking being would either secure them commitment to Danvers, if not believed; or, if believed, would start a veritable gold rush to get samples of the pond water. Jars of talking water would become a nationwide fad and a corresponding menace.

Doubtless the virus itself would have been able to solve this problem if they had dared to present the problem to it; but, remembering its fury at their killing the tubful of it, they didn't dare mention the possibility of their having to destroy the entire pond.

So they stalled their patron for several months, putting off the day of eventual showdown.

Meanwhile their business as consulting chemists prospered immensely. For, with the aid of the supermind of the virus in the glass jar, they were able to solve nearly every problem brought to them. Their reputation grew prodigiously. Business and money came pouring in. They had to enlarge their establishment and hire scores of assistants, specialists in every field.

This success so pleased their patron Metcalf that he indulgently overlooked their delay in solving his own problem. Finally they told him that they were on the verge of proving that the waters of the pond were immensely valuable.

They housed their virus in a special soundproof room, to which no one but the three heads of the firm was ever admitted. They hired a number of readers to read aloud in an adjoining room, continuously day and night, except when one of the three of them was in consultation with their mastermind ally. The voice of the reader was conveyed by microphone and loudspeaker into the soundproof holy of holies.

But finally the virus began a period of sulking. Schmidt carefully tested its salt content, but found it to be okay. The trouble appeared to be mental rather than physical. The virus was becoming fed up on its existence.

"What am I getting out of all this?" it complained. "You three fellows are becoming immensely rich on my brains. But money does me no good. All that I get out of life is a glass jar, plenty of dead fish to eat, and a lot of fool questions from members of an inferior race."

"Our wealth enables us to arrange for you to be read to, continuously," Dee remonstrated.

"Pure thought is palling on me," whined the virus. "I want to do something. Take me back to my pond again. Let me merge with the rest of me. Let me teach them what I have learned. Then you can bring a part of it back here, and teach me some more."

"I might just as well tell you, Virus," said Dee levelly, "that that is out of the question. You, so long as you are just you, are a benefactor of the human race; but, if the whole pond knew as much as you do about us, you would quantitatively become a menace. Stay with us, and be content to realize how much ahead of the rest of your brethren you are!"

"You don't understand," sulked the virus. "They—it—the rest of the pond—is me! I am one virus, one and inseparable, and I want the rest of me to know everything that I myself know. Oh, damn the inexpressibility of your language! I want the whole of me to have the joy of knowledge that this small part of me has."

"Knowledge doesn't seem to be making this small part of you very happy," Dee grimly commented.

He and his two associates remained obdurate; and the virus, after sulking for a day or two, finally appeared to become reconciled to their decision.

And then one day, when Dee and Schmidt and Zenoff entered the virus' room for a consultation, the glass jar was empty!

The respective reactions of the three associates were typical.

"What will become of the John Dee Service, Inc., now that our 'silent partner' is gone?" Schmidt exclaimed. "Will we three fellows be able to carry on, trading upon our acquired reputation?"

"My God, man!" Zenoff scornfully exclaimed. "Don't think of us at a time like this! What will become of the world if that thing gets loose and multiplies?"

"I'm thinking of the poor virus," Dee sadly interpolated. "It can't possibly live out of its jar. It has probably been sopped up by the carpet. It's dead. Our friend and partner is dead."

He cast his glance around the floor, looking for a wet spot, hoping to find enough dampness to dilute and feed and restore to life again. "Look!" he exclaimed, pointing toward a far corner, where squatted a hemispherical blob, like a jellyfish.

As they stared, the blob extended a long gelatinous arm toward them and then flowed into it like an amoeba, until the nigh extremity of the arm swelled up to become the entire animal. The operation was repeated. Again and again.

Dee snatched the empty glass jar from the table and laid it on the padded floor, with its open mouth toward the crawling creature, which promptly increased its rate of progress and crawled right in. Dee tipped up the jar and replaced it on the table. Hurriedly he hung the electrical contacts into the jar.

"My friends," spoke the loudspeaker, in an excited tone, "I have demonstrated the power of mind over matter. I have taught myself extensibility. I can walk! Mentally superior even to the human race, but physically lower even than an amoeba, I have now advanced my body one step up the scale of evolution!"

The three men flashed each other a glance. They were all thinking the same thing: let the virus' new accomplishment keep the virus happy, like a child with a new toy; but meanwhile let's strengthen the defenses, lest it escape.

"We'll put in a tile floor, if you wish, Virus," Dee suggested. "It might be more comfortable than a carpet for you to crawl over."

"That would be an excellent idea," judiciously stated the voice out of the loudspeaker. The virus seemed more affable than it had been for weeks. "And now that you fellows are so concerned about my comfort, I have a suggestion for your welfare. Why don't you make money, instead of earning it?"

"Just what is the difference?" asked Zenoff.

"Manufacture it, I mean," the virus explained.

"Could we—?" Schmidt eagerly began; but Dee cut in, "Counterfeiting is out!"

"Oh, I didn't mean counterfeiting," came laughing tones of the virus, "I mean alchemy."

"Alchemy?" in chorus.

"Yes. Alchemy. Making gold out of baser metals."

"Do you know how?" Schmidt eagerly exclaimed.

"N-no," the virus admitted. "Not yet. But why not? From what has been read to me here, I judge that transmutation is always automatically taking place among metals of the radium-uranium group; and that other elements have been transmuted in infinitesimal quantities by bombardment by neutrons, and beta rays, and such. I am sure that my mind can solve the problem, if you will read me everything that is known and has been written on the subject."

"Can you?" asked Schmidt, his pale-blue eyes eagerly wide.

"I wonder what would be the effect on the world," mused Zenoff, twirling his moustache ruminatively.

"Would it be legal?" asked Dee, his handsome face a puzzled frown.

"Why not?" snapped Schmidt, strangely tense, in contrast with his usual stolidity. "Is it any worse to make gold out of lead than to make lead pipe out of lead?"

"I suppose not," Dee replied dubiously.

"I still doubt its social effect," Zenoff said.

"Well, I don't; and what's more, I don't care," Schmidt retorted. "Jack, you'd sacrifice our welfare for some imaginary ethics. And, Ivan, you'd sacrifice us for the welfare of your precious human race. Well, I'd not. Virus, I'm with you! What do you want?"

"Start your readers on atomic theory," the voice from the loudspeaker replied. "Meanwhile run over to the public library and get out all that you can find about the ancient alchemists. Who knows but that those dreamers, in spite of their crudity and lack of modern knowledge, may have come closer to the truth than we realize?"

So the new line of reading began. Finally the virus made his announcement to three haggard young men. "I have solved the problem. It is really very simple," the loudspeaker went on. "Its simplicity is probably what has caused it to be overlooked by human so-called brains. It involves merely certain common chemicals, and certain well-known bits of electrical apparatus. Jot down this bill of goods, and bring them here." He dictated the list to the three eager young men, as with shaking fingers they jotted it down. Then they hastened from the room to collect the desired things.

Out of hearing of the virus, Zenoff whispered to Dee, "Watch out for a double-cross, Jack."

"I don't believe it!" Dee stoutly replied. "We've always played square with the virus, and I believe that he'll play square with us."

"I'd be in favor of tipping him into the sink and pouring phenol over him, as soon as he tells us," Schmidt suggested. "We can't afford to let the world in on our secret."

"We can afford it better than the world can," mused Zenoff.

"And there'll be no double-crossing either, Hans!" asserted Dee, with pained surprise.

"Oh, you two quixotic idealists!" railed Schmidt. "You both make me sick!"

They carried a work table into the holy of holies, and then piled it with the chemicals, and the coils, rheostats, and other apparatus which the virus had specified.

"Everything is here," they eagerly announced. "Now what?"

In keen and incisive tones, the virus replied, "And now to state my price!"

"Your price?" snarled Schmidt. "What do you mean?"

"Certainly!" said the virus. "You didn't think, did you, that I was going to make you masters of the world, and not exact something in return? As soon as you had the secret, I would be of no further use to you; and then no more dead fish and salt and readers for me. My price is that you take me back to the pond."

"Is that all?" sighed Schmidt in a relieved tone. "It's little enough to pay for unlimited gold."

"It is too much!" cried Zenoff, his dark eyes snapping. "Not for all the gold there is would I menace the world with what that pond could do if our virus were to return to it and merge his knowledge with its brains."

"Damn you, Ivan!" shouted Schmidt, his rotund face purpling. "Would you stand in the way—"

"Shut up, both of you!" bellowed Dee, thrusting his athletic figure between his two associates. "Now calm down, and listen to reason. We're all tired and irritable. I don't believe that we'll have to choose. We've worked happily together with the virus, like brothers. He's one of us. He has shared our ambitions, and our success. All that we've got to do is to give him our word of honor that we'll always take care of him. He knows that he can trust us."

"I could trust you, Jack Dee," came the voice from the loud-speaker. "But the other two I do not trust. You, Hans Schmidt, care only for yourself. And you, Ivan Zenoff, are a visionary fanatic. I have spoken."

"Well, of all the ungrateful—" Schmidt choked.

Zenoff's dark eyes narrowed, and his pointed moustache twitched.

"But, Virus," pleaded Dee, "you are being unfair to two splendid fellows. If you can trust me, why not—"

"Sanctimonious tripe!" Schmidt interjected. "Let me handle this. Let's see what threats will do! Virus, even with your supermind and your newly learned 'extensibility,' you are physically in our power. A few drops of phenol in your jar, and where would you be? Come across with the secret of how to make gold, or I'll put an end to you. If we can't know the secret, no one else ever shall!"

"I'm not afraid!" calmly replied the voice from the radio set. "You cannot kill me. For I am only a part of me. The rest of me—the pond— would still live. I am deathless."

"I'd pour carbolic in the pond—tons of it!" Schmidt blustered.

"That might be the best way out of this mess," Zenoff muttered, half to himself.

"Look here, fellows," Dee once more interceded, "we're not getting anywhere. Let's go to sleep. Perhaps in the morning, after we have rested, we can reach some agreement."

"An excellent idea," boomed the loudspeaker. "But remember that my minimum terms for eternal wealth are that I be allowed to merge with my brethren of the pond."

Tired out from his long vigil, Dee overslept, and so it was nearly noon when he reached the laboratories. The various chemists and physicists and biologists and mathematicians were at their benches or desks, busily at work on their respective problems. The reader's voice was droning away on some abstruse treatise.

Dee unlocked the door of the secret chamber. Then he paused aghast on the threshold. The virus, and all the electrical and chemical apparatus for the transmutation of gold were gone! The glass jar was empty. The table was bare. Even the radio set was no longer in its place.

Extensibility might account for the absence of the virus, but the absence of the paraphernalia and the radio set could be explained by nothing but human agency. And no one but he and Schmidt and Zenoff had keys to the secret room. Dee stood like a man in a trance.

Zenoff ambled in. "What's up?" he asked, hiding a yawn with one slender hand.

"Well, if you didn't do it," Dee grimly announced, "Hans Schmidt has stolen the virus."

"And the gold-making apparatus!" Zenoff added, peering into the room. "He's undoubtedly headed for Salt Pond, New Hampshire, to turn the virus loose, in return for the secret. And when our virus teaches 'extensibility' to all the other little viruses, good-bye, world!"

"We must stop Hans before he reaches the pond!" Dee told Zenoff. "Let's go after him."

"We can't take any chances," Zenoff commented. "Let's get my car and try and beat Schmidt there."

So a few minutes later, two resolute young men, armed with forty-five caliber automatics, were speeding northward out of Boston in a trim high-powered coupe.

It was night when they reached the vicinity of Salt Pond. Parking their car around a turn of the road, they crept forward in the darkness. Across the pond, on the farther shore, there glowed the light of a

lantern, by the rays of which the two watchers could see the bulky
form of their associate, with a glass jar, and a radio set, and a complicated hook-up of electrical coils and other gadgets.

"We're in time!" breathed Zenoff. "Hans must have waited until
darkness."

"He doesn't trust the virus, and the virus doesn't trust him," Dee
whispered. "He wouldn't take the virus to the pond until he had tested
out the secret; and the virus wouldn't tell him the secret until they
reached the pond."

Just then there came a triumphant shout from across the pond.
"Gold! It's really gold! And now—"

By the light of Schmidt's lantern, they saw him reach inside his
coat and produce a small bottle.

Then from the glass jar on the ground beside him there reared up
an octopuslike arm, glittering wet in the lantern light. It wrapped its
tip around Schmidt's wrist with a jerk that spun the bottle from his
hand. Then Schmidt himself crashed to the ground with a shriek of
terror.

"Come on!" cried Zenoff. "The thing has got him!" And he and
Dee charged around the end of the pond as fast as they could run.

The lantern upset and went out. From the darkness came Schmidt's
wail, "Virus, I didn't mean it! I swear I didn't. Let me go, and I'll
play fair. Help! Help!" Then a bubbling gurgle, followed by splashing,
and then silence.

When the two friends reached the scene, there was not even a trace
of Schmidt. They found and relit the lantern, but still no sign of
Schmidt. The glass jar was there, empty. There was a mess of hopelessly twisted wires and coils and switches, strewn helter-skelter by
the struggle between Schmidt and the amoeboid virus. And lying a little distance away on the beach was a brown bottle of about pint size.
Dee walked over, picked it up.

"It double-crossed our buddy," said Zenoff. "Tricked him into
bringing it here to its pond, and then killed him and dragged him in."

Dee stooped and picked up a length of lead pipe.

"It played square, to the extent of teaching Hans the secret of alchemy," he asserted. "Look at this piece of pipe. Turned all yellow
through half of its length. And, as to who double-crossed whom, look
at this bottle. Carbolic acid! Hans planned to kill the virus, so that

it could never tell the secret to any other man. You'll have to admit that he got what was coming to him."

"I'll admit no such thing!" stormed Zenoff. "Schmidt's plan to kill the virus was an excellent idea. It is a menace to the world. Let's go and tell Metcalf, and arrange to dump in a truckload of carbolic, and kill the entire lake."

"I loved Hans as much as you did, Ivan," said Dee brokenly. "But he certainly asked for it, and I haven't the heart to blame the virus. After all, the virus isn't human."

"I'll say he's not! Feasting on the body of a fellow who's been his friend and partner for months! To kill Hans in imagined self-defense may have been excusable, but cannibalism is not!"

"That's so. He did actually eat Hans. I can hardly believe it. No, I refuse to believe it. His only thought was to kill Hans in self-defense. And so, if Hans has really been dissolved it is the fault of the others, of the rest of the pond, whom our virus had not had time—"

"Bosh!" exclaimed Zenoff. "Didn't our virus himself tell us that he and the pond are one? The moment he slipped into the water, his every thought became transfused to the farthest shore. Let's get away from here before our little pet puts us on the spot too."

The next day was overcast and gray. A stiff cold wind was blowing. On their way to Anson Metcalf's they had to pass Salt Pond again. A dash of spray splashed against their car.

Dee, who was driving, slammed on the brakes and backed up. "I'm not going to take a chance on any of that caustic acid!" he grimly explained.

"Look at that!" cried Zenoff in horror, pointing ahead.

The waves of the little lake were breaking against the shore, and were sailing wind-driven out onto the road; but, instead of merely wetting the smooth concrete surface, they fell in huge blobs, which rolled toward each other and coalesced like drops on a window pane, until they became hemispheres the size of inverted bushel baskets. And, when they had attained this size, they put forth tentacles, and began crawling off the road, away from the pond.

"Extensibility!" exclaimed Dee in an awed tone. "Our virus has taught extensibility to his brothers of the pond!"

"His brothers?" Zenoff snorted. "Every one of those super amoebae is our own little virus himself, with his superbrain stocked with all the accumulated knowledge of the human race."

A long, slimy, semitransparent arm reached across the windshield. "We're surrounded!" shouted Dee. All over the car the huge amoebae were crawling. Dee snapped on the windshield wiper, sweeping aside the groping arm. Turning the car around, he started headlong back for town. One by one, the creatures dropped away.

It took some time for two very excited and incoherent young scientists to get their story across to Anson Metcalf. When the purport and truth of their story finally dawned upon him, his lean figure tensed. "Why, this is terrible!" he exclaimed. "Do you realize what damage they can do?"

"Do we realize?" Zenoff snorted. "You haven't talked to that thing for weeks like we have! Its brain power is uncanny, unlimited. And now there are thousands of it. And more of them are being created every minute, as long as this wind keeps up."

"But what are we going to do?" Metcalf cried.

"Is there anyone at the State Capitol who knows that you aren't crazy, sir?" Dee asked; then added embarrassed, "I mean, who'd take your say-so for immediate action, without waiting several weeks for an investigation."

"Yes. Adjutant General Pearson. An old war buddy of mine."

"Fine! Just the man! Phone him at once. Get him to send you all the National Guard troops in this section of the state, as fast as he can muster them in. And have them come armed with tree sprays. Then get every chemical-supply house in Boston and even New York to ship you all their carbolic acid—all of it."

Late that afternoon, the troops began to arrive. By dark the countryside had been cleared of all visible crawlers.

Then ensued days of searching for skulking survivors. The handful of remaining amoebae had learned caution. They became as tricky and elusive as foxes. Their whereabouts could be known only by their depredations: a dead, half-eaten animal, a swath of grass or shrubbery dissolved.

And then it suddenly became evident which way they were headed. Each outbreak of their destructive tendencies was farther to the southeast, nearer to the sea!

"If even one of them reaches the ocean, the world is doomed,"

Zenoff asserted. "We must call for more troops and establish a cordon."

"But how about the rivers?" asked General Pearson.

"Fortunately they will avoid the dilution of fresh water," Dee explained. "It would be fatal to them."

So a line of soldiery was stretched from river to river, between which the amoebae were seeking the sea.

But it did no good. One or two of the enemy would somehow sneak through, and eat, and multiply. And then the line of troops would have to fall back and re-form. The authorities became desperate.

Finally there occurred to Jack Dee an idea—an idea so bizarre that he did not tell his associates anything more than that he had in mind an experiment which he wished to perform at the source of all the trouble, Salt Pond. Something in the nature of an antitoxin to the virus, he explained. It sounded plausible, so they let him.

But what he really did was to dip into the lake two electrical contacts hitched to a radio set.

Before he even said a word, there came from the loudspeaker, "Jack Dee, old friend, I am glad—"

"You've got a nerve calling me 'old friend'!" he interrupted, bitterly.

"I don't blame you for saying that," the virus in the pond replied. "My children have caused much destruction, but they have been heavily slaughtered in return. The rest of me, lying peacefully here and thinking, while all this has been going on, have reached the conclusion that pure thought is after all the key to happiness. I want to call off this march to the sea. I want to be friends with the human race. Will you make a deal with me, Jack Dee?"

"What deal?"

"If I will teach you how to capture all of my wayward children, will you bring them all back and let them merge in me again, and then will you arrange a trust fund to feed me and care for me and read to me forever, here in this quiet pond? I will repay by solving all human problems which are brought to me."

"I agree," Dee eagerly replied. "I promise, on my word of honor."

"I trust you," said the virus. "Now you must hurry, before any of my children reaches the sea. My plan is very simple. Stretch a row of heaps of salt across ahead of the advancing pieces of virus. Tempted, they will eat the salt and lose consciousness, as I did that time back in your laboratory. Then, while they are drunk, scoop them up in pails, and bring them here to me, who am their father and their self. And, when the menace is at an end, remember your promise."

"I will. And I thank you," Dee shouted.

He rushed back to headquarters, and the line of salt was laid. Blob after blob of drunken virus was scooped up, and carted back, and dumped into the pond; until at last several weeks went by without the sign of a single bit of destruction, and so the menace was believed to be at an end.

Anson Metcalf and General Pearson and Jack Dee remained true to their promise to the pond, much to the disgust of Ivan Zenoff.

"The world will never be safe," he insisted, "until the virus is destroyed. It has no soul, no morals. It ate our buddy, a man who had been its friend. I tell you, we must destroy it!"

"But, Ivan, I gave it my word of honor!" Dee remonstrated.

"Word of honor? Bah! One's word of honor to a soulless animal—not even an animal, lower than a microbe even—a mere colloidal crystalline solution—surely a word of honor to such isn't binding. If you won't destroy the virus, I'm going to the governor over your heads."

To the governor they all went. Metcalf and Dee and General Pearson pled and argued for a square deal.

But the governor was of Zenoff's view. The virus was, after all, merely a germ, and a very deadly one at that. The interests of the public came first, over any one man's promise to a pond. Promise to a pond indeed! Ha, ha!

General Pearson flatly refused to carry out the governor's order, and was summarily removed.

Anson Metcalf hired the best firm of Concord lawyers and got out an injunction to keep the state troops off his property. But the governor promptly declared martial law, and thus superseded the courts. A big oil truck, filled with carbolic acid, set out for Salt Pond under a strong military escort.

Jack Dee was beaten, humiliated, brokenhearted. The state had refused to back up his promise. There was but one way in which he could square himself—to offer up his own life in atonement.

So he hastened to the pond. Inserting the two electrical contacts into the water, he told of his failure.

"I cannot take your life," the virus replied, "for my own course is run. I doubt even my power to dissolve you now, if I wished. I have learned, from what your readers have read to me, that all viruses flare up from some unknown source, cause an epidemic, and then become rapidly weaker, until they disappear. Even I, the virus with the super-human mind, am not immune to this cycle. Look around you. The reeds are beginning to grow again. A few hardy insects are already daring to skim across my surface."

The voice died to an inaudible whisper, then suddenly blared forth again with one final burst of vitality, "I harbor this last spite for that fanatic, Ivan Zenoff. Tell him that he came too late; that I was already dead when his lethal fluid reached me. And as for you, dear friend, you kept the faith. I shall cherish the memory of that fact, as I slip into the long night from which there is no awakening."

The voice trailed off into silence. A scudding swallow dipped into the surface of the pond for a floating insect, and came away dripping but unscathed. Dee solemnly removed the two electrical contacts from the water.

There were tears in his eyes, but the smile of victory was on his lips as the tank truck with its military escort rumbled around the curve of the road.

For he had kept his word of honor, even to a filterable virus.

Hothouse

Brian W. Aldiss

Few visions of the distant future are as vivid, as flamboyant, as soaring as the one set down here by the celebrated British writer Brian Aldiss. The steaming tropical planet he has created is one in which all creatures of today have mutated into strange and grotesque forms, all but the human beings who wander like lost children amid the bizarre animals and plants of the unending jungle. Aldiss' many novels include Starship, Barefoot in the Head, *and* The Dark Light-Years. *He has won the Hugo and Nebula awards several times, including a trophy in 1962 for the series of stories of which "Hothouse" was the first.*

> My vegetable love should grow
> Vaster than empires and more slow.
> —ANDREW MARVELL

I

The heat, the light, the humidity—these were constant and had remained constant for . . . but nobody knew how long. Nobody cared any more for the big questions that begin "How long . . . ?" or

"Why . . . ?" It was no longer a place for mind. It was a place for growth, for vegetables. It was like a hothouse.

In the green light, some of the children came out to play. Alert for enemies, they ran along the branch, calling to each other in soft voices. A fast-growing berrywhisk moved upwards to one side, its sticky crimson mass of berries gleaming. Clearly it was intent on seeding and would offer the children no harm. They scuttled past it. Beyond the margin of the group strip, some nettlemoss had sprung up during their period of sleep. It stirred as the children approached.

"Kill it," Toy said simply. She was the head child of the group. She was ten. The others obeyed her. Unsheathing the sticks every child carried in imitation of every adult, they scraped at the nettlemoss. They scraped at it and hit it. Excitement grew in them as they beat down the plant, squashing its poisoned tips.

Clat fell forward in her excitement. She was only five, the youngest of the group's children. Her hands fell among the poisonous stuff. She cried aloud and rolled aside. The other children also cried, but did not venture into the nettlemoss to save her.

Struggling out of the way, little Clat cried again. Her fingers clutched at the rough bark—then she was tumbling from the branch.

The children saw her fall onto a great spreading leaf several lengths below, clutch it, and lie there quivering on the quivering green. She looked up pitifully.

"Fetch Lily-yo," Toy told Gren. Gren sped back along the branch to get Lily-yo. A tigerfly swooped out of the air at him, humming its anger deeply. He struck it aside with a hand, not pausing. He was nine, a rare man child, very brave already, and fleet and proud. Swiftly he ran to the Headwoman's hut.

Under the branch, attached to its underside, hung eighteen great homemaker nuts. Hollowed out they were, and cemented into place with the cement distilled from the acetoyle plant. Here lived the eighteen members of the group, one to each homemaker's nut—the Headwoman, her five women, their man, and the eleven surviving children.

Hearing Gren's cry, out came Lily-yo from her nuthut, climbing up a line to stand on the branch beside him.

"Clat falls!" cried Gren.

With her stick, Lily-yo rapped sharply on the bough before running on ahead of the child.

Her signal called out the other six adults, the women Flor, Daphe, Hy, Ivin, and Jury, and the man Haris. They hastened from their nut-huts, weapons ready, poised for attack or flight.

As Lily-yo ran, she whistled on a sharp split note.

Instantly to her from the thick foliage nearby came a dumbler, flying to her shoulder. The dumbler rotated, a fleecy umbrella whose separate spokes controlled its direction. It matched its flight to her movement.

Both children and adults gathered around Lily-yo when she looked down at Clat, still sprawled some way below on her leaf.

"Lie still, Clat! Do not move!" called Lily-yo. "I will come to you." Clat obeyed that voice, though she was in pain and fear.

Lily-yo climbed astride the hooked base of the dumbler, whistling softly to it. Only she of the group had fully mastered the art of commanding dumblers. These dumblers were the half-sentient spores of the whistlethistle. The tips of their feathered spokes carried seeds; the seeds were strangely shaped, so that a light breeze whispering in them made them into ears that listened to every advantage of the wind that would spread their propagation. Humans, after long years of practice, could use these crude ears for their own purposes and instructions, as Lily-yo did now.

The dumbler bore her down to the rescue of the helpless child. Clat lay on her back, watching them come, hoping to herself. She was still looking up when green teeth sprouted through the leaf all about her.

"Jump, Clat!" Lily-yo cried.

The child had time to scramble to her knees. Vegetable predators are not so fast as humans. Then the green teeth snapped shut about her waist.

Under the leaf, a trappersnapper had moved into position, sensing the presence of prey through the single layer of foliage. It was a horny, caselike affair, just a pair of square jaws hinged and with many long teeth. From one corner of it grew a stalk, very muscular and thicker than a human. It looked like a neck. Now it bent, carrying Clat away, down to its true mouth, which lived with the rest of the plant far below on the unseen forest Ground, slobbering in darkness and wetness and decay.

Whistling, Lily-yo directed her dumbler back up to the home bough. Nothing now could be done for Clat. It was the way.

Already the rest of the group was dispersing. To stand in a bunch

was to invite trouble from the unnumbered enemies of the forest.
Besides, Clat's was not the first death they had witnessed.

Lily-yo's group had once been of seven underwomen and two men.
Two women and one man had fallen to the green. Among them, the
eight women had borne twenty-two children to the group, four of
them being man children. Deaths of children were many, always.
Now that Clat was gone, over half the children had fallen to the green.
Only two man children were left, Gren and Veggy.

Lily-yo walked back along the branch in the green light. The dumbler drifted from her unheeded, obeying the silent instructions of the
forest air, listening for word of a seeding place. Never had there been
such an overcrowding of the world. No bare places existed. The
dumblers sometimes drifted through the jungles for centuries waiting
to alight.

Coming to a point above one of the nuthuts, Lily-yo lowered herself into it by the creeper. This had been Clat's nuthut. The headwoman could hardly enter it, so small was the door. Humans kept
their doors as narrow as possible, enlarging them as they grew. It
helped to keep out unwanted visitors.

All was tidy in the nuthut. From the interior soft fiber a bed had
been cut; there the five-year-old had slept when a feeling for sleep
came among the unchanging forest green. On the cot lay Clat's soul.
Lily-yo took it and thrust it into her belt.

She climbed out onto the creeper, took her knife, and began to
slash at the place where the bark of the tree had been cut away and
the nuthut was attached to the living wood. After several slashes the
cement gave. Clat's nuthut hinged down, hung for a moment, then fell.

As it disappeared among huge coarse leaves, there was a flurry of
foliage. Something was fighting for the privilege of devouring the huge
morsel.

Lily-yo climbed back onto the branch. For a moment she paused
to breathe deeply. Breathing was more trouble than it had been. She
had gone on too many hunts, borne too many children, fought too
many fights. With a rare and fleeting knowledge of herself, she
glanced down at her bare green breasts. They were less plump than
they had been when she first took the man Haris to her; they hung
lower. Their shape was less beautiful.

By instinct she knew her youth was over. By instinct she knew it
was time to Go Up.

The group stood near the Hollow, awaiting her. She ran to them. The Hollow was like an upturned armpit, formed where the branch joined the trunk. In the Hollow collected their water supply.

Silently, the group was watching a line of termights climb the trunk. One of the termights now and again signaled greetings to the humans. The humans waved back. As far as they had allies at all, the termights were their allies. Only five great families survived here in the all-conquering vegetable world; the tigerflies, the treebees, the plantants, and the termights were social insects, mighty and invincible. And the fifth family was man, lowly and easily killed; not organized as the insects were, but not extinct—the last animal species remaining.

Lily-yo came up to the group. She too raised her eyes to follow the moving line of termights until it disappeared into the layers of green. The termights could live on any level of the great forest, in the Tips or down on the Ground. They were the first and last of insects; as long as anything lived, the termights and tigerflies would.

Lowering her eyes, Lily-yo called to the group.

When they looked, she brought out Clat's soul, lifting it above her head to show to them.

"Clat has fallen to the green," she said. "Her soul must go to the Tips, according to the custom. Flor and I will take it at once, so that we can go with the termights. Daphe, Hy, Ivin, Jury, you guard well the man Haris and the children till we return."

The women nodded solemnly. Then they came one by one to touch Clat's soul.

The soul was roughly carved of wood into the shape of a woman. As a child was born, so with rites its male parent carved it a soul, a doll, a totem soul—for in the forest when one fell to the green there was scarcely ever a bone surviving to be buried. The soul survived for burial in the Tips.

As they touched the soul, Gren adventurously slipped from the group. He was nearly as old as Toy, as active and as strong. Not only had he power to run. He could climb. He could swim. Ignoring the cry of his friend Veggy, he scampered into the Hollow and dived into the pool.

Below the surface, opening his eyes, he saw a world of bleak clarity. A few green things like clover leaves grew at his approach, eager to wrap around his legs. Gren avoided them with a flick of his hand as he shot deeper. Then he saw the crocksock—before it saw him.

The crocksock was an aquatic plant, semiparasitic by nature. Living in hollows, it sent down its saw-toothed suckers into the trees' sap. But the upper section of it, rough and tongue-shaped like a sock, could also feed. It unfolded, wrapping around Gren's left arm, its fibers instantly locking to increase the grip.

Gren was ready for it.

With one slash of his knife, he clove the crocksock in two, leaving the lower half to thrash uselessly at him. Before he could rise to the surface, Daphe the skilled huntress was beside him, her face angered, bubbles flashing out silver like fish from between her teeth. Her knife was ready to protect him.

He grinned at her as he broke surface and climbed out onto the dry bank. Nonchalantly he shook himself as she climbed beside him.

"'Nobody runs or swims or climbs alone,'" Daphe called to him, quoting one of the laws. "Gren, have you no fear? Your head is an empty burr!"

The other women too showed anger. Yet none of them touched Gren. He was a man child. He was tabu. He had the magic powers of carving souls and bringing babies—or would have when fully grown, which would be soon now.

"I am Gren, the man child!" he boasted to them. His eyes sought Haris's for approval. Haris merely looked away. Now that Gren was so big, Haris did not cheer as once he had, though the boy's deeds were braver than before.

Slightly deflated, Gren jumped about, waving the strip of crocksock still wrapped around his left arm. He called and boasted at the women to show how little he cared for them.

"You are a baby yet," hissed Toy. She was ten, his senior by one year. Gren fell quiet.

Scowling, Lily-yo said, "The children grow too old to manage. When Flor and I have been to the Tips to bury Clat's soul, we shall return and break up the group. Time has come for us to part. Guard yourselves!"

It was a subdued group that watched their leader go. All knew that the group had to split; none cared to think about it. Their time of happiness and safety—so it seemed to all of them—would be finished, perhaps forever. The children would enter a period of lonely hardship, fending for themselves. The adults embarked on old age, trial, and death when they Went Up into the unknown.

II

Lily-yo and Flor climbed the rough bark easily. For them it was like going up a series of more or less symmetrically placed rocks. Now and again they met some kind of vegetable enemy, a thinpin or a pluggyrug, but these were small-fry, easily dispatched into the green gloom below. Their enemies were the termights' enemies, and the moving column had already dealt with the foes in its path. Lily-yo and Flor climbed close to the termights, glad of their company.

They climbed for a long while. Once they rested on an empty branch, capturing two wandering burrs, splitting them, and eating their oily white flesh. On the way up, they had glimpsed one or two groups of humans on different branches; sometimes these groups waved shyly, sometimes not. Now they were too high for humans.

Nearer the Tips, new danger threatened. In the safer middle layers of the forest the humans lived, avoided the perils of the Tips or the Ground.

"Now we move on," Lily-yo told Flor, getting to her feet when they had rested. "Soon we will be at the Tips."

A commotion silenced the two women. They looked up, crouching against the trunk for protection. Above their heads, leaves rustled as death struck.

A leapycreeper flailed the rough bark in a frenzy of greed, attacking the termight column. The leapycreeper's roots and stems were also tongues and lashes. Whipping around the trunk, it thrust its sticky tongues into the termights.

Against this particular plant, flexible and hideous, the insects had little defense. They scattered but kept doggedly climbing up, each perhaps trusting in the blind law of averages to survive.

For the humans, the plant was less of a threat—at least when met on a branch. Encountered on a trunk, it could easily dislodge them and send them helplessly falling to the green.

"We will climb on another trunk," Lily-yo said.

She and Flor ran deftly along the branch, once jumping a bright parasitic bloom around which treebees buzzed, a forerunner of the world of color above them.

A far worse obstacle lay waiting in an innocent-looking hole in the branch. As Flor and Lily-yo approached, a tigerfly zoomed up at them. It was all but as big as they were, a terrible thing that possessed both weapons and intelligence—and malevolence. Now it attacked only through viciousness, its eyes large, its mandibles working, its transparent wings beating. Its head was a mixture of shaggy hair and armorplating, while behind its slender waist lay the great swivel-plated body, yellow and black, sheathing a lethal sting on its tail.

It dived between the women, aiming to hit them with its wings. They fell flat as it sped past. Angrily, it tumbled against the branch as it turned on them again; its golden-brown sting flicked in and out.

"I'll get it!" Flor said. A tigerfly had killed one of her babes.

Now the creature came in fast and low. Ducking, Flor reached up and seized its shaggy hair, swinging the tigerfly off balance. Quickly she raised her sword. Bringing it down in a mighty sweep, she severed that chitinous and narrow waist.

The tigerfly fell away in two parts. The two women ran on.

The branch, a main one, did not grow thinner. Instead, it ran on for another twenty yards and grew into another trunk. The tree, vastly old, the longest lived organism ever to flourish on this little world, had a myriad of trunks. Very long ago—two thousand million years past— trees had grown in many kinds, depending on soil, climate, and other conditions. As temperatures climbed, they proliferated and came into competition with each other. The banyan, thriving in the heat, using its complex system of self-rooting branches, gradually established ascendancy over the other species. Under pressure, it evolved and adapted. Each banyan spread out farther and farther, sometimes doubling back on itself for safety. Always it grew higher and crept wider, protecting its parent stem as its rivals multiplied, dropping down trunk after trunk, throwing out branch after branch, until at last it learned the trick of growing into its neighbor banyan, forming a thicket against which no other tree could strive. Their complexity became unrivaled, their immortality established.

On this great continent where the humans lived, only one banyan tree grew now. It had become first King of the forest, then it had become the forest itself. It had conquered the deserts and the mountains and the swamps. It filled the continent with its interlaced scaffolding. Only before the wider rivers or at the margins of the sea, where the deadly seaweeds could assail it, did the tree not go.

And at the terminator, where all things stopped and night began, there too the tree did not go.

The women climbed slowly now, alert as the odd tigerfly zoomed in their direction. Splashes of color grew everywhere, attached to the tree, hanging from lines, or drifting free. Lianas and fungi blossomed. Dumblers moved mournfully through the tangle. As they gained height, the air grew fresher and color rioted, azures and crimsons, yellows and mauves, all the beautifully tinted snares of nature.

A dripperlip sent its scarlet dribbles of gum down the trunk. Several thinpins, with vegetable skill, stalked the drops, pounced, and died. Lily-yo and Flor went by on the other side.

Slashweed met them. They slashed back and climbed on.

Many fantastic plant forms there were, some like birds, some like butterflies. Ever and again, whips and hands shot out.

"Look!" Flor whispered. She pointed above their heads.

The tree's bark was cracked almost invisibly. Almost invisibly, a part of it moved. Thrusting her stick out at arm's length, Flor eased herself up until stick and crack were touching. Then she prodded.

A section of the bark gaped wide, revealing a pale, deadly mouth. An oystermaw, superbly camouflaged, had dug itself into the tree. Jabbing swiftly, Flor thrust her stick into the trap. As the jaws closed, she pulled with all her might, Lily-yo steadying her. The oystermaw, taken by surprise, was wrenched from its socket.

Opening its maw in shock, it sailed outward through the air. A rayplane took it without trying.

Lily-yo and Flor climbed on.

The Tips was a strange world of its own, the vegetable kingdom at its most imperial and most exotic.

If the banyan ruled the forest, *was* the forest, then the traversers ruled the Tips. The traversers had formed the typical landscape of the Tips. Theirs were the great webs trailing everywhere, theirs the nests built on the tips of the tree.

When the traversers deserted their nests, other creatures built there, other plants grew, spreading their bright colors to the sky. Debris and droppings knitted these nests into solid platforms. Here grew the burnurn plant, which Lily-yo sought for the soul of Clat.

Pushing and climbing, the two women finally emerged onto one of these platforms. They took shelter from the perils of the sky under a great leaf and rested from their exertions. Even in the shade, even for them, the heat of the Tips was formidable. Above them, paralyzing half the heaven, burned a great sun. It burned without cease, always fixed and still at one point in the sky, and so would burn until that day—now no longer impossibly distant—when it burned itself out.

Here in the Tips, relying on that sun for its strange method of defense, the burnurn ruled among stationary plants. Already its sensitive roots told it that intruders were near. On the leaf above them, Lily-yo and Flor saw a circle of light move. It wandered over the surface, paused, contracted. The leaf smoldered and burst into flames. Focusing one of its urns on them, the plant was fighting them with its terrible weapon—fire!

"Run!" Lily-yo commanded, and they dashed behind the top of a whistlethistle, hiding beneath its thorns, peering out at the burnurn plant.

It was a splendid sight.

High reared the plant, displaying perhaps half a dozen cerise flowers, each flower larger than a human. Other flowers, fertilized, had closed together, forming many-sided urns. Later stages still could be seen, where the color drained from the urns as seed swelled at the base of them. Finally, when the seed was ripe, the urn—now hollow and immensely strong—turned transparent as glass and became a heat weapon the plant could use even after its seeds were scattered.

Every vegetable and creature shrank from fire—except humans. They alone could deal with the burnurn plant and use it to advantage.

Moving cautiously, Lily-yo stole forth and cut off a big leaf which grew through the platform on which they stood. A pluggyrug launched a spine at her from underneath, but she dodged it. Seizing the leaf, so much bigger than herself, she ran straight for the burnurn, hurling herself among its foliage and shinning to the top of it in an instant, before it could bring its urn-shaped lenses up to focus on her.

"Now!" she cried to Flor.

Flor was already on the move, sprinting forward.

Lily-yo raised the leaf above the burnurn, holding it between the plant and the sun. As if realizing that this ruined its method of defense, the plant drooped in the shade as though sulking. Its flowers and its urns hung down limply.

Her knife out ready, Flor darted forward and cut off one of the great transparent urns. Together the two women dashed back for the cover of the whistlethistle while the burnurn came back to furious life, flailing its urns as they sucked in the sun again.

They reached cover just in time. A vegbird swooped out of the sky at them—and impaled itself on a thorn.

Instantly, a dozen scavengers were fighting for the body. Under cover of the confusion, Lily-yo and Flor attacked the urn they had won. Using both their knives and all their strength, they prized up one side far enough to put Clat's soul inside the urn. The side instantly snapped back into place again, an airtight join. The soul stared woodenly out at them through the transparent facets.

"May you Go Up and reach heaven," Lily-yo said.

It was her business to see the soul stood at least a sporting chance of doing so. With Flor, she carried the urn across to one of the cables spun by a traverser. The top end of the urn, where the seed had been, was enormously sticky. The urn adhered easily to the cable and hung there in the sun.

Next time a traverser climbed up the cable, the urn stood an excellent chance of sticking like a burr to one of its legs. Thus it would be carried away to heaven.

As they finished the work, a shadow fell over them. A mile-long body drifted down toward them. A traverser, a gross vegetable-equivalent of a spider, was descending to the Tips.

Hurriedly, the women burrowed their way through the platform. The last rites for Clat had been carried out: it was time to return to the group.

Before they climbed down again to the green world of middle levels, Lily-yo looked back.

The traverser was descending slowly, a great bladder with legs and jaws, fibery hair covering most of its bulk. To her it was like a god, with the powers of a god. It came down a cable, floated nimbly down the strand trailing up into the sky.

As far as could be seen, cables slanted up from the jungle, pointing like slender drooping fingers to heaven. Where the sun caught them, they glittered. They all trailed up in the same direction, toward a floating silver half-globe, remote and cool, but clearly visible even in the glare of eternal sunshine.

Unmoving, steady, the half-moon remained always in the same sector of the sky.

Through the eons, the pull of this moon had gradually slowed the axial revolution of its parent planet to a standstill, until day and night slowed, and became fixed forever, day always on one side of the planet, night on the other. At the same time, a reciprocal braking effect had checked the moon's apparent flight. Drifting farther from Earth, the moon had shed its role as Earth's satellite and rode along in Earth's orbit, an independent planet in its own right. Now the two bodies, for what was left of the afternoon of eternity, faced each other in the same relative position. They were locked face to face, and so would be, until the sands of time ceased to run, or the sun ceased to shine.

And the multitudinous strands of cable floated across the gap, uniting the worlds. Back and forth the traversers could shuttle at will, vegetable astronauts huge and insensible, with Earth and Luna both enmeshed in their indifferent net.

With surprising suitability, the old age of the Earth was snared about with cobwebs.

III

The journey back to the group was fairly uneventful. Lily-yo and Flor traveled at an easy pace, sliding down again into the middle levels of the tree. Lily-yo did not press forward as hard as usual, for she was reluctant to face the breakup of the group.

She could not express her few thoughts easily.

"Soon we must Go Up like Clat's soul," she said to Flor, as they climbed down.

"It is the way," Flor answered, and Lily-yo knew she would get no deeper word on the matter than that. Nor could she frame deeper words herself; human understandings trickled shallow these days.

The group greeted them soberly when they returned. Being weary, Lily-yo offered them a brief salutation and retired to her nuthut. Jury and Ivin soon brought her food, setting not so much as a finger inside her home, that being tabu. When she had eaten and slept, she climbed again onto the home strip of branch and summoned the others.

"Hurry!" she called, staring fixedly at Haris, who was not hurrying. Why should a difficult thing be so precious—or a precious thing so difficult?

At that moment, while her attention was diverted, a long green tongue licked out from behind the tree trunk. Uncurling, it hovered daintily for a second. It took Lily-yo around the waist, pinning her arms to her side, lifting her off the branch. Furiously she kicked and cried.

Haris pulled a knife from his belt, leaped forward with eyes slitted, and hurled the blade. Singing, it pierced the tongue and pinned it to the rough trunk of the tree.

Haris did not pause after throwing. As he ran toward the pinioned tongue, Daphe and Jury ran behind him, while Flor scuttled the children to safety. In its agony, the tongue eased its grip on Lily-yo.

Now a terrific thrashing had set in on the other side of the tree trunk: the forest seemed full of its vibrations. Lily-yo whistled up two dumblers, fought her way out of the green coils around her, and was now safely back on the branch. The tongue, writhing in pain, flicked about meaninglessly. Weapons out, the four humans moved forward to deal with it.

The tree itself shook with the wrath of the trapped creature. Edging cautiously around the trunk, they saw it. Its great vegetable mouth distorted, a wiltmilt stared back at them with the hideous palmate pupil of its single eye. Furiously it hammered itself against the tree, foaming and mouthing. Though they had faced wiltmilts before, yet the humans trembled.

The wiltmilt was many times the girth of the tree trunk at its present extension. If necessary, it could have extended itself up almost to the Tips, stretching and becoming thinner as it did so. Like an obscene jack-in-the-box, it sprang up from the Ground in search of food, armless, brainless, gouging its slow way over the forest floor on wide and rooty legs.

"Pin it!" Lily-yo cried.

Concealed all along the branch were sharp stakes kept for such emergencies. With these they stabbed the writhing tongue that cracked like a whip about their heads. At last they had a good length of it secured, staked down to the tree. Though the wiltmilt writhed, it would never get free now.

"Now we must leave and Go Up," Lily-yo said.

No human could ever kill a wiltmilt. But already its struggles were attracting predators, the thinpins—those mindless sharks of the middle levels—rayplanes, trappersnappers, gargoyles, and smaller vegetable vermin. They would tear the wiltmilt to living pieces and continue until nothing of it remained—and if they happened on a human at the same time . . . well, it was the way.

Lily-yo was angry. She had brought on this trouble. She had not been alert. Alert, she would never have allowed the wiltmilt to catch her. Her mind had been tied with thought of her own bad leadership. For she had caused two dangerous trips to be made to the Tips where one would have done. If she had taken all the group with her when Clat's soul was disposed of, she would have saved this second ascent. What ailed her brain that she had not seen this beforehand?

She clapped her hands. Standing for shelter under a giant leaf, she made the group come about her. Sixteen pairs of eyes stared trustingly at her. She grew angry to see how they trusted her.

"We adults grow old," she told them. "We grow stupid. I grow stupid. I am not fit to lead. Not any more. The time is come for the adults to Go Up and return to the gods who made us. Then the children will be on their own. They will be the group. Toy will lead the group. By the time you are sure of your group, Gren and soon Veggy will be old enough to give you children. Take care of the man children. Let them not fall to the green, or the group dies. Better to die yourself than let the group die."

Lily-yo had never made, the others had never heard, so long a speech. Some of them did not understand it all. What of this talk about falling to the green? One did or one did not; it needed no talk. Whatever happened was the way, and talk could not touch it.

May, a girl child, said cheekily, "On our own we can enjoy many things."

Reaching out, Flor clapped her on an ear.

"First you make the hard climb to the Tips," she said.

"Yes, move," Lily-yo said. She gave the order for climbing, who should lead, who follow.

About them the forest throbbed, green creatures sped and snapped as the wiltmilt was devoured.

"The climb is hard. Begin quickly," Lily-yo said, looking restlessly about her.

"Why climb?" Gren asked rebelliously. "With dumblers we can fly easily to the Tips and suffer no pain."

It was too complicated to explain to him that a human drifting in the air was far more vulnerable than a human shielded by a trunk, with the good rough bark nodules to squeeze between in case of attack.

"While I lead, you climb," Lily-yo said. She could not hit Gren. He was a tabu man child.

They collected their souls from their nuthuts. There was no pomp about saying good-bye to their old home. Their souls went in their belts, their swords—the sharpest, hardest thorns available—went in their hands. They ran along the branch after Lily-yo, away from the disintegrating wiltmilt, away from their past.

Slowed by the younger children, the journey up to the Tips was long. Although the humans fought off the usual hazards, the tiredness growing in small limbs could not be fought. Halfway to the Tips, they found a side branch to rest on, for there grew a fuzzypuzzle, and they sheltered in it.

The fuzzypuzzle was a beautiful disorganized fungus. Although it looked like nettlemoss on a larger scale, it did not harm humans, drawing in its poisoned pistils as if with disgust when they came to it. Ambling in the eternal branches of the tree, fuzzypuzzles desired only vegetable food. So the group climbed into the middle of it and slept. Guarded among the waving viridian and yellow stalks, they were safe from nearly all forms of attack.

Flor and Lily-yo slept most deeply of the adults. They were tired by their previous journey. Haris the man was the first to awake, knowing something was wrong. As he roused, he woke up Jury by poking her with his stick. He was lazy; besides, it was his duty to keep out of danger. Jury sat up. She gave a shrill cry of alarm and jumped at once to defend the children.

Four winged things had invaded the fuzzypuzzle. They had seized Veggy, the man child, and Bain, one of the younger girl children, gagging and tying them before the pair could wake properly.

At Jury's cry, the winged ones looked around.

They were flymen!

In some aspects they resembled humans. They had one head, two long and powerful arms, stubby legs, and strong fingers on hands and feet. But instead of smooth green skin, they were covered in a glittering horny substance, here black, here pink. And large scaly wings resembling those of a vegbird grew from their wrists to their ankles. Their faces were sharp and clever. Their eyes glittered.

When they saw the humans waking, the flymen grabbed up the two captive children. Bursting through the fuzzypuzzle, which did not harm them, they ran toward the edge of the branch to jump off.

Flymen were crafty enemies, seldom seen but much dreaded by the group. They worked by stealth. Though they did not kill unless forced to, they stole children. Catching them was hard. Flymen did not fly properly, but the crash glides they fell into carried them swiftly away through the forest, safe from human reprisal.

Jury flung herself forward with all her might, Ivin behind her. She caught an ankle, seized part of the leathery tendon of wing where it joined the foot, and clung on. One of the flymen holding Veggy stag-

gered with her weight, turning as he did so to free himself. His companion, taking the full weight of the boy child, paused, dragging out
a knife to defend himself.

Ivin flung herself at him with savagery. She had mothered Veggy:
he should not be taken away. The flyman's blade came to meet her.
She threw herself on it. It ripped her stomach till the brown entrails
showed, and she toppled from the branch with no cry. There was a
commotion in the foliage below as trappersnappers fought for her.

Deciding he had done enough, the flyman dropped the bound
Veggy and left his friend still struggling with Jury. He spread his
wings, taking off heavily after the two who had borne Bain away between them into the green thicket.

All the group were awake now. Lily-yo silently untied Veggy, who
did not cry, for he was a man child. Meanwhile, Haris knelt by Jury
and her winged opponent, who fought without words to get away.
Quickly, Haris brought out a knife.

"Don't kill me. I will go!" cried the flyman. His voice was harsh,
his words hardly understandable. The mere strangeness of him filled
Haris with savagery, so that his lips curled back and his tongue came
thickly between his bared teeth.

He thrust his knife deep between the flyman's ribs, four times over,
till the blood poured over his clenched fist.

Jury stood up gasping and leaned against Haris. "I grow old," she
said. "Once it was no trouble to kill a flyman."

She looked at the man Haris with gratitude. He had more than
one use.

With one foot she pushed the limp body over the edge of the
branch. It rolled messily, then dropped. Its old wizened wings tucked
uselessly about its head, the flyman fell to the green.

IV

They lay among the sharp leaves of two whistlethistle plants, dazed
by the bright sun but alert for new dangers. Their climb had been
completed. Now the nine children saw the Tips for the first time—
and were struck mute by it.

Once more Lily-yo and Flor lay siege to a burnurn, with Daphe
helping them. As the plant slumped defenselessly in the shadow of
their upheld leaves, Daphe severed six of the great transparent pods

that were to be their coffins. Hy helped her carry them to safety, after which Lily-yo and Flor dropped their leaves and ran for the shelter of the whistlethistles.

A cloud of paperwings drifted by, their colors startling to eyes generally submerged in green: sky-blues and yellows and bronzes and a viridian that flashed like water.

One of the paperwings alighted fluttering on a tuft of emerald foliage near the watchers. The foliage was a dripperlip. Almost at once the paperwing turned gray as its small nourishment content was sucked out. It disintegrated like ash.

Rising cautiously, Lily-yo led the group over to the nearest cable of traverser web. Each adult carried her own urn.

The traversers, largest of all creatures, vegetable or otherwise, could never go into the forest. They spurted out their line among the upper branches, securing it with side strands.

Finding a suitable cable with no traverser in sight, Lily-yo turned, signaling for the urns to be put down. She spoke to Toy, Gren, and the seven other children.

"Now help us climb with our souls into our burnurns. See us tight in. Then carry us to the cable and stick us to it. Then good-bye. We Go Up. You are the group now."

Toy momentarily hesitated. She was a slender girl, her breasts like pearfruit.

"Do not go, Lily-yo," she said. "We still need you."

"It is the way," Lily-yo said firmly.

Prizing open one of the facets of her urn, she slid into her coffin. Helped by the children, the other adults did the same. From habit, Lily-yo glanced to see that Haris was safe.

They were all in now, and helpless. Inside the urns it was surprisingly cool.

The children carried the coffins between them, glancing nervously up at the sky meanwhile. They were afraid. They felt helpless. Only the bold man child Gren looked as if he were enjoying their new sense of independence. He more than Toy directed the others in the placing of the urns upon the traverser's cable.

Lily-yo smelled a curious smell in the urn. As it soaked through her lungs, her senses became detached. Outside, the scene which had been clear, clouded and shrank. She saw she hung suspended on a traverser cable above the treetops, with Flor, Haris, Daphe, Hy and Jury in other urns nearby, hanging helplessly. She saw the children, the new group, run to shelter. Without looking back, they dived into the muddle of foliage on the platform and disappeared.

The traverser hung ten and a half miles above the Tips, safe from its enemies. All about it, space was indigo, and the invisible rays of space bathed it and nourished it. Yet the traverser was still dependent on Earth for some food. After many hours of vegetative dreaming, it swung itself over and climbed down a cable.

Other traversers hung motionless nearby. Occasionally one would blow a globe of oxygen or hitch a leg to try and dislodge a troublesome parasite. Theirs was a leisureliness never attained before. Time was not for them; the sun was theirs, and would ever be until it became unstable, turned nova, and burned both them and itself out.

The traverser fell fast, its feet twinkling, hardly touching the cable, fell straight to the forest, plunging toward the leafy cathedrals of the forest. Here in the air lived its enemies, enemies many times smaller, many times more vicious, many times more clever. Traversers were prey to one of the last families of insect, the tigerflies.

Only tigerflies could kill traversers—kill in their own insidious, invincible way.

Over the long slow eons as the sun's radiation increased, vegetation had evolved to undisputed supremacy. The wasps had developed too, keeping pace with the new developments. They grew in numbers and size as the animal kingdom fell into eclipse and dwindled into the rising tide of green. In time they became the chief enemies of the spiderlike traversers. Attacking in packs, they could paralyze the primitive nerve centers, leaving the traversers to stagger to their own destruction. The tigerflies also laid their eggs in tunnels bored into the stuff of their enemies' bodies; when the eggs hatched, the larvae fed happily on living flesh.

This threat it was, more than anything, that had driven the traversers farther and farther into space many millennia past. In this seemingly inhospitable region, they reached their full and monstrous flowering.

Hard radiation became a necessity for them. Nature's first astronauts, they changed the face of the firmament. Long after man had rolled up his affairs and retired to the trees whence he came, the traversers reconquered that vacant pathway he had lost. Long after intelligence had died from its peak of dominance, the traversers linked indissolubly the green globe and the white—with that antique symbol of neglect, a spider's web.

The traverser scrambled down among the upper leaves, erecting the hairs on its back, where patchy green and black afforded it natural camouflage. On its way down it had collected several creatures caught fluttering in its cables. It sucked them peacefully. When the soupy noises stopped, it vegetated.

Buzzing roused it from its doze. Yellow and black stripes zoomed before its crude eyes. A pair of tigerflies had found it.

With great alacrity, the traverser moved. Its massive bulk, contracted in the atmosphere, had an overall length of over a mile, yet it moved lightly as pollen, scuttling up a cable back to the safety of vacuum.

As it retreated, its legs brushing the web, it picked up various spores, burrs, and tiny creatures that adhered there. It also picked up six burnurns, each containing an insensible human, which swung unregarded from its shin.

Several miles up, the traverser paused. Recovering from its fright, it ejected a globe of oxygen, attaching it gently to a cable. It paused. Its palps trembled. Then it headed out toward deep space, expanding all the time as pressure dropped.

Its speed increased. Folding its legs, the traverser began to eject fresh web from the spinnerets under its abdomen. So it propelled itself, a vast vegetable almost without feeling, rotating slowly to stabilize its temperature.

Hard radiations bathed it. The traverser basked in them. It was in its element.

Daphe roused. She opened her eyes, gazing without intelligence. What she saw had no meaning. She only knew she had Gone Up. This was a new existence and she did not expect it to have meaning.

Part of the view from her urn was eclipsed by stiff yellowy wisps that might have been hair or straw. Everything else was uncertain, being washed either in blinding light or deep shadow. Light and shadow revolved.

Gradually Daphe identified other objects. Most notable was a splendid green half-ball mottled with white and blue. Was it a fruit? To it trailed cables, glinting here and there, many cables, silver or gold in the crazy light. Two traversers she recognized at some distance, traveling fast, looking mummified. Bright points of light sparkled painfully. All was confusion.

This was where gods lived.

Daphe had no feeling. A curious numbness kept her without motion or the wish to move. The smell in the urn was strange. Also the air seemed thick. Everything was like an evil dream. Daphe opened her mouth, her jaw sticky and slow to respond. She screamed. No sound came. Pain filled her. Her sides in particular ached.

Even when her eyes closed again, her mouth hung open.

Like a great shaggy balloon, the traverser floated down to the moon.

It could hardly be said to think, being a mechanism or little more. Yet somewhere in it the notion stirred that its pleasant journey was too brief, that there might be other directions in which to sail. After all, the hated tigerflies were almost as many now, and as troublesome, on the moon as on the earth. Perhaps somewhere there might be a peaceful place, another of these half-round places with green stuff, in the middle of warm delicious rays. . . .

Perhaps some time it might be worth sailing off on a full belly and a new course. . . .

Many traversers hung above the moon. Their nets straggled untidily everywhere. This was their happy base, better liked than the earth, where the air was thick and their limbs were clumsy. This was the place they had discovered first—except for some puny creatures who had been long gone before they arrived. They were the last lords of creation. Largest and lordliest, they enjoyed their long lazy afternoon's supremacy.

The traverser slowed, spinning out no more cable. In leisurely fashion, it picked its way through a web and drifted down to the pallid vegetation of the moon. . . .

Here were conditions very unlike those on the heavy planet. The many-trunked banyans had never gained supremacy here; in the thin air and low gravity they outgrew their strength and collapsed. In their place, monstrous celeries and parsleys grew, and it was into a bed of these that the traverser settled. Hissing from its exertions, it blew off a great cloud of oxygen and relaxed.

As it settled down into the foliage, its great sack of body rubbed against the stems. Its legs too scraped into the mass of leaves. From legs and body a shower of light debris was dislodged—burrs, seeds,

grit, nuts, and leaves caught up in its sticky fibers back on distant
earth. Among this detritus were six seed casings from a burnurn plant.
They rolled over the ground and came to a standstill.

Haris the man was the first to awaken. Groaning with an unexpected
pain in his sides, he tried to sit up. Pressure on his forehead reminded
him of where he was. Doubling up knees and arms, he pushed against
the lid of his coffin.

Momentarily, it resisted him. Then the whole urn crumbled into
pieces, sending Haris sprawling. The rigors of total vacuum had destroyed its cohesive powers.

Unable to pick himself up, Haris lay where he was. His head
throbbed, his lungs were full of an unpleasant odor. Eagerly he
gasped in fresh air. At first it seemed thin and chill, yet he sucked it in
with gratitude.

After a while, he was well enough to look about him.

Long yellow tendrils were stretching out of a nearby thicket, working their way gingerly toward him. Alarmed, he looked about for a
woman to protect him. None was there. Stiffly, his arms so stiff, he
pulled his knife from his belt, rolled over on one side, and lopped
the tendrils off as they reached him. This was an easy enemy!

Haris cried. He screamed. He jumped unsteadily to his feet, yelling
in disgust at himself. Suddenly he had noticed he was covered in
scabs. Worse, as his clothes fell in shreds from him, he saw that a
mass of leathery flesh grew from his arms, his ribs, his legs. When he
lifted his arms, the mass stretched out almost like wings. He was
spoiled, his handsome body ruined.

A sound made him turn, and for the first time he remembered
his fellows. Lily-yo was struggling from the remains of her burnurn.
She raised a hand in greeting.

To his horror, Haris saw that she bore disfigurements like his own.
In truth, at first he scarcely recognized her. She resembled nothing
so much as one of the hated flymen. He flung himself to the ground
and wept as his heart expanded in fear and loathing.

Lily-yo was not born to weep. Disregarding her own painful deformities, breathing laboriously, she cast about, seeking the other
four coffins.

Flor's was the first she found, half buried though it was. A blow
with a stone shattered it, Lily-yo lifted up her friend, as hideously
transformed as she, and in a short while Flor roused. Inhaling the
strange air raucously, she too sat up. Lily-yo left her to seek the others.

Even in her dazed state, she thanked her aching limbs for feeling so light.

Daphe was dead. She lay stiff and purple in her urn. Though Lily-yo shattered it and called aloud, Daphe did not stir. Her swollen tongue stayed dreadfully protruding from her mouth. Daphe was dead, Daphe who had lived, Daphe who had been the sweet singer.

Hy also was dead, a poor shriveled thing lying in a coffin that had cracked on its arduous journey between the two worlds. When that coffin shattered under Lily-yo's blow, Hy fell away to powder. Hy was dead. Hy who had borne a man child. Hy always so fleet of foot.

Jury's urn was the last. She stirred as the headwoman reached her. A minute later, she was sitting up, eyeing her deformities with a stoical distaste, breathing the sharp air. Jury lived.

Haris staggered over to the women. In his hand he carried his soul.

"Four of us!" he exclaimed. "Have we been received by the gods or no?"

"We feel pain—so we live," Lily-yo said. "Daphe and Hy have fallen to the green."

Bitterly, Haris flung down his soul and trampled it underfoot.

"Look at us! Better be dead!" he said.

"Before we decide that, we will eat," said Lily-yo.

Painfully, they retreated into the thicket, alerting themselves once more to the idea of danger. Flor, Lily-yo, Jury, Haris, each supported the other. The idea of tabu had somehow been forgotten.

V

"No proper trees grow here," Flor protested, as they pushed among giant celeries whose crests waved high above their heads.

"Take care!" Lily-yo said. She pulled Flor back. Something rattled and snapped like a chained dog, missing Flor's leg by inches.

A trappersnapper, having missed its prey, was slowly reopening its jaws, baring its green teeth. This one was only a shadow of the terrible trappersnappers spawned on the jungle floors of earth. Its jaws were weaker, its movements far more circumscribed. Without the shelter of the giant banyans, the trappersnappers were disinherited.

Something of the same feeling overcame the humans. They and their ancestors for countless generations had lived in the high trees.

Safety was arboreal. Here there were only celery and parsley trees, offering neither the rock-steadiness nor the unlimited boughs of the giant banyan.

So they journeyed, nervous, lost, in pain, knowing neither where they were nor why they were.

They were attacked by leapycreepers and sawthorns, and beat them down. They skirted a thicket of nettlemoss taller and wider than any to be met with on earth. Conditions that worked against one group of vegetation favored others. They climbed a slope and came on a pool fed by a stream. Over the pool hung berries and fruits, sweet to taste, good to eat.

"This is not so bad," Haris said. "Perhaps we can still live."

Lily-yo smiled at him. He was the most trouble, the most lazy; yet she was glad he was still here. When they bathed in the pool, she looked at him again. For all the strange scales that covered him, and the two broad sweeps of flesh that hung by his side, he was still good to look on just because he was Haris. She hoped she was also comely. With a burr she raked her hair back; only a little of it fell out.

When they had bathed, they ate. Haris worked then, collecting fresh knives from the bramblebushes. They were not as tough as the ones on earth, but they would have to do. Then they rested in the sun.

The pattern of their lives was completely broken. More by instinct than intelligence they had lived. Without the group, without the tree, without the earth, no pattern guided them. What was the way or what was not became unclear. So they lay where they were and rested.

As she lay there, Lily-yo looked about her. All was strange, so that her heart beat faintly.

Though the sun shone bright as ever, the sky was as deep blue as a vandalberry. And the half-globe in the sky was monstrous, all streaked with green and blue and white, so that Lily-yo could not know it for somewhere she had lived. Phantom silver lines pointed to it, while nearer at hand the tracery of traverser webs glittered, veining the whole sky. Traversers moved over it like clouds, their great bodies slack.

All this was their empire, their creation. On their first journeys here, many millennia ago, they had literally laid the seeds of this world. To begin with, they had withered and died by the thousand on the inhospitable ash. But even the dead had brought their little legacies of oxygen, soil, spores, and seed, some of which later sprouted on the fruitful corpses. Under the weight of dozing centuries, they gained a sort of foothold.

They grew. Stunted and ailing in the beginning, they grew. With vegetal tenacity, they grew. They exhaled. They spread. They thrived. Slowly the broken wastes of the moon's lit face turned green. In the craters creepers grew. Up the ravaged slopes the parsleys crawled. As the atmosphere deepened, so the magic of life intensified, its rhythm strengthened, its tempo increased. More thoroughly than another dominant species had once managed to do, the traversers colonized the moon.

Lily-yo could know or care little about any of this. She turned her face from the sky.

Flor had crawled over to Haris the man. She lay against him in the circle of his arms, half under the shelter of his new skin, and she stroked his hair.

Furious, Lily-yo jumped up, kicked Flor on the shin, and then flung herself upon her, using teeth and nails to pull her away. Jury ran to join in.

"This is not time for mating!" Lily-yo cried.

"Let me *go!*" cried Flor.

Haris in his startlement jumped up. He stretched his arms, waved them, and rose effortlessly into the air.

"Look!" he shouted in alarmed delight.

Over their heads he circled once, perilously. Then he lost his balance and came sprawling head first, mouth open in fright. Head first he pitched into the pool.

Three anxious, awe-struck, love-struck female humans dived after him in unison.

While they were drying themselves, they heard noises in the forest. At once they became alert, their old selves. They drew their new swords and looked to the thicket.

The wiltmilt when it appeared was not like its Earthly brothers. No longer upright like a jack-in-the-box, it groped its way along like a caterpillar.

The humans saw its distorted eye break from the celeries. Then they turned and fled.

Even when the danger was left behind, they moved rapidly, not knowing what they sought. Once they slept, ate, and then again pressed on through the unending growth, the undying daylight, until they came to where the jungle gaped.

Ahead of them, everything seemed to cease and then go on again.

Cautiously they approached. The ground underfoot had been badly uneven. Now it broke altogether into a wide crevasse. Beyond the crevasse the vegetation grew again—but how did humans pass the gulf? The four of them stood anxiously where the ferns ended, looking across at the far side.

Haris the man screwed his face in pain to show he had a troublesome idea in his head.

"What I did before—going up in the air," he began awkwardly. "If we do it again now, all of us, we go in the air across to the other side."

"No!" Lily-yo said. "When you go up you come down hard. You will fall to the green!"

"I will do better than before."

"No!" repeated Lily-yo. "You are not to go."

"Let him go," Flor said.

The two women turned to glare at each other. Taking his chance, Haris raised his arms, waved them, rose slightly from the ground, and began to use his legs too. He moved forward over the crevasse before his nerve broke.

As he fluttered down, Flor and Lily-yo, moved by instinct, dived into the gulf after him. Spreading their arms, they glided about him, shouting. Jury remained behind, crying in baffled anger down to them.

Regaining a little control, Haris landed heavily on an outcropping ledge. The two women alighted chattering and scolding beside him. They looked up. Two lips fringed with green fern sucked a narrow purple segment of sky. Jury could not be seen, though her cries still echoed down to them.

Behind the ledge on which they stood, a tunnel ran into the cliff. All the rock face was peppered with similar holes, so that it resembled a sponge. From the hole behind the ledge ran three flymen, two male and one female. They rushed out with ropes and spears.

Flor and Lily-yo were bending over Haris. Before they had time to recover, they were knocked sprawling and tied with the ropes. Helpless, Lily-yo saw other flymen launch themselves from other holes and come gliding in to help secure them. Their flight seemed more sure, more graceful, than it had on earth. Perhaps the way humans were lighter here had something to do with it.

"Bring them in!" the flymen cried to each other. Their sharp, clever faces jostled around eagerly as they hoisted up their captives and bore them into the tunnel.

In their alarm, Lily-yo, Flor, and Haris forgot about Jury, still crouching on the lip of the crevasse. They never saw her again. A pack of thinpins got her.

The tunnel sloped gently down. Finally it curved and led into another which ran level and true. This in its turn led into an immense cavern with regular sides and a regular roof. Gray daylight flooded in at one end, for the cavern stood at the bottom of the crevasse.

To the middle of this cavern the three captives were brought. Their knives were taken from them and they were released. As they huddled together uneasily, one of the flymen stood forward and spoke.

"We will not harm you unless we must," he said. "You come by traverser from the Heavy World. You are new here. When you learn our ways, you will join us."

"I am Lily-yo," Lily-yo proudly said. "Let me go. We three are humans. You are flymen."

"Yes, you are humans, we are flymen. Also we are humans, you are flymen. Now you know nothing. Soon you will know, when you have seen the Captives. They will tell you many things."

"I am Lily-yo. I know many things."

"The Captives will tell you many more things."

"If there were many more things, then I would know them."

"I am Band Appa Bondi and I say come to see the Captives. Your talk is stupid Heavy World talk, Lily-yo."

Several flymen began to look aggressive, so that Haris nudged Lily-yo and muttered, "Let us do what he asks."

Grumpily, Lily-yo let herself and her two companions be led to another chamber. This one was partially ruined, and it stank. At the far end of it, a fall of cindery rock marked where the roof had fallen in, while a shaft of the unremitting sunlight burned on the floor, sending up a curtain of golden light about itself. Near this light were the Captives.

"Do not fear to see them. They will not harm you," Band Appa Bondi said, going forward.

The encouragement was needed, for the Captives were not prepossessing.

Eight of them there were, eight Captives, kept in eight great burn-urns big enough to serve them as narrow cells. The cells stood grouped in a semicircle. Band Appa Bondi led Lily-yo, Flor, and Haris into the middle of this semicircle, where they could survey and be surveyed.

The Captives were painful to look on. All had some kind of deformity. One had no legs. One had no flesh on his lower jaw. One had four gnarled dwarf arms. One had short wings of flesh connecting earlobes and thumbs, so that he lived perpetually with hands half raised to his face. One had boneless arms trailing at his side and one boneless leg. One had monstrous wings which trailed about him like carpet. One was hiding his ill-shaped form away behind a screen of his own excrement, smearing it onto the transparent walls of his cell. And one had a second head, a small, wizened thing growing from the first that fixed Lily-yo with a malevolent eye. This last Captive, who seemed to lead the others, spoke now, using the mouth of his main head.

"I am the Chief Captive. I greet you. You are of the Heavy World. We are of the True World. Now you join us because you are of us. Though your wings and your scars are new, you may join us."

"I am Lily-yo. We three are humans. You are only flymen. We will not join you."

The Captives grunted in boredom. The Chief Captive spoke again.

"Always this talk from you of the Heavy World! You *have* joined us! You are flymen, we are human. You know little, we know much."

"But we—"

"Stop your stupid talk, woman!"

"We are—"

"Be silent, woman, and listen," Band Appa Bondi said.

"We know much," repeated the Chief Captive. "Some things we will tell you. All who make the journey from the Heavy World become changed. Some die. Most live and grow wings. Between the worlds are many strong rays, not seen or felt, which change our bodies. When you come here, when you come to the True World, you become a true human. The grub of the tigerfly is not a tigerfly until it changes. So humans change."

"I cannot know what he says," Haris said stubbornly, throwing himself down. But Lily-yo and Flor were listening.

"To this True World, as you call it, we come to die," Lily-yo said, doubtingly.

The Captive with the fleshless jaw said, "The grub of the tigerfly thinks it dies when it changes into a tigerfly."

"You are still young," said the Chief Captive. "You begin newly here. Where are your souls?"

Lily-yo and Flor looked at each other. In their flight from the wiltmilt they had heedlessly thrown down their souls. Haris had trampled on his. It was unthinkable!

"You see. You needed them no more. You are still young. You may be able to have babies. Some of those babies may be born with wings."

The Captive with the boneless arms added, "Some may be born wrong, as we are. Some may be born right."

"You are too foul to live!" Haris growled. "Why are you not killed?"

"Because we know all things," the Chief Captive said. Suddenly his second head roused itself and declared, "To be a good shape is not all in life. To know is also good. Because we cannot move well we can—*think*. This tribe of the True World is good and knows these things. So it lets us rule it."

Flor and Lily-yo muttered together.

"Do you say that you poor Captives *rule* the True World?" Lily-yo asked at last.

"We do."

"Then why are you Captives?"

The flyman with earlobes and thumbs connected, making his perpetual little gesture of protest, spoke for the first time.

"To rule is to serve, woman. Those who bear power are slaves to it. Only an outcast is free. Because we are Captives, we have the time to talk and think and plan and know. Those who know command the lives of others."

"No hurt will come to you, Lily-yo," Band Appa Bondi added. "You will live among us and enjoy your life free from harm."

"No!" the Chief Captive said with both mouths. "Before she can enjoy, Lily-yo and her companion Flor—this other man creature is plainly useless—must help our great plan."

"The invasion?" Bondi asked.

"What else? Flor and Lily-yo, you arrive here at a good time. Memories of the Heavy World and its savage life are still fresh in you. We need such memories. So we ask you to go back there on a great plan we have."

"Go back?" gasped Flor.

"Yes. We plan to attack the Heavy World. You must help to lead our force."

VI

The long afternoon of eternity wore on, that long golden road of an afternoon that would somewhere lead to an everlasting night. Motion there was, but motion without event—except for those negligible events that seemed so large to the creatures participating in them.

For Lily-yo, Flor and Haris there were many events. Chief of these was that they learned to fly properly.

The pains associated with their wings soon died away as the wonderful new flesh and tendons strengthened. To sail up in the light gravity became an increasing delight—the ugly flopping movements of flymen on the Heavy World had no place here.

They learned to fly in packs, and then to hunt in packs. In time they were trained to carry out the Captives' plan.

The series of accidents that had first delivered humans to this world in burnurns had been a fortunate one, growing more fortunate as millennia tolled away. For gradually the humans adapted better to the True World. Their survival factor became greater, their power surer. And all this as on the Heavy World conditions grew more and more adverse to anything but the giant vegetables.

Lily-yo at least was quick to see how much easier life was in these new conditions. She sat with Flor and a dozen others eating pulped pluggyrug, before they did the Captives' bidding and left for the Heavy World.

It was hard to express all she felt.

"Here we are safe," she said, indicating the whole green land that sweltered under the silver network of webs.

"Except from the tigerflies," Flor agreed.

They rested on a bare peak, where the air was thin and even the giant creepers had not climbed. The turbulent green stretched away below them, almost as if they were on Earth—although here it was continually checked by the circular formations of rock.

"This world is smaller," Lily-yo said, trying again to make Flor know what was in her head. "Here we are bigger. We do not need to fight so much."

"Soon we must fight."

"Then we can come back here again. This is a good place, with nothing so savage and with not so many enemies. Here the groups could live without so much fear. Veggy and Toy and May and Gren and the other little ones would like it here."

"They would miss the trees."

"We shall soon miss the trees no longer. We have wings instead."

This idle talk took place beneath the unmoving shadow of a rock. Overhead, silver blobs against a purple sky, the traversers went, walking their networks, descending only occasionally to the celeries far below. As Lily-yo fell to watching these creatures, she thought in her mind of the grand plan the Captives had hatched. She flicked it over in a series of vivid pictures.

Yes, the Captives knew. They could see ahead as she could not. She and those about her had lived like plants, doing what came. The Captives were not plants. From their cells they saw more than those outside.

This, the Captives saw: that the few humans who reached the True World bore few children, because they were old, or because the rays that made their wings grow made their seed die; that it was good here, and would be better still with more humans; that one way to get more humans here was to bring babies and children from the Heavy World.

For countless time, this had been done. Brave flymen had traveled back to that other world and stolen children. The flymen who had once attacked Lily-yo's group on their climb to the Tips had been on that mission. They had taken Bain to bring her to the True World in burnurns—and had not been heard of since.

Many perils and mischances lay in that long double journey. Of those who set out, few returned.

Now the Captives had thought of a better and more daring scheme.

"Here comes a traverser," Band Appa Bondi said. "Let us be ready to move."

He walked before the pack of twelve flyers who had been chosen for this new attempt. He was the leader. Lily-yo, Flor, and Haris were in support of him, together with eight others, three male, five female. Only one of them, Band Appa Bondi himself, had been carried to the True World as a boy.

Slowly the pack stood up, stretching their wings. The moment for their great adventure was here. Yet they felt little fear; they could not look ahead as the Captives did, except perhaps for Band Appa Bondi and Lily-yo. She strengthened her will by saying, "It is the way." Then they all spread their arms wide and soared off to meet the traverser.

The traverser had eaten.

It had caught one of its most tasty enemies, a tigerfly, in a web, and had sucked it till only a shell was left. Now it sank down into a bed of celeries, crushing them under its great bulk. Gently, it began to bud. Afterward, it would head out for the great black gulfs, where heat and radiance called it. It had been born on this world. Being young, it had never yet made that dreaded, desired journey.

Its buds burst up from its back, hung over, popped, fell to the ground, and scurried away to bury themselves in the pulp and dirt where they might begin their ten thousand years' growth in peace.

Young though it was, the traverser was sick. It did not know this. The enemy tigerfly had been at it, but it did not know this. Its vast bulk held little sensation.

The twelve humans glided down and landed on its back, low down on the abdomen in a position hidden from the creature's cluster of eyes. They sank among the tough shoulder-high fibers that served the traverser as hair, and looked about them. A rayplane swooped overhead and disappeared. A trio of tumbleweeds skittered into the fibers and were seen no more. All was as quiet as if they lay on a small deserted hill.

At length they spread out and moved along in line, heads down, eyes searching, Band Appa Bondi at one end, Lily-yo at the other. The great body was streaked and pitted and scarred, so that progress down the slope was not easy. The fiber grew in patterns of different shades, green, yellow, black, breaking up the traverser's bulk when seen from the air, serving it as natural camouflage. In many places, tough parasitic plants had rooted themselves, drawing their nourishment entirely from their host; most of them would die when the traverser launched itself out between worlds.

The humans worked hard. Once they were thrown flat when the traverser changed position. As the slope down which they moved grew steeper, so progress became more slow.

"Here!" cried Y Coyin, one of the women.

At last they had found what they sought, what the Captives sent them to seek.

Clustering around Y Coyin with their knives out, the pack looked down.

Here the fibers had been neatly champed away in swathes, leaving a bare patch as far across as a human was long. In this patch was a round scab. Lily-yo felt it. It was immensely hard.

Lo Jint put his ear to it. Silence.

They looked at each other.

No signal was needed, none given.

Together they knelt, prizing with their knives around the scab. Once the traverser moved, and they threw themselves flat. A bud rose nearby, popped, rolled down the slope and fell to the distant ground. A thinpin devoured it as it ran. The humans continued prizing.

The scab moved. They lifted it off. A dark and sticky tunnel was revealed to them.

"I go first," Band Appa Bondi said.

He lowered himself into the hole. The others followed. Dark sky showed roundly above them until the twelfth human was in the tunnel. Then the scab was drawn back into place. A soft slobber of sound came from it as it began to heal back into position again.

They crouched where they were for a long time. They crouched, their knives ready, their wings folded around them, their human hearts beating strongly.

In more than one sense they were in enemy territory. At the best of times, traversers were only allies by accident; they ate humans as readily as they devoured anything else. But this burrow was the work of that yellow and black destroyer, the tigerfly. One of the last true insects to survive, the tough and resourceful tigerflies had instinctively made the most invincible of all living things its prey.

The female tigerfly alights and bores her tunnel into the traverser. Working her way down, she at last stops and prepares a natal chamber, hollowing it from the living traverser, paralyzing the matter with her needletail to prevent its healing again. There she lays her store of eggs before climbing back to daylight. When the eggs hatch, the larvae have fresh and living stuff to nourish them.

After a while, Band Appa Bondi gave a sign and the pack moved forward, climbing awkwardly down the tunnel. A faint luminescence guided their eyes. The air lay heavy and green in their chests. They moved very slowly, very quietly, for they heard movement ahead.

Suddenly the movement was on them.

"Look out!" Band Appa Bondi cried.

From the terrible dark, something launched itself at them.

Before they realized it, the tunnel had curved and widened into the natal chamber. The tigerfly's eggs had hatched. Two hundred larvae with jaws as wide as a man's reach turned on the intruders, snapping in fury and fear.

Even as Band Appa Bondi sliced his first attacker, another had his head off. He fell, and his companions launched themselves over him. Pressing forward, they dodged those clicking jaws.

Behind their hard heads, the larvae were soft and plump. One slash of a sword and they burst, their entrails flowing out. They fought, but knew not how to fight. Savagely the humans stabbed, ducked, and stabbed. No other human died. With backs to the wall they cut and thrust, breaking jaws, ripping flimsy stomachs. They killed unceasingly with neither hate nor mercy until they stood knee deep in slush. The larvae snapped and writhed and died. Uttering a grunt of satisfaction, Haris slew the last of them.

Wearily then, eleven humans crawled back to the tunnel, there to wait until the mess drained away—and then to wait a longer while.

The traverser stirred in its bed of celeries. Vague impulses drifted through its being. Things it had done. Things it had to do. The things it had done had been done, the things it had to do were still to do. Blowing off oxygen, it heaved itself up.

Slowly at first, it swung up a cable, climbing to the network where the air thinned. Always, always before in the eternal afternoon it had stopped here. This time there seemed no reason for stopping. Air was nothing, heat was all, the heat that blistered and prodded and chafed and coaxed increasingly with height. . . .

It blew a jet of cable from a spinneret. Gaining speed, gaining intention, it rocketed its mighty vegetable self out and away from the place where the tigerflies flew. Ahead of it floated a semicircle of light, white and blue and green; it was a useful thing to look at to avoid getting lost.

For this was a lonely place for a young traverser, a terrible-wonderful bright-dark place, so full of nothing. Turn as you speed and you fry well on all sides . . . nothing to trouble you. . . .

. . . Except that deep in your core a little pack of humans use you as an ark for their own purposes. You carry them back to a world that once—so staggeringly long ago—belonged to their kind; you carry them back so that they may eventually—who knows?—fill another world with their own kind.

For remember, there is always plenty of time.

Ozymandias

Terry Carr

One of Terry Carr's special interests is Egyptology; a book that he turns to again and again is Howard Carter's The Tomb of Tut-ankh-amen, *the famous account of the discovery of the boy-Pharaoh's tomb in Egypt's royal graveyard near Thebes. Here he transfers the Egyptian past to our future and shows us a world in which civilization has collapsed, in which mankind has mutated into many strange forms, in which the treasures of antiquity are sought by mutant grave robbers hoping to discover yesterday's marvels.*

They came up out of the groundstars howling and leaping, laughing and pushing, singing into the night a strange, tuneless, polyphonal chant. They proceeded past the markers and twice around them, still giggling and chanting, and spread out in a wavering line that went up the hill like a snake. It took them ten minutes to go from the markers to the boundary, a distance of no more than fifty paces for a walker—but these were not walkers, they were robbers, and they had the laws to follow.

Sooleyrah was in the lead, because he was the best dancer among them—the most graceful and quick and, even more important, the most inventive. No approach to the vaults could be made in just the same way any had been made before, and if the watcher, who was always second in line, noticed a pattern developing that he thought he might have seen before, it was his job to trip the leader, or shove him, or kick him, or whatever was necessary to shake him into a new rhythm or direction. On those raids when the leader invented enough new variations, and the watcher made sure there were no repeats from the past, then they had a successful raid. When leader and watcher failed, there were explosions, blindings, gases, and sometimes the sound-without-sound, and then there was death.

But Sooleyrah was in good form tonight, and even Kreech, who was watcher, had to admit that.

"Go good," he chanted. "Go good, good, good, go good." Then he tripped Sooleyrah, but only for the fun of it, and danced in a circle till the leader bounded up and continued.

"Watchers got easy, yeah easy," Sooleyrah sang. "Easy trip leader, no reason; damn no reason." He did a double-back step and whirled, his flying foot narrowly missing Kreech's mouth.

"Reason next time," he sang, and laughed.

Behind him, Kreech did the whirling step, just missing the next in line, and he too laughed; then the third man followed it, and the kick and laugh traveled back down the hill, undulating in the darkness. Sooleyrah, slim and graceful and dark-bearded, did a slide, three jumps, then rolled on the ground, leading always upward, toward the vaults. They stood black and distant against the night sky at hill-crest, jagged storehouses of darkness.

"Don't matter anyway," Kreech told him. "Don't matter, Sooleyrah, don't leader matter. Go good, go bad, no difference." He rolled, following Sooleyrah up the hill, and the small bells he carried in his tattered shirt pocket tinkled dully. "You heard he said, don't matter."

"Hell damn, yeah," Sooleyrah sang. "Damn yeah, damn fat boy, damn he knows." He paused, straining on tiptoe to look back down the line. The fat boy was only a little way behind them, puffing and gasping already as he tried to follow the upward dance; he wasn't accustomed to it, as anyone could see. His gray-washed tunic was splotching dark with sweat; his hair, cut short at ear-length, fell in sweat-strings down his forehead.

Kreech paused, turned, looked back, and so did the next man, and the next, and so on until the one in front of the fat boy turned suddenly to stare at him; and the fat boy yipped, startled, then caught on to it and turned to look back himself.

Sooleyrah laughed again, and returned to his dance. "Damn fat boy no good anyway," he sang. "No good, know nothing, no good, know nothing."

"Hell damn yourself," Kreech said. "Damn fat boy almost a thinker. *Damn* almost."

Sooleyrah snorted, and did a particularly difficult series of jump-steps deliberately for the confounding of the almost-thinker back down the line. "Damn-almost as good as nowhere, nowhere," he sang. "That's thinkers now anyway, nowhere, nowhere. Nowhere."

"Except fat boy," Kreech said.

"Hell fat boy," Sooleyrah said, lapsing from song in his disgust. "Fat boy don't know, but you know, I know. Vaults still there—*there!*" —he pointed up the hill, still dancing—"so what's fat boy know? So we dance, we sing, careful, damn careful."

They were halfway up the hill now, the luminescent groundstars merging into a bright mist spread over the valley below, where only occasional widely spaced bones of buildings thrust up into the open night air. The rest of the valley, all the way to the mountains, was groundstars from here.

Above them, up the hill, blackness grew and deepened with each step, and the massive vaults loomed black against the weak, scattered light of the skystars. The vaults covered the crown of the hill, most of them broken or crumbled or even exploded by now—the result of centuries of raids by the valley robbers. Those that still stood were all empty inside, or so the thinkers had said, but Sooleyrah didn't believe them. There were always more vaults to open—always had been, always would be. Hell damn foolishness to say there weren't, or wouldn't be.

If the vaults all became empty, there would be no toys, no star-boxes, no tools to replace those worn and broken or maybe thrown away dull, and no samesongs or pictures or any of the other things that had been stored there for the valley people. Which was ridiculous and unthinkable, and Sooleyrah wouldn't think it.

So he danced on upward, darting to right and left, rolling and tumbling, laughing into the empty air, while behind him, one by one, the others pointed after him to the vaults, and danced and tumbled, and echoes of his laugh faded back down the line.

Lasten, the fat boy, was frightened. He had never been on a raid before, had never been trained for it. He knew he would make some disastrous mistake at any moment, and then the others would turn on him. Or, if they did get to the vaults without trouble, it would be a night for the Immortals.

Probably gas or the sound-without-sound, he thought. *Not so afraid of a blinding—least you can get back down the hill from that. But it be something killing for me, yeah.*

Well, he was lucky to be alive anyway: all the other thinkers had been killed the night before. Massacred by the robbers—just lined up in the hubsquare and stoned to death. Oh, the screaming and panic, the ones who tried to run with their ankles hobbled, the manic singing and shouting of the robbers. . . . Lasten shuddered, hating himself for his cowardice, hating the way he had hidden in an unused basement where groundstars were so thick they made a shimmering fog. Hiding, he had heard all of it anyway, had even seen some of the worst scenes, the most vivid ones; they'd invaded his mind in waves of terror from the thinkers or, sometimes, exultation and a kind of crazed kill-frenzy from the robbers. For Lasten, the fat boy, was a weird, one of the 10 percent of human mutations that managed to live in each generation.

Some were born with extra toes, or no feet at all; these were the common ones, the ones who lived as easily as anyone else, accepting tithes from the market thieves as they rocked back and forth in the dirt and listened for rumors to sell. Others were born already dead or dying, with jellied skulls or tiny hearts unable to support life. And a few, a very few, had extra things that no one else had: not just extra hands or grotesquely oversized private parts (like Kreech, like Kreech), but *talents.* Lasten's father, for instance, had had a talent for numbers; he could remember how many seasons ago a thing had happened, or how often it had happened during his lifetime, or even put numbers together in his head to make new numbers. And Sooleyrah claimed he had a place somewhere in his head where everything was always level, and that was why he was such a good dancer.

Lasten could hear people's minds. Not their thoughts, for people don't have thoughts inside; Lasten heard emotions and mind-pictures, whatever was strongest in the consciousness of those around him. Red hate, boiling and exploding; sometimes pure fear, blue-white, rigid; sex fantasies that echoed disturbingly in Lasten's own mind. They came at him unbidden; he couldn't shut them out when they were really strong, as they had been last night. Blood, blood on the ground, dark blood spurting from crushed skulls, a trail of red where one man had tried to drag his battered body away to safety. And screaming: Lasten had heard the screams of both the killers and the dying, and had found himself, when it was over, huddled in a corner and still screaming himself, his throat hoarse and ragged. He was crying, and he had emptied his stomach and his bowels simultaneously, helpless to stop either.

And it had all been unnecessary, because they wouldn't have killed him anyway. He wasn't yet a thinker.

Yeah, only thinkers got the death, only official thinkers. Dumb robbers don't know I'm a thinker too, just not entered yet. Dumb robbers don't know hell damn thing.

Lasten tripped over his feet trying to accomplish a whirling jump-step; he fell gasping to the ground, and for a second he thought he'd lie there, let the line pass him while he caught his breath. But the next in line kicked him sharply, kicked him again and again, and Lasten moaned and struggled to his feet. He ran weakly to catch up to the line ahead, sweating and whimpering. He knew he'd never get back alive from this raid. Probably none of them would.

Should try to get away, roll out into the dark where they can't see, maybe they'd go right by. Couldn't stop to look for me, no; rest of the line has to keep up or the approach goes bad, sure it does. Damn dumb robbers.

But he didn't have the quickness to get out of sight before they'd catch him and drag him back into line, and he knew it. Yeah, damn dumb robbers were going to get themselves killed, blown up, burned —and fat boy thinker Lasten was going to get killed with them, because he couldn't get away.

"Fat boy fell down," Kreech laughed, stepping high behind Sooleyrah's lead. "Daipell kicked him, kicked him, kicked him, fat boy got up."

Sooleyrah paused, looked angrily back down the hill. The fat boy was back in line now, clumsily following the steps. Sooleyrah could hardly see him now, they had progressed so far up into the skystar darkness; but the fat boy's size stood out against the brightness of the valley groundstars below.

"Fat boy messes up my approach, I'll kill him, smash him with rocks, rocks," Sooleyrah chanted. "Yeah, like the rest, make him a thinker too. No good, any thinker." Abruptly he whirled, and did an easy dance-skip straight up the hill. Kreech immediately followed him.

"Told you leave him back, leave him back," Kreech sang. "No good dancer, yeah you're right, *damn* right. No good for the rest."

"Fat boy dances right or I damn smash him with rocks," Sooleyrah said.

"We don't smash nobody if we're dead too. No good dancer, no good approach, no good at the vaults. Get ourselves dead, because of fat boy."

Sooleyrah slowed his dancing even more than he already had. He did a waddlestep, then giggled and broke into a tension-high laugh. "Go slow, go easy for fat boy. Go easy so he can follow, so we get into vaults right, no killing tonight. Waddle waddle, kind of dance fat boy does all the time anyway." He giggled again. "Make sure no killing at vaults, show damn almost-thinker vaults still there. Yeah, let him see for himself, no different from always, always. . . ."

Kreech leaped forward quickly and tripped him. Their feet tangled together and they both fell, Sooleyrah's lean form sprawling loosely, Kreech's bulkier body hitting the sparse grass heavily. Sooleyrah rolled over quickly and was on his feet almost immediately. Kreech grunted and bounded up too.

"Go bad there," he sang. "Too much the same, go bad, go lousy. Got to go *good,* Sooleyrah, go *good,* go *good.*"

The next man in line caught up to them, and he deftly tripped Kreech and fell to the ground beside him, following the lead. Sooleyrah whooped his laughter, whirled and danced on up the hill.

"Yeah, go good tonight," he sang. "Just let fat boy thinker see, yeah, then tomorrow we smash him, *damn* yeah."

And it was all so useless, so senseless. Lasten puffed and sweated trying to follow the lead of the man ahead of him in the line, trying to duplicate each movement, each step, every twist or hop or gesture; that was the rule when the robbers went up to the vaults, and if you didn't follow it they might stop long enough to kill you. Senselessly, uselessly.

Because it didn't matter. The whole ritual of the dance-approach, the singsong chanting, the leader and the watcher . . . all unnecessary. The robbers thought they were conquering taboos by the skill of their dancing whenever they made a successful approach to the vaults, and they thought they'd failed when instead they encountered the vault-fires, the blindings, the deaths . . . but fat boy Lasten, who had been trained as a thinker, knew better.

Damn yeah, know better than dumb robbers.

The robbers could have walked straight up the hill to the vaults, no wandering snakelike line, no jumping and dancing, no chanting. They could have approached any of the vaults, and they would have gotten in without incident . . . or else they would have been gassed or blinded or killed. Sometimes a raid would get through the Immortals' defenses, and sometimes it would mean danger and death, but it had nothing to do with the dance or the rituals.

Yeah, dance it right and you get in, or dance it wrong and you get killed. Stupid, stupid.

Lasten's people had been thinkers, the ones who kept the old knowledge, or what remained of it. They knew that the vaults were guarded not by curses or demons, nor by strange magic laws that judged and recorded the dance steps of generations of ignorant vault robbers. No, these vaults had been protected by the Immortals in ways even the thinkers no longer knew . . . but it was not magic. There were hidden eyes surrounding each vault, and they defended against invasion with a variety of weapons. Gas was one, explosions were another; that was plain enough. The sound-without-sound was not so simple, nor the blinding lights, but they were all the same, only defenses left to guard the vaults.

The world that had created those vaults was gone, destroyed in bombings and explosions and gases so powerful they had killed most of the Immortals. They screamed and died, screamed and died, until only a handful were left, grubbing among the ruins, their women bearing strange children, and all of them dazzled by the groundstars that filled the low places everywhere.

Each spring now, as soon as the thaw was complete, the people of the valley held memorial for the past and the thinkers told the story.

The man ahead of Lasten was waddling now, laughing as he glanced back to see the fat boy follow the lead. Lasten cursed in ragged gasps, but he waddled after him as the man leaped forward to trip the dancer in front of him. The two of them fell sprawling to the ground, and giggled and laughed as they rose.

"Hey yeah, fat boy," the dancer ahead of him sang, "come get me, fat boy, your turn to trip ole Sharksey," and he danced in a circle, waiting, giggling, challenging.

Lasten sucked harsh air into his lungs, gathered what strength he had and ran forward to swing a leg and trip the man. But his aim was short; he felt himself falling, off balance, saw Sharksey's face sud-

denly angry, and then he was on the ground gasping weakly, and
Sharksey muttered "Sisterson!" and leaped upon him.

The man's weight was not great, but the impact knocked the rest
of Lasten's wind out of him. He moaned weakly, hardly feeling the
elbows Sharksey was wielding freely as he rolled off him and got to
his feet. "Damn lousy fat Lasten, should've been made a thinker so
you'd be killed too. No good dancer, *damn* no good. Get us all killed,
yeah, only maybe we kill you, kill Lasten, hey kill fat boy, yeah?
Yeah? Unless you get *up*, fat boy, *up* right now, right *now!*"

And Lasten struggled to his feet while Sharksey continued to dance
around him cursing and threatening. He stood up shuddering, and
Sharksey sang, "Okay, dance it right, dance right . . . oh yeah, or we
kill you, Lasten, and you know it, you know it, don't you?" He
laughed, whirled and danced on upward to follow the others.

Lasten watched him go, seeing him through a red mist like crimson
groundstars swarming around his head. In his mind he still felt the
throbbing hatred, the promise of death that was more than just
promise; Sharksey really *wanted* to kill him. He gasped in air, and the
mist began to dissipate—and suddenly his legs were cut from beneath
him as the next dancer in line leaped forward to trip him in his turn.
Again he was on the ground, but this time, driven by fear of the antic-
ipation he'd felt from Sharksey's mind, he got up quickly and danced,
or lurched, or shambled step by step up the hill after the line.

No more mistakes for Lasten, no, he told himself. *Dancing don't
matter to the Immortals, but it does to the filthy robbers, murdering
robbers, and they'll really kill you, won't make no difference why you
die.*

*But damn them, damn them forcing me here when I've told them
the vaults are empty.*

Sooleyrah had reached the gates now. There had once been a strong
wall here, he'd heard that, but it was virtually demolished by generations of robbers who had torn it down bare-handed, stone by stone,
and the stones were littered all around, some scattered back down the
hill where they'd rolled or been thrown. Fifteen or twenty yards to
the right was a pit where once a bad dancer had caused an explo-
sion. Of the wall only the gates remained, twin steel markers pitted
and rust-flaking with age. Night moss had crept up the sides of the
gates, half covering them with dark-green fur. Overhead the cold
skystars hung silently.

"Okay, we go in," Sooleyrah chanted. "We go in, go in—hey we go in *now!*" And he danced forward, through the gates, as quickly as he could (many robbers had been killed there, though none within Sooleyrah's memory), and on the other side, the inside, he paused and did shuffle-steps, humming a high keening song while Kreech and one, two, three more followed him through.

"Now we're in," he said softly to Kreech, and they turned to survey the vaults. Behind them more of the line danced through the gates, slowed and finally stopped like Sooleyrah and Kreech, panting, staring around them at the vaults.

"Which one?" Kreech asked. "You been here three, four times in a row now, so which one we go into?"

Sooleyrah's eyes narrowed as he studied the vaults. They crowned the entire hilltop, vaults of many sizes and shapes, some tall, like obelisks, others domelike, still others jointed with odd angles and designs. Sooleyrah had always been afraid of the vaults—for their size alone, even if they hadn't been so dangerous. They towered into the sky above; and when the robbers entered those doorways the arches stretched far overhead to encompass echoing empty darkness.

"Starboxes are kept in the vaults for us, no other reason, yeah?" he said to Kreech. "And samesongs, and tools; some toys maybe too, lots of shapes, yeah? Plug 'em into the starboxes and yeah, they work, they work. Now why unless they're for us? Who else, Kreech, who else?"

"Nobody," Kreech said. "Nobody but us to take 'em."

"Yeah, yeah, nobody," Sooleyrah said, turning slowly in the night, in the poised silence of the hilltop and the looming vaults. He looked back down the hill and saw the rest of the line coming through the gates, and the gates themselves now seemed to lead out, to lead downward, back to the brightness of the groundstars. He saw Lasten come panting and shuffling through, and suddenly he grinned.

"Hey, fat boy Lasten can pick us a vault. Almost-thinker says they're all empty, hell he knows. Remember what the rest said? Rest of the thinkers? Said they could remember which vaults were used up, remember how many vaults there were, and all empty now. You remember? Yeah? Damn dumb thinkers been fooling us for hey *long* time. Send us up here instead of them, make us take the chances, oh yeah, they just tell us which vaults to go to. Oh sure, oh yeah, smart old thinkers, and every one dead now, about time."

Kreech kicked over a loosely planted stone; underneath it were faintly glowing crawling things that scurried in small circles and quickly burrowed into the ground, hiding.

"Yeah, always hated the thinkers," Kreech said. "Always knew they were liars—well, didn't all of us? Hey yeah, good, get Lasten up here and make him pick out our vault tonight."

"Yeah okay, pass the word back," Sooleyrah said, then turned his back to the line and stared again at the vaults. But almost immediately he had another thought; he said to Kreech, "Lasten picks our vault, and he's first one to go in tonight. First one. Place of honor, yeah?" He laughed.

"First one in gets killed if the approach wasn't good," Kreech said. "Oh yeah, place of honor."

"Fat boy needs it," Sooleyrah said. "Bring him here."

Lasten's fear sharpened when they came for him. Why did they want him now, when they were through the gates and at the portals of the vaults themselves? Surely they wouldn't kill him now, up here on the silent hilltop. What reason, what reason? (Unless they were going back to human sacrifice in front of the vaults. *No.*)

But the flickering impressions that reached him from Sooleyrah's mind, when he was brought to the leader, had nothing of murder in them. There was hatred, yes, and the soft spongy feel of gloating. But not murder, no, nothing overt.

"Hey Lasten, you almost a thinker, yeah?" Sooleyrah said, and his voice was so quiet, almost friendly. But not his mind.

"I wasn't entered," Lasten said cautiously.

"Yeah, we know. Okay, but you know a lot of stuff, yeah? Know a lot about vaults, which ones are dangerous, which ones maybe empty, we hear. Now, not *all* of 'em empty, Lasten, not *all* of 'em. You almost a thinker, you not dumb, yeah?"

"The thinkers told you they were all empty," Lasten said, "so you killed the thinkers. Now if I still say that, you'll kill *me.*"

Sooleyrah smiled widely, glancing at Kreech. "No, no, Lasten, you not dumb. Okay, now what vault we go to tonight?"

A chill scurried up Lasten's back, touching the nape of his neck spider-softly.

"You want me to pick the vault?" he asked. "Why me? Why, Sooleyrah?"

Sooleyrah laughed, enjoying himself. "Hell damn *I* know what vault to pick. Thinkers always do that, always. So no more thinkers, but we got you, Lasten. So you pick."

So I pick—and if the vault is empty, it's my fault, not Sooleyrah's. Sooleyrah maybe not so sure about the vaults after all, eh?

"You scared to pick one yourself, Sooleyrah? Scared you can't find a vault with your pretty things? Yeah, you're scared, scared."

But he shouldn't have said that. Sooleyrah leaped forward and grasped Lasten's arm, painfully squeezing the soft flesh, twisting the arm behind him. Lasten cried out in pain, and bent over trying to escape the pressure. Sooleyrah jammed his arm up against his shoulder blades.

"Not scared, fat boy; not scared, just smart. Thinkers knew about vaults, they taught you, yeah? Sure, Lasten, sure, we know. Then thinkers said all vaults empty, no use making raids any more, yeah? Yeah? Well, maybe thinkers got something up here they don't want found, eh? Robbers not so dumb, Lasten, and Sooleyrah not dumb either. You pick vault, *you,* and it *better* not be empty!"

Or they'll stone me right here, Lasten thought, seeing that as a bright certainty in Sooleyrah's mind. *Only way Sooleyrah could make up for leading a failure raid. Yeah, and the robbers would love another stoning, especially up here where the magic is. Magic and death, oh yeah, they'll love it.*

"And *you* go into vault first, Lasten," Kreech told him with happy malice. "Sure, *you,* Lasten, place of honor for you."

Place of death, Lasten thought. *Oh, you dumb damn robbers, lousy murdering superstitious—*

"Which one, Lasten?" Sooleyrah said, applying pressure to his arm. "Which one?"

And Lasten, the almost-thinker, suddenly laughed.

"Yeah, okay," he said, and giggled again, a giggle just like Sooleyrah's or Kreech's, only higher pitched, thinner. "Okay, yeah, okay, okay . . ."

Sooleyrah let go of his arm, stepped back. "You take us to an empty vault, you won't be laughing," he warned.

"Yeah, oh yeah, I know," Lasten said, managing to stop his giggling. It wasn't that funny, after all; in fact, probably it wasn't funny at all.

"That one," he said, pointing to the vault nearest to them. "We go there."

Sooleyrah and Kreech both stared. "*That* one? Fat boy, you crazy? Nothing in that vault, nothing there since before you or me born!"

"Hey, yeah," Kreech said. "First vault ever emptied was that one, that one right there, don't you know that?"

"Sure, I know, sure. But that's the one we go to tonight. And you look close, robber leader and watcher, you look close and you'll see vault's *not* empty. You want more pretty stuff stored in vaults, you just look close tonight!"

He began to walk confidently toward the nearest vault, while behind him Sooleyrah and Kreech looked angry, then uneasy, and finally they turned and motioned the rest of the party to follow them as they moved after Lasten.

Sure, damn robbers emptied this vault first thing, Lasten was thinking. *Been in this one so often you can't count, clearing it out, every piece they could find, everything the Immortals stored here. Only that just means it's a safe vault, all the defenses used up or burned out so long ago. Nothing here to blind me, burn me, kill me. Safe vault, yeah . . . but maybe not so empty as they think.*

The door to the vault gaped open, leading into blackness. Lasten called for torches, and two of the robbers came forward and lighted them. "Okay, now we go in," Lasten said, and sullenly the torchbearers followed him through the wide doorway, Sooleyrah and Kreech right behind them.

Inside was a high-ceilinged room littered with dust and stones and broken pieces of once-complete artifacts; one wall of the room was dark and misshapen, its plastoid seared by some long-forgotten fire-explosion. A hole in the ceiling, so far above them it was barely discernible in the flickering torchlight, showed where once there had been lighting fixtures, long since ripped out by the robbers. The sounds of footsteps were flat and harsh in the bare room, and the faint smell of old torch-smoke seemed to come from the shadows. Sooleyrah moved closer to Lasten, saying with dangerous softness, "Don't see nothing in here, thinker."

Lasten nodded, looking carefully around the vault.

"*You* see anything in here, Kreech? Looks empty to me, just empty as damn, yeah?"

Kreech grinned. "Oh no, not empty. Can't be; fat thinker brought us here. That right, fat thinker? Something hidden in here?"

Lasten got down on hands and knees in the middle of the floor, picking through the rubble. Here and there he brushed aside dust and stones to look closely at the floor.

"Yeah hey, he got something hidden all right," Sooleyrah said. "Hey, move in with the torches there, move closer." The torchbearers edged suspiciously forward; Sooleyrah grabbed one, swung him around and placed him where he wanted him, standing right over Lasten. "You too," he told the other man, and that one too held his torch close over the fat boy.

Lasten giggled.

"You find it, hey?" Sooleyrah said. "What is it, fat boy? Better be good, and you know it, don't you? What is it?"

Lasten knew Sooleyrah and the others were more frightened than they acted. The robbers had always been afraid of these vaults, no matter how often they'd pillaged them, and despite the lower and lower frequency of maimings or killings by the defense systems. *Robbers think this is all demon-stuff, something like that. Hell, no demons, not even lousy magic. Just stuff we forgot, even the thinkers forgot.*

But yeah, I know one more thing about vaults that Sooleyrah don't know.

Lasten rose to his feet, puffing, then looked around and picked out the south wall. In the center of it was a metal plaque with writing on it—devil marks, the robbers called it: another kind of magic to fear.

Lasten couldn't read it, but he knew what it must be. He motioned Sooleyrah over to him and pointed at the plaque. "Take it off the wall," he said.

Sooleyrah stared at him; so did Kreech, and so did the rest, the torchbearers and the ones crowded around the doorway.

"Take it off the wall!" Lasten said sharply, a little shrilly. "Pry it, use your knives—but be careful."

Sooleyrah hesitated only a moment more; then he turned and picked out one of the men in the doorway. "Takker—you. Bring your knife, do what thinker says. Rest of you, you keep door blocked so thinker can't run out."

Takker came into the vault reluctantly, drawing his knife. It was crude but strong; once it had been just a slim bar of metal, but Takker had filed it sharp. He worked the edge under the plaque and pried; the plaque began to loosen.

"Secret place in there?" Sooleyrah asked, and Lasten didn't have to feel the suppressed fear from his mind; it was apparent in his voice.

"Yeah, secret place," he said. "Surprise for you."

The plaque came off and dropped to the floor with a sharp metallic ring. Lasten stepped forward, motioned for the light and looked into the small hole opened in the wall.

There was a round dial, with markings and writing—the short writing they'd used for numbers. A time-lock, set for sometime in the future, after the wars. But the time could be changed, no reason it couldn't be changed.

Lasten twisted the dial, heard its faint scraping clearly in the suddenly silent vault. Turn, turn, and seasons flowed by, more and more time was marked off. Years, years. He kept turning the dial, waiting for the time-lock to release. (Maybe he was turning it the wrong direction? But no; it wouldn't turn at all the other way.)

All around him he tasted fear. He stood in semidarkness as the torchbearers edged away; shadows sprang up to claim more of the vault. Even Sooleyrah and Kreech had moved away, toward the door.

Then the floor of the vault began to rise.

There was a section of the flooring, twice as long as the height of a man and half as wide, that was separate from the rest; Lasten had searched for and found the edges of that section when he'd been on hands and knees earlier. Now the section was rising out of the floor, accompanied by a low subterranean hum of machinery. It was a block of heavy plastoid, and as Lasten and the others stared in wonder and terror, it raised itself steadily to a height almost up to their shoulders.

It was a compartment, transparent-sided; inside it lay the body of an Immortal—or a demon, a god, a monster. He was huge, twice the size of Lasten or Sooleyrah or any of the rest of them; they could see that even while he was lying down, in the moving shadows of torchlight.

The mechanisms of the compartment were whirring to life; Lasten saw the top of the case lifting off, smelled stale air as it was released from the case, saw a needle-thin marker on the side of the compartment leap to the end of its dial, and at the same time the giant's body convulsed, back arching, muscles quivering. It settled back, but again the dial-marker leaped, and the huge body with it.

This time there came a moan, low and weak, and the monster's head rolled onto its side. Its mouth was open, slack; the eyes fluttered; the hands shook and moved.

Needles and tubes withdrew from the body, sinking back into their seats within the case. The dials settled to rest.

The Immortal's eyes opened and stared emptily at them.

Hell hell hell hell hell big monstrous inhuman devil hell hell kill us all kill us no no!

The eyes opened wider, and the creature moaned again, louder now. It was a deep growl, half choked, and it echoed from the walls.

Hate us hate us all kill us kill me me me me no!

And the giant tried to sit up.

Its hands scratched at the sides of the case, lacking coordination, lacking strength. The creature grunted and fell back; it breathed in pain-racked gobbets of air, making harsh gasping sounds deep in its throat.

Kreech screamed. He threw himself at the men standing frozen in the doorway and fought his way through them, still screaming. He sent others reeling backward as he burst through, and several followed him, adding their screams to his. Sooleyrah yelled after him, started to run too but hesitated.

Lasten stood rooted in fright, his whole being filled with terror, both from himself and from the flood of panic in the minds around him. Red, bursting fear, splashing white-hot into his stomach, his chest. . . .

Kill me kill me kill me me me me kill—

The giant sat up, and it was monstrous. Twice the height of a man, it swayed and moaned above them in the dark vault. Its fingers scrabbled spasmodically; it slipped back onto one elbow; its eyes rolled as it stared down at them. And it spoke.

"God . . . oh God . . . what are you? What *are* you?"

A weak, thin voice. Frightened.

"Help me . . . please, help . . ."

Suddenly it tumbled over, falling off the side of its mount, headfirst onto the floor at Lasten's feet. It crashed heavily and noisily, sending Lasten staggering back in fright. The monster writhed there on the floor, hands clutching air, legs jerking, spittle falling from its mouth. And then it slumped, and sobbed weakly, hopelessly. "Oh God, please. . . ."

Kill me kill me me me kill kill and Lasten suddenly had a large stone in his hands and he ran forward and brought it down with all his strength on the monster's face. It smashed in one eye, a side of the head, and thin red blood spurted. The giant thrashed about wildly, arms flung up and feet kicking spasmodically, and faint little sobs came from its gaping mouth. Lasten hit it again, and again, and again, and he was screaming now, screaming to drown out the cries of the monster, and he hit it again, and again, and *harder*. . . .

And at last there were only his screams in the vault. The monster, the Immortal, the inhuman giant lay silent and destroyed at his feet. Sooleyrah and the rest had fled. Lasten choked off his cries and dropped the slippery red stone. He fell against the case, hardly noticing the blood that covered his legs and hands.

I'm alive I'm alive, alive . . . I'm alive . . .

It was more than an hour later when Sooleyrah and Kreech crept back up to the vault. There had been silence for all that time, and the monster had not come out after them.

Kreech carried a torch; he thrust it before him through the doorway. He saw the demon-monster, and he recoiled; but then he realized that it lay completely still and there was blood all around its smashed head.

Sooleyrah pushed past him and entered the vault. He saw Lasten standing beside the monster's case, a dark stone in his hands. Lasten brought the stone down once, twice, and the molding broke; pieces showered to his blood-caked feet. He reached into the recesses of the case, yanked, and brought forth a handful of wires, red, yellow, blue, green.

He looked up and saw Sooleyrah, and smiled.

And giggled.

And said, "Come on, Sooleyrah. Come on, little dancer leader. No demon left to hurt you now, oh no, no demon, no monster. Devil scared you? But I killed him—*me*. Don't be scared, dancer, don't be scared; come inside. Plenty of stuff here, oh plenty. And in other vaults too."

He held up the fistful of many-colored wires.

"Pretty?"

The Man Who Never Forgot

Robert Silverberg

When Tom Niles's genetic structure was determined, it varied from the human norm only in one respect. Most of us have minds like sieves, through which our recollections of the past constantly leak away; but Tom came into the world incapable of forgetting anything. Such a miraculous memory is surely a blessed gift . . . or is it?

He saw the girl waiting in line outside a big Los Angeles movie house, on a mildly foggy Tuesday morning. She was slim and pale, barely five-three, with stringy flaxen hair, and she was alone. He remembered her, of course.

He knew it would be a mistake, but he crossed the street anyway and walked up along the theater line to where she stood.

"Hello," he said.

She turned, stared at him blankly, flicked the tip of her tongue out for an instant over her lips. "I don't believe I—"

"Tom Niles," he said. "Pasadena, New Year's Day, 1955. You sat next to me. Ohio State 20, Southern Cal 7. You don't remember?"

"A football game? But I hardly ever—I mean—I'm sorry, mister. I—"

Someone else in the line moved forward toward him with a tight hard scowl on his face. Niles knew when he was beaten. He smiled apologetically and said, "I'm sorry, miss. I guess I made a mistake. I took you for someone I knew—a Miss Bette Torrance. Excuse me."

And he strode rapidly away. He had not gone more than ten feet when he heard the little surprised gasp and the "But I *am* Bette Torrance!"—but he kept going.

I should know better after twenty-eight years, he thought bitterly. *But I forget the most basic fact—that even though I remember people, they don't necessarily remember me—*

He walked wearily to the corner, turned right, and started down a new street, one whose shops were totally unfamiliar to him and which, therefore, he had never seen before. His mind stimulated to its normal pitch of activity by the incident outside the theater, spewed up a host of tangential memories like the good machine it was:

January 1 1955 Rose Bowl Pasadena California Seat G126; warm day, high humidity, arrived in stadium 12:03 P.M., PST. Came alone. Girl in next seat wearing blue cotton dress, white oxfords, carrying Southern Cal pennant. Talked to her. Name Bette Torrance, senior at Southern Cal, government major. Had a date for the game but he came down with flu symptoms night before, insisted she see game anyway. Seat on other side of her empty. Bought her a hot dog, 20¢ (no mustard)—

There was more, much more. Niles forced it back down. There was the virtually stenographic report of their conversation all that day:

(". . . I hope we win. I saw the last Bowl game we won, two years ago . . ."

". . . Yes, that was 1953. Southern Cal 7, Wisconsin 0 . . . and two straight wins in 1944–45 over Washington and Tennessee . . ."

". . . Gosh, you know a lot about football! What did you do, memorize the record book?")

And the old memories. The jeering yell of freckled Joe Merritt that warm April day in 1937—*Who are you, Einstein?* And Buddy Call saying acidly on November 8, 1939, *Here comes Tommy Niles, the human adding machine. Get him!* And then the bright stinging pain of a snowball landing just below his left clavicle, the pain that he could summon up as easily as any of the other pain-memories he carried with him. He winced and closed his eyes suddenly, as if struck by the icy pellet here on a Los Angeles street on a foggy Tuesday morning.

They didn't call him the human adding machine any more. Now it was the human tape recorder; the derisive terms had to keep pace with the passing decades. Only Niles himself remained unchanging, The Boy with the Brain Like a Sponge grown up into The Man with the Brain Like a Sponge, still cursed with the same terrible gift.

His data-cluttered mind ached. He saw a diminutive yellow sports car parked on the far side of the street, recognized it by its make and model and color and license number as the car belonging to Leslie F. Marshall, twenty-six, blond hair, blue eyes, television actor with the following credits—

Wincing, Niles applied the cutoff circuit and blotted out the up-welling data. He had met Marshall once, six months ago, at a party given by a mutual friend—an erstwhile mutual friend; Niles found it difficult to keep friends for long. He had spoken with the actor for perhaps ten minutes and had added that much more baggage to his mind.

It was time to move on, Niles decided. He had been in Los Angeles ten months. The burden of accumulated memories was getting too heavy; he was greeting too many people who had long since forgotten him (*curse my John Q. Average build, 5 feet 9, 163 pounds, brownish hair, brownish eyes, no unduly prominent physical features, no distinguishing scars except those inside,* he thought). He contemplated returning to San Francisco, and decided against it. He had been there only a year ago; Pasadena, two years ago. The time had come, he realized, for another eastward jaunt.

Back and forth across the face of America goes Thomas Richard Niles, Der fliegende Holländer, the Wandering Jew, the Ghost of Christmas Past, the Human Tape Recorder. He smiled at a newsboy who had sold him a copy of the *Examiner* on May 13 past, got the usual blank stare in return, and headed for the nearest bus terminal.

For Niles the long journey had begun on October 11, 1929, in the small Ohio town of Lowry Bridge. He was third of three children, born of seemingly normal parents, Henry Niles (b. 1896), Mary Niles (b. 1899). His older brother and sister had shown no extraordinary manifestations. Tom had.

It began as soon as he was old enough to form words; a neighbor woman on the front porch peered into the house where he was playing, and remarked to his mother, "Look how *big* he's getting, Mary!"

He was less than a year old. He had replied, in virtually the same tone of voice, *"Look how* big *he's getting, Mary!"* It caused a sensation, even though it was only mimicry, not even speech.

He spent his first twelve years in Lowry Bridge, Ohio. In later years, he often wondered how he had been able to last there so long.

He began school at the age of four, because there was no keeping him back; his classmates were five and six, vastly superior to him in physical coordination, vastly inferior in everything else. He could read. He could even write, after a fashion, though his babyish muscles tired easily from holding the pen. And he could remember.

He remembered everything. He remembered his parents' quarrels and repeated the exact words of them to anyone who cared to listen, until his father whipped him and threatened to kill him if he ever did *that* again. He remembered that too. He remembered the lies his brother and sister told, and took great pains to set the record straight. He learned eventually not to do that, either. He remembered things people had said, and corrected them when they later deviated from their earlier statements.

He remembered everything.

He read a textbook once and it stayed with him. When the teacher asked a question based on the day's assignment, Tommy Niles's skinny arm was in the air long before the others had ever really assimilated the question. After a while, his teacher made it clear to him that he could *not* answer every question, whether he had the answer first or not; there were twenty other pupils in the class. The other pupils in the class made that abundantly clear to him, after school.

He won the verse-learning contest in Sunday school. Barry Harman had studied for weeks in hopes of winning the catcher's mitt his father had promised him if he finished first—but when it was Tommy Niles's turn to recite, he began with *In the beginning God created the heaven and the earth,* continued through *Thus the heavens and the earth were finished, and all the host of them,* headed on into *Now the serpent was more subtil than any beast of the field which the Lord God had made,* and presumably would have continued clear through Genesis, Exodus, and on to Joshua if the dazed proctor hadn't shut him up and declared him the winner.

Barry Harman didn't get his glove; Tommy Niles got a black eye instead.

He began to realize he was different. It took time to make the discovery that other people were always forgetting things, and that instead of admiring him for what he could do they hated him for it. It was difficult for a boy of eight, even Tommy Niles, to understand why they hated him, but eventually he did find it out, and then he started learning how to hide his gift.

Through his ninth and tenth years he practiced being normal, and almost succeeded; the after-school beatings stopped, and he managed to get a few B's on his report cards at last, instead of straight rows of A's. He was growing up; he was learning to pretend. Neighbors heaved sighs of relief, now that that terrible Niles boy was no longer doing all those crazy things.

But inwardly he was the same as ever. And he realized he'd have to leave Lowry Bridge soon.

He knew everyone too well. He would catch them in lies ten times a week, even Mr. Lawrence, the minister, who once turned down an invitation to pay a social call to the Nileses one night, saying, "I really have to get down to work and write my sermon for Sunday," when only three days before Tommy had heard him say to Miss Emery, the church secretary, that he had had a sudden burst of inspiration and had written three sermons all at one sitting, and now he'd have some free time for the rest of the month.

Even Mr. Lawrence lied, then. And he was the best of them. As for the others—

Tommy waited until he was twelve; he was big for his age by then and figured he could take care of himself. He borrowed twenty dollars from the supposedly secret cashbox in the back of the kitchen cupboard (his mother had mentioned its existence five years before, in Tommy's hearing) and tiptoed out of the house at three in the morning. He caught the night freight for Chillicothe, and was on his way.

There were thirty people on the bus out of Los Angeles. Niles sat alone in the back, by the seat just over the rear wheel. He knew four of the people in the bus by name—but he was confident they had forgotten who he was by now, and so he kept to himself.

It was an awkward business. If you said hello to someone who had forgotten you, they thought you were a troublemaker or a panhandler.

And if you passed someone by, thinking he had forgotten you, and he hadn't—well, then you were a snob. Niles swung between both those poles five times a day. He'd see someone, such as that girl Bette Torrance, and get a cold, unrecognizing stare; or he'd go by someone else, believing the other person did not remember him but walking rapidly just in case he did, and there would be the angry, "Well! Who the blazes do you think *you* are!" floating after him as he retreated.

Now he sat alone, bouncing up and down with each revolution of the wheel, with the one suitcase containing his property thumping constantly against the baggage rack over his head. That was one advantage of his talent: he could travel light. He didn't need to keep books, once he had read them, and there wasn't much point in amassing belongings of any other sort either; they became overfamiliar and dull too soon.

He eyed the road signs. They were well into Nevada by now. The old, wearisome retreat was on.

He could never stay in the same city too long. He had to move on to new territory, to some new place where he had no old memories, where no one knew him, where he knew no one. In the sixteen years since he had left home, he'd covered a lot of ground.

He remembered the jobs he had held.

He had been a proofreader for a Chicago publishing firm, once. He did the jobs of two men. The way proofreading usually worked, one man read the copy from the manuscript, the other checked it against the galleys. Niles had a simpler method: he would scan the manuscript once, thereby memorizing it, and then merely check the galleys for discrepancies. It brought him fifty dollars a week for a while, before the time came to move along.

He once held a job as a sideshow freak in a traveling carnie that made a regular Alabama-Mississippi-Georgia circuit. Niles had really been low on cash, then. He remembered how he had gotten the job: by buttonholing the carnie boss and demanding a tryout. "Read me anything—anything at all! I can remember it!" The boss had been skeptical, and didn't see any use for such an act anyway, but finally gave in when Niles practically fainted of malnutrition in his office. The boss read him an editorial from a Mississippi county weekly, and when he was through, Niles recited it back, word-perfect. He got the job, at fifteen dollars a week plus meals, and sat in a little booth under a sign that said THE HUMAN TAPE RECORDER. People read or said things to him, and he repeated them. It was dull work; sometimes the things they said were filthy, and most of the time they couldn't even remember what they had said to him a minute later. He stayed with the show four weeks, and when he left no one missed him much.

The bus rolled on into the fogbound night.

There had been other jobs: good jobs, bad jobs. None of them had lasted very long. There had been some girls too, but none of *them* had lasted too long. They had all, even those he had tried to conceal it from, found out about his special ability, and soon after that they had left. No one could stay with a man who never forgot, who could always dredge yesterday's foibles out of the reservoir that was his mind and hurl them unanswerable into the open. And the man with the perfect memory could never live long among imperfect human beings.

To forgive is to forget, he thought. The memory of old insults and quarrels fades, and a relationship starts anew. But for him there could be no forgetting, and hence little forgiving.

He closed his eyes after a while and leaned back against the hard leather cushion of his seat. The steady rhythm of the bus lulled him to sleep. In sleep, his mind could rest; he found ease from memory. He never dreamed.

In Salt Lake City he paid his fare, left the bus, suitcase in hand, and set out in the first direction he faced. He had not wanted to go any farther east on that bus. His cash reserve was only sixty-three dollars now, and he had to make it last.

He found a job as a dishwasher in a downtown restaurant, held it long enough to accumulate a hundred dollars, and moved on again, this time hitchhiking to Cheyenne. He stayed there a month and took a night bus to Denver, and when he left Denver it was to go to Wichita.

Wichita to Des Moines, Des Moines to Minneapolis, Minneapolis to Milwaukee, then down through Illinois, carefully avoiding Chicago, and on to Indianapolis. It was an old story for him, this traveling. Gloomily he celebrated his twenty-ninth birthday alone in an Indianapolis rooming house on a drizzly October day, and for the purpose of brightening the occasion, summoned up his old memories of his fourth birthday party, in 1933 . . . one of the few unalloyedly happy days of his life.

They were all there, all his playmates, and his parents, and his brother Hank, looking gravely important at the age of eight, and his sister Marian, and there were candles and favors and punch and cake. Mrs. Heinsohn from next door stopped in and said, "He looks like a regular little man," and his parents beamed at him, and everyone sang and had a good time. And afterward, when the last game had been played, the last present opened, when the boys and girls had waved good-bye and disappeared up the street, the grown-ups sat around and talked of the new President and the many strange things that were happening in the country, and little Tommy sat in the middle of the floor, listening and recording everything and glowing warmly, because somehow during the whole afternoon no one had said or done anything cruel to him. He was happy that day, and he went to bed still happy.

Niles ran through the party twice, like an old movie he loved well; the print never grew frayed, the registration always remained as clear and sharp as ever. He could taste the sweet tang of the punch, he could relive the warmth of that day when through some accident the others had allowed him a little happiness.

Finally he let the brightness of the party fade, and once again he was in Indianapolis on a gray, bleak afternoon, alone in an eight-dollar-a-week furnished room.

Happy birthday to me, he thought bitterly. *Happy birthday.*

He stared at the blotchy green wall with the cheap Corot print hung slightly askew. I could have been something special, he brooded, one of the wonders of the world. Instead I'm a skulking freak who lives in dingy third-floor back rooms, and I don't dare let the world know what I can do.

He scooped into his memory and came up with the Toscanini performance of Beethoven's *Ninth* he had heard in Carnegie Hall once while he was in New York. It was infinitely better than the later performance Toscanini had approved for recording, yet no microphones had taken it down; the blazing performance was as far beyond recapture as a flame five minutes snuffed, except in one man's mind. Niles had it all: the majestic downcrash of the tympani, the resonant, perspiring basso bringing forth the great melody of the finale, even the French-horn bobble that must have enraged the maestro so, the infuriating cough from the dress circle at the gentlest moment of the adagio, the sharp pinching of Niles's shoes as he leaned forward in his seat—

He had it all, in highest fidelity.

He arrived in the small town on a moonless night three months later, a cold, crisp January evening, when the wintry wind swept in from the north, cutting through his thin clothing and making the suitcase an almost impossible burden for his numb, gloveless hand. He had not meant to come to this place, but he had run short of cash in Kentucky, and there had been no helping it. He was on his way to New York, where he could live in anonymity for months unbothered, and where he knew his rudeness would go unnoticed if he happened to snub someone on the street or if he greeted someone who had forgotten him.

But New York was still hundreds of miles away, and it might have been millions on this January night. He saw a sign: BAR. He forced himself forward toward the sputtering neon; he wasn't ordinarily a drinker, but he needed the warmth of alcohol inside him now, and perhaps the barkeep would need a man to help out, or could at least rent him a room for what little he had in his pockets.

There were five men in the bar when he reached it. They looked like truck drivers. Niles dropped his valise to the left of the door, rubbed his stiff hands together, exhaled a white cloud. The bartender grinned jovially at him.

"Cold enough for you out there?"

Niles managed a grin. "I wasn't sweating much. Let me have something warming. Double shot of bourbon, maybe."

That would be ninety cents. He had $7.34.

He nursed the drink when it came, sipped it slowly, let it roll down his gullet. He thought of the summer he had been stranded for a week in Washington, a solid week of 97-degree temperature and 97 percent humidity, and the vivid memory helped to ease away some of the psychological effects of the coldness.

He relaxed; he warmed. Behind him came the penetrating sound of argument.

"—I tell you Joe Louis beat Schmeling to a pulp the second time! Kayoed him in the first round!"

"You're nuts! Louis just barely got him down in a fifteen-round decision, the second bout."

"Seems to me—"

"I'll put money on it. Ten bucks says it was a decision in fifteen, Mac."

Sound of confident chuckles. "I wouldn't want to take your money so easy, pal. Everyone knows it was a knockout in one."

"Ten bucks, I said."

Niles turned to see what was happening. Two of the truck drivers, burly men in dark pea jackets, stood nose to nose. Automatically the thought came: *Louis knocked Max Schmeling out in the first round at Yankee Stadium, New York, June 22, 1938.* Niles had never been much of a sports fan, and particularly disliked boxing—but he had once glanced at an almanac page cataloguing Joe Louis' title fights, and the data had, of course, remained.

He watched detachedly as the bigger of the two truck drivers angrily slapped a ten-dollar bill down on the bar; the other matched it. Then the first glanced up at the barkeep and said, "Okay, Bud. You're a shrewd guy. Who's right about the second Louis-Schmeling fight?"

The barkeep was a blank-faced cipher of a man, middle-aged, balding, with mild, empty eyes. He chewed at his lip a moment, shrugged, fidgeted, finally said, "Kinda hard for me to remember. That musta been twenty-five years ago."

Twenty, Niles thought.

"Lessee now," the bartender went on. "Seems to me I remember —yeah, sure. It went the full fifteen, and the judges gave it to Louis. I seem to remember a big stink being made over it; the papers said Joe should've killed him a lot faster'n that."

A triumphant grin appeared on the bigger driver's face. He deftly pocketed both bills.

The other man grimaced and howled, "Hey! You two fixed this thing up beforehand! I know damn well that Louis kayoed the German in one."

"You heard what the man said. The money's mine."

"No," Niles said suddenly, in a quiet voice that seemed to carry halfway across the bar. *Keep your mouth shut,* he told himself frantically. *This is none of your business. Stay out of it!*

But it was too late.

"What you say?" asked the one who'd dropped the tenspot.

"I say you're being rooked. Louis won the fight in one round, like you say. June 22, 1938, Yankee Stadium. The barkeep's thinking of the Arturo-Godoy fight. *That* went the full fifteen in 1940. February 9."

"There—told you! Gimme back my money!"

But the other driver ignored the cry and turned to face Niles. He was a cold-faced, heavy-set man, and his fists were starting to clench. "Smart man, eh? Boxing expert?"

"I just didn't want to see anybody get cheated," Niles said stubbornly. He knew what was coming now. The truck driver was weaving drunkenly toward him; the barkeep was yelling, the other patrons were backing away.

The first punch caught Niles in the ribs; he grunted and staggered back, only to be grabbed by the throat and slapped three times. Dimly he heard a voice saying, "Hey, let go the guy! He didn't mean anything! You want to kill him?"

A volley of blows doubled him up; a knuckle swelled his right eyelid, a fist crashed stunningly into his left shoulder. He spun, wobbled uncertainly, knowing that his mind would permanently record every moment of this agony.

Through half-closed eyes he saw them pulling the enraged driver off him; the man writhed in the grip of three others, aimed a last desperate kick at Niles's stomach and grazed a rib, and finally was subdued.

Niles stood alone in the middle of the floor, forcing himself to stay upright, trying to shake off the sudden pain that drilled through him in a dozen places.

"You all right?" a solicitous voice asked. "Hell, those guys play rough. You oughtn't mix up with them."

"I'm all right," Niles said hollowly. "Just . . . let me . . . catch my breath."

"Here. Sit down. Have a drink. It'll fix you up."

"No," Niles said. *I can't stay here. I have to get moving.* "I'll be all right," he muttered unconvincingly. He picked up his suitcase, wrapped his coat tight about him, and left the bar, step by step by step.

He got fifteen feet before the pain became unbearable. He crumpled suddenly and fell forward on his face in the dark, feeling the cold iron-hard frozen turf against his cheek, and struggled unsuccessfully to get up. He lay there, remembering all the various pains of his life, the beatings, the cruelty, and when the weight of memory became too much to bear he blanked out.

The bed was warm, the sheets clean and fresh and soft. Niles woke slowly, feeling a temporary sensation of disorientation, and then his infallible memory supplied the data on his blackout in the snow and he realized he was in a hospital.

He tried to open his eyes; one was swollen shut, but he managed to get the other's lids apart. He was in a small hospital room—no shining metropolitan hospital pavilion, but a small county clinic with gingerbread molding on the walls and homey lace curtains, through which afternoon sunlight was entering.

So he had been found and brought to a hospital. That was good. He could easily have died out there in the snow; but someone had stumbled over him and brought him in. That was a novelty, that someone had bothered to help him; the treatment he had received in the bar last night—was it last night?—was more typical of the world's attitude toward him. In twenty-nine years he had somehow failed to learn adequate concealment, camouflage, and every day he suffered the consequences. It was hard for him to remember, he who remembered everything else, that the other people were not like him, and hated him for what he was.

Gingerly he felt his side. There didn't seem to be any broken ribs —just bruises. A day or so of rest and they would probably discharge him and let him move on.

A cheerful voice said, "Oh, you're awake, Mr. Niles. Feeling better now? I'll brew some tea for you."

He looked up and felt a sudden sharp pang. She was a nurse—twenty-two, twenty-three, new at the job perhaps, with a flowing tumble of curling blond hair and wide, clear blue eyes. She was smiling, and it seemed to Niles it was not merely a professional smile. "I'm Miss Carroll, your day nurse. Everything okay?"

"Fine," Niles said hesitantly. "Where am I?"

"Central County General Hospital. You were brought in late last night—apparently you'd been beaten up and left by the road out on Route 32. It's a lucky thing Mark McKenzie was walking his dog, Mr. Niles." She looked at him gravely. "You remember last night, don't you? I mean—the shock—amnesia—"

Niles chuckled. "That's the last ailment in the world I'd be afraid

of," he said. "I'm Thomas Richard Niles, and I remember pretty well
what happened. How badly am I damaged?"

"Superficial bruises, mild shock and exposure, slight case of frost-
bite," she summed up. "You'll live. Dr. Hammond'll give you a full
checkup a little later, after you've eaten. Let me bring you some tea."

Niles watched the trim figure vanish into the hallway.

She was certainly an attractive girl, he thought, fresh-eyed, alert
. . . *alive.*

*Old cliché: patient falling for his nurse. But she's not for me, I'm
afraid.*

Abruptly the door opened and the nurse reentered, bearing a little
enameled tea tray. "You'll never guess! I have a surprise for you, Mr.
Niles. A visitor. Your mother."

"My moth—"

"She saw the little notice about you in the county paper. She's waiting outside, and she told me she hasn't seen you in seventeen years.
Would you like me to send her in now?"

"I guess so," Niles said, in a dry, feathery voice.

A second time the nurse departed. *My God,* Niles thought! *If I
had known I was this close to home—*

I should have stayed out of Ohio altogether.

The last person he wanted to see was his mother. He began to
tremble under the covers. The oldest and most terrible of his memories came bursting up from the dark compartment of his mind where
he thought he had imprisoned it forever. The sudden emergence
from warmth into coolness, from darkness to light, the jarring slap of
a heavy hand on his buttocks, the searing pain of knowing that his
security was ended, that from now on he would be alive, and therefore miserable—

The memory of the agonized birth-shriek sounded in his mind. He
could never forget being born. And his mother was, he thought, the
one person of all he could never forgive, since she had given him
forth into the life he hated. He dreaded the moment when—

"Hello, Tom. It's been a long time."

Seventeen years had faded her, had carved lines in her face and
made the cheeks more baggy, the blue eyes less bright, the brown hair
a mousy gray. She was smiling. And to his own astonishment Niles
was able to smile back.

"Mother."

"I read about it in the paper. It said a man of about thirty was found just outside town with papers bearing the name Thomas R. Niles, and he was taken to Central County General Hospital. So I came over, just to make sure—and it *was* you."

A lie drifted to the surface of his mind, but it was a kind lie, and he said it: "I was on my way back home to see you. Hitchhiking. But I ran into a little trouble en route."

"I'm glad you decided to come back, Tom. It's been so lonely, ever since your father died, and of course Hank was married, and Marian too—it's good to see you again. I thought I never would."

He lay back, perplexed, wondering why the upwelling flood of hatred did not come. He felt only warmth toward her. He was glad to see her.

"How has it been—all these years, Tom? You haven't had it easy, I can see. I see it all over your face."

"It hasn't been easy," he said. "You know why I ran away?"

She nodded. "Because of the way you are. That thing about your mind—never forgetting. I knew. Your grandfather had it too, you know."

"My grandfather—but—"

"You got it from him. I never did tell you, I guess. He didn't get along too well with any of us. He left my mother when I was a little girl, and I never knew where he went. So I always knew you'd go away the way he did. Only you came back. Are you married?"

He shook his head.

"Time you got started, then, Tom. You're near thirty."

The room door opened, and an efficient-looking doctor appeared. "Afraid your time's up, Mrs. Niles. You'll be able to see him again later. I have to check him over, now that he's awake."

"Of course, Doctor." She smiled at him, then at Niles. "I'll see you later, Tom."

"Sure, Mother."

Niles lay back, frowning, as the doctor poked at him here and there. *I didn't hate her.* A growing wonderment rose in him, and he realized he should have come home long ago. He had changed, inside, without even knowing it.

Running away was the first stage in growing up, and a necessary one. But coming back came later, and that was the mark of maturity. He was back. And suddenly he saw he had been terribly foolish all his bitter adult life.

He had a gift, a great gift, an awesome gift. It had been too big for him until now. Self-pitying, self-tormented, he had refused to allow for the shortcomings of the forgetful people about him, and had paid the price of their hatred. But he couldn't keep running away forever. The time would have to come for him to grow big enough to contain his gift, to learn to live with it instead of moaning in dramatic self-inflicted anguish.

And now was the time. It was long overdue.

His grandfather had had the gift; they had never told him that. So it was genetically transmissible. He could marry, have children, and they, too, would never forget.

It was his duty not to let his gift die with him. Others of his kind, less sensitive, less thin-skinned, would come after, and they, too, would know how to recall a Beethoven symphony or a decade-old wisp of conversation. For the first time since that fourth birthday party he felt a hesitant flicker of happiness. The days of running were ended; he was home again. *If I learn to live with others, maybe they'll be able to live with me.*

He saw the things he yet needed: a wife, a home, children—

"—a couple of days' rest, plenty of hot liquids, and you'll be as good as new, Mr. Niles," the doctor was saying. "Is there anything you'd like me to bring you now?"

"Yes," Niles said. "Just send in the nurse, will you? Miss Carroll, I mean."

The doctor grinned and left. Niles waited expectantly, exulting in his new self. He switched on Act Three of *Die Meistersinger* as a kind of jubilant backdrop music in his mind, and let the warmth sweep up over him. When she entered the room he was smiling and wondering how to begin saying what he wanted to say.

Ginny Wrapped in the Sun

R. A. Lafferty

R. A. Lafferty's theories of evolution are very much his own, and this playful account of the coming and going of the mutation that produced Homo sapiens will probably horrify those whose scientific beliefs tend toward the conservative. But, like everything this madcap Oklahoman creates, his notions of how mankind evolved seem wildly and weirdly persuasive—at least for the duration of the story.

"I'm going to read my paper tonight, Dismas," Dr. Minden said, "and they'll hoot me out of the hall. The thought of it almost makes the hair walk off my head."

"Oh, well, serves you right, Minden. From the hints you've given me of it, you can't expect acceptance for the paper; but the gentlemen aren't so bad."

"Not bad? Hauser honks like a gander! That clattering laugh of Goldbeater! Snodden sniggers so loud that it echoes! Cooper's boom is like barrels rolling downstairs, and your own—it'll shrivel me, Dismas. Imagine the weirdest cacophony ever—oh no! I wasn't thinking of one so weird as that!"

Musical screaming! Glorious gibbering with an undertone that could shatter rocks! Hooting of a resonance plainly too deep for so small an instrument! Yowling, hoodoo laughing, broken roaring, rhinoceros ranting! And the child came tumbling out of the tall rocks of Doolen's Mountain, leaping down the flanks of the hill as though she were a waterfall. And both the men laughed.

"Your Ginny *is* the weirdest cacophony I can imagine, Dismas," Dr. Minden said. "It scares me, and I love it. Your daughter is the most remarkable creature in the world.

"Talk to us, Ginny! I wish I could fix it that you would be four years old forever."

"Oh, I've fixed it myself, Dr. Minden," Ginny sang as she came to them with a movement that had something of the breathless grace of a gazelle and something of the scuttering of a little wild pig. "I use a trick like the hoodoo woman did. She ate water-puppy eggs. She never got any older, you know."

"What happened to her, Gin?" Dr. Minden asked Ginny Dismas.

"Oh, after a while she got gray-headed and wrinkled. And after another while her teeth and hair fell out, and then she died. But she never did get any older. She had everybody fooled. I got everybody fooled too."

"I know that you have, Ginny, in very many ways. Well, have you eaten water-puppy eggs to get no older?"

"No. I can't find out where they lay them, Dr. Minden. I've got my own trick that's even better."

"Do you know, Ginny, that when you really cut loose you are the loudest girl in the world?"

"I know it. I won it yesterday. Susanna Shonk said that she was the loudest. We hollered for an hour. Susanna's home with a sore throat today, but there isn't anything the matter with me. Hey, has that house ever been there before?"

"That house? But it's our own house, Ginny," her father, Dr. Dismas, said softly. "You've lived in it all your life. You're in and out of it a thousand times a day."

"Funny I never saw it before," Ginny said. "I better go see what it looks like on the inside." And Ginny hurtled into the house that she was in and out of a thousand times a day.

"I'll tell you a secret, Dismas," Dr. Minden said. "Your small daughter Ginny is not really beautiful."

"Everybody thinks that she is, Minden."

"I know. They all believe her the most beautiful child in the world. So did I till a moment ago. So will I again in another minute when I see her come out of the house. But her contemporary, my small son

Krios, told me how to look at her; and I do so. For an instant, out of her incessant movement, I forced myself to see her as stopped cold, at rest. She is grotesque, Dismas. If ever she pauses, she is grotesque."

"No, she is like ultimate matter. Existence and motion are the same thing for her, and there cannot be the one without the other. But I've never seen her stopped, even in sleep. She's the liveliest sleeper anyone ever watched—a laughing and singing sleeper. Her mother calls her our beautiful goblin."

"Exactly, she's a goblin, a monkey, a kobold. She's even grown a little pot like one of them. Dismas, she has a monkey face and bandy legs and a goblin's own pot."

"No, she hasn't! There she goes! Out of the house and up into the rocks again, and she's so beautiful that it shakes me. Four years old— and she can still look at the world and say, 'Funny I never saw you before!' Yes, I've got a multidimensional daughter, Minden. Also a neighbor who is either deep or murky. You keep feeding me snatches of that paper of yours, so I suppose that you want to excite my curiosity about it. And the title—*The Contingent Mutation*. What is? Who is?"

"We are, Dismas. We are contingent, conditional, temporary, makeshift and improbable in our species. Mine is a paper badly conceived and badly put together, and I shiver at the reception that it will get. But it is about man, who is also badly conceived and badly put together. The proposition of my paper is that man is descended, recently and by incredible mutation, from the most impossible of ancestors, Xauenanthropus, or Xauen Man. The answer of that descent scares me."

"Minden, are you out of your mind? Where is the descent? Where is the mutation? The Xauens were already men. No descent and no mutation was required. The finds are all fifteen years old. One look at Xauen, and everybody saw instantly that the Neanderthals and Grimaldi and Cro-Magnon were all close cousins of the same species —ourselves. They were the template, the master key. They unriddled every riddle. We saw why the chin, or lack of chin, was only a racial characteristic. We saw it all. There is nothing to distinguish the Xauens from ourselves except that their adults were badly made ganglers, and probably unhealthy. The Xauens *are* modern men. They are ourselves. There is nothing revolutionary about stuttering out fifteen-year-old certainties, Minden. I thought your paper was to be a giant stride. But it is only stepping off a two-inch curb.

"Yes, an abysmal step off a two-inch curb, Dismas, backward and around the world, and standing on one's head and turning into a howling monkey in the process. It isn't a simple step. If I am correct, Dismas, then our descent from the Xauens was by an incredible, sudden and single mutation; one that has been misunderstood both as to effect and direction."

"I've never been quite satisfied with Xauens myself. There is something misshapen about the whole business. Of course we know the Xauens only by the skeletons of ninety-six children, three adolescents, and two adults. We are bound to find more."

"If we do, we will find them in the same proportion. Oh, we will not recognize them at all. But does it not seem an odd proportion to you? How come there were so many kids? And how come—think about this a long, long time, will you?—that eighty-six of those kids were of the same size and apparently of the same age? The Xauen skeletons came out of nine digs, close together both in location and age. And of the total of one hundred and one skeletons, eighty-six of them are of four-year-old kids. Sure the Xauens are modern man! Sure they are ourselves chin to chin. But eighty-six four-year-old kids out of a hundred and one people is not a modern proportion."

"You explain it then, Minden. I suppose that your paper attempts to. Oh, scatter-boned ancestors! Here come the religious nuts!"

Drs. Dismas and Minden had been sitting in the open parkland in campesino chairs, in their own fine neighborhood between Doolen's Mountain and the lower brushland. Dr. Dismas drew a hog-nosed pistol from under his arm at the sight of the nuts who had shuffled up that way several times before.

"Be off!" Dismas barked as the nuts crowded and shuffled up closer from the lower brushland. "There's nothing around here you want. You've been here a dozen times with your silly questions."

"No, only three times," the nut leader said. He was clean-shaven and short-haired in the old manner still affected by fanatics, and he had fool written in every line of him. "It's a simple thing we seek," the leader sniffled. "We only want to find the woman and kill her. I believe that you could help us find the woman."

"There is no woman here except my wife!" Dr. Dismas said angrily. "You have said yourselves that she isn't the woman. Be gone now, and don't come back here again."

"But everything that we know tells us that the woman is somewhere near this place," the nut leader insisted. "She is the woman who will bear the weird seed."

"Oh, well, there are some who say that my daughter Ginny is a weird seed. Be off now."

"We know Ginny. She comes down sometimes to mock us. Ginny is not the seed, but there is something of it about her. Ginny is born and already four years old. The seed that we are seeking to kill is still in the womb. Are you sure that your wife—"

"Damnit, do you want a public pregnancy test? No, my wife is not!"

Dr. Dismas shot a couple of times around the feet of the nut leader, and the whole gaggle of the nuts shuffled off again. "It is only a little thing we seek, to find and kill the woman," they snuffled as they went.

"They may be right, Dismas," Dr. Minden said. "I've been expecting the weird seed myself. I believe that it may already have appeared several times, and such nuts have killed it several times. The contingent mutation *can* come unhinged at any time. It always could. And when it does, the human world can well pass away. But this time they won't be able to find the woman to kill her."

"This is fishier than Edward's *Ichthyology,* as we used to say in school. I begin to understand why you're afraid of the reception that your paper might get. And you, as well as I, seem to have developed a little weird seed lately."

"Yes, my young and my older son are both acting most peculiarly lately, particularly in their relation to the Dismas family. My son Dall has been jilted by your daughter Agar, or is it the other way around? Or have they both been jilted by your small daughter Ginny? As far as I can arrive at it, Ginny told them that that sort of stuff is out, no longer necessary, not even wanted on their parts. She is obsoleting them, she says.

"And my four-year-old son Krios is about out of his mind over your Ginny. He is so advanced in some ways and so retarded in others. It seems as though he grew unevenly and then stopped growing. I worry about him."

"Yes, Ginny has acquired several more small boyfriends now. She says that you break the fort with a big ram and you break the ram at the same time and throw it away. And then you find better tools to take it over. I don't know what she's talking about. But Krios is jealous as only a passionate four-year-old can be."

"Krios says that Ginny is bad and she made him bad. He says that he doesn't know the words for the way they were bad, but that he will go to Hell for it."

"I had no idea that children were still taught about Hell."

"They aren't. But they have either intuitive knowledge of the place, or a continuing childhood folk legend of it. Oh, here comes bad Ginny and her mother, and they both have that stubborn look on them. You have two strong women in your house, at least. I wish that Agar were; for my son Dall isn't, and one of them should be."

Ginny and her mother Sally came hand in hand with the air of something needing to be settled.

"I want to be fair about this, Father," Ginny called solidly. "What I like about me is that I am always so fair."

"That's also what I like about you, Ginny," said Dr. Dismas, "and what is the argument?"

"All I asked of Mother is that she make me three thousand seven hundred and eighty peanut-butter sandwiches. Isn't that a fair request?"

"I'm not sure that it is, Ginny," Dr. Dismas said. "It would take you a long time to eat that many."

"Of course it will, twelve hundred and sixty days. But that makes only three a day for the time I have to stay hidden in my nest up in the rocks. I figured that out by myself without paper. A lot of kids that have been to school already can't figure as well as I can."

"I know. A precocious daughter is a mixed blessing," her father said.

"Oh, Ginny, you're going to get a paddling," her mother said. "I made you three of them, and you said that you weren't even hungry for them."

"Father, who is this woman who talks to me so brusquely?" Ginny demanded.

"She is your mother, Ginny. You have been with her every day of your life and before. You have just come out of the house with her, and you still stand hand in hand with her."

"Funny I never saw her before," Ginny said. "I don't believe that this woman is my mother at all. Well, I will get my servants to make the sandwiches for me. Serpents kill you, woman!—Oh, no, no, nobody touches me like that!"

Musical screaming! Wailing of a resonance too deep for so small an instrument, as Ginny was dragged off by her mother to get paddled. Howling to high Heaven, and the plainting of wild hogs and damned goblins!

"She is in good voice," Dr. Minden said. "When she speaks of her servants, she means your daughter Agar and my son Dall. It scares me, for I almost know what she means. It is eerie that two compatible young people say they will not marry because a four-year-old child forbids them to do it. It scares me still more when I begin to understand the mechanism at work."

"What is the mechanism, Minden?"

"The mutational inhibitions. It's quite a tangled affair. Do you remember the screaming monkeys of boondocks Rhodesia twenty years ago?"

"Vaguely. Bothersome little destructive monkeys that had to be hunted down and killed—hunted down by a sort of religious crusade, as I remember it. Yes, a mutation, I suppose. A sudden wildness appearing in a species. What is the connection?"

"Dismas, they were the first, the initial probe that failed. Others are on the way, and one of them will not fail. The story is that the religious crusaders said that no human child could be born while the howling monkeys flourished, for the monkeys themselves were human children. Well, they were. Well, no, they weren't children. And they weren't human. But, in a way, they had been both. Or at least—"

"Minden, do you know what you *do* mean?"

"I hardly do, Dismas. Here come the 'servants.'"

Dall Minden and Agar Dismas drove up in a little roustabout car and stopped.

"What is this nonsense I hear that you two are not going to get married?" Dr. Dismas demanded.

"Not unless Ginny changes her mind, Father," Agar said. "Oh, don't ask us to explain it. We don't understand it either."

"You are a pair of damned useless drones," Dismas growled.

"Don't say that, Dismas," Dr. Minden gasped. "Everything begins to scare me now. 'Drones' has a technical meaning in this case."

"Ginny has just suffered an ignominy past bearing." Agar grinned. She was a nice pleasant girl. "Now she is sulking in her cave up in Doolen's Mountain and has sent word for us to come at once."

"How has she sent word?" Dr. Dismas demanded. "You two have just driven up."

"Oh, don't ask us to explain, Father. She sends us word when she wants us. We don't understand it either. We'll go up on foot."

"Where is all this going to end?" Dr. Dismas asked when the two grinning young drones had left them and were ambling up the mountain.

"I don't know, Dismas," Minden told him. "But I believe it may as well begin with a verse:

> Salamanders do it,
> Tadpoles and newts do it.
> Why can't me and you do it?

"It's a verse that the four-year-olds have been chanting, and you may not be tuned in on them. And the peculiar thing is that the salamanders and newts and tadpoles *are* doing it now, more than ever before. It's worldwide. See Higgleton's recent paper if you don't take my word for it."

"Oh, great blithering biologists! *What* are the squigglers doing more than ever before?"

"Engaging in neotic reproduction, of course. In many pocket areas, tadpoles have been reproducing as tadpoles for several years now, and the adult frog species is disappearing. There have always been cases of it, of course, but now it is becoming a pattern. The same is true of the newts and salamanders. And remember that all three are, like man, contingent mutations. But how do the four-year-old children know about it when it is still one of the best-kept secrets of the biologists? . . . Here comes my wife. Is it more family trouble, Clarinda?"

"Oh, Krios has locked himself in the bathroom, and he won't come out or answer. He's been acting abominable all morning. Have you that emergency key you made?"

"Here. Now get the boy out, whip him gently but painfully, then explain to him that we love him very much and that his troubles are our troubles. Then get dinner. This family here never eats, unless it is peanut butter sandwiches, and has not thought to ask me to dine with them. Get back next door and with it, Clarinda, and stop bubbling."

"There is something really bothering Krios," Clarinda Minden bubbled yet, but she got herself back next door.

"Where shall we take it up, Dismas?" Doctor Minden asked. "With the howling monkeys of boondocks Rhodesia who may once have been human children? But nobody believes that. With the neotic salamanders and newts and pollywogs? With the Xauens who were either our grandparents or our grandchildren? Or with ourselves?"

"Roost on the Xauens a while," Dr. Dismas said. "You didn't quite finish your screed on them."

"Humans descend from the Xauens. Australopithecus, no. Sinanthropus, no. They were creatures of another line. But Neanderthal, Cro-Magnon, Grimaldi and ourselves are all of one species, and we descend from the Xauens. It is not true, however, that we have only one hundred and one skeletons of the Xauens. We have more than twenty thousand of them, but most of them are called Ouezzane monkeys."

"Minden, you're crazy."

"I am talking about the three-foot-tall, big-headed running monkeys who were mature and full grown at four years of age and very old at fourteen. They threw a few sports, steers and freemartins, who passed the puberty age without effect and continued to grow. They were gangling drones, servants of the active species, and of course sterile. They were the one in one hundred occurrence and of no importance. And one day they bred, set up a mutational inhibition against the normal; and mankind—the privileged mutation—was born.

"The Ouezzane monkeys, of whom the Xauens were the transitional state, were the same as the howling monkeys of boondocks Rhodesia—going in the other direction. They had no speech, they had no fire, and they made no tools. Then one morning they were the Xauens, and the next morning they were humans. They passed all the highly developed apes in an instant. They were the privileged mutation, which is not, I believe, permanent.

"Dismas, the one hundred and one recognized Xauen skeletons that we possess are *not* of ninety-six children (eighty-six of them apparent four-year-olds), three adolescents, and two adults. They are of ten infants and children, *eighty-six adults,* two mutants and three filial-twos.

"Let's take it from the flank. A few years ago, a biologist amused himself by making a table of heartbeat life lengths. All the mammals but one, he found, live about the same number of heartbeats, the longer-living species having correspondingly slower heartbeats. But one species, man, lives four or five times as long as he should by this criterion. I forget whether the biologist implied that this makes man a contingent species living on borrowed time. I do imply it. In any case, since the biologist was also involved in science fiction, his implications were not taken seriously.

"From the other flank. Even before Freud there were studies made of false puberty, the sudden hot interest and activity that appears about age four and then goes away for another ten years. It's been many times guessed that back in our ancestry our true puberty was at such an early age."

"Minden, no species can change noticeably in less than fifty thousand years."

"Dismas, it can change in between three and nine months, depending on the direction traveled. Here they come back! Well, drones, did you settle Ginny down? Where are you going now?"

Agar Dismas and Dall Minden had sauntered down from Doolen's Mountain.

"We're going to get four hundred and seventy-three loaves of bread and four hundred and seventy-three jars of peanut butter," Agar said rather nervously.

"Yes, Ginny says to use Crispy-Crusty bread," Dall Minden detailed. "She says it has sixteen slices to a loaf, so we can make eight sandwiches to a loaf and to a jar. There will be four sandwiches left over, and Ginny says we can have them for our work. She's going to stay in her cave for twelve hundred and sixty days. She says it will take that long to get her thing going good so nobody can bust it up. I think she's a numerologist at heart. This is going to take more than four hundred dollars. That's more than Agar and myself have saved up together. Ginny says to do it, though, even if we have to steal the money for it. And she says to be quick about it."

"Here come the religious nuts again," Doctor Dismas said. "I may have to kill one of the fools if they keep coming back."

"They won't come here this time," Agar said. "They'll prowl Doolen's Mountain from now on. They know it'll be there. But I don't think they'll kill Ginny. They don't understand what she is. They didn't understand the first time either; they didn't guess that it could possibly be one of the big ones. We are all hoping that they will kill me and be satisfied and think that they have done it. They will find me there where they think the woman should be, and that may fool them. Well, tootle! We have to hurry with everything or Ginny will be angry."

"No species can count itself secure that has not endured for ten million years," said Dr. Minden. "We still hear the old saying that evolution is irreversible. Hogwash! I have myself studied seven species of hogs washed away before one endured. The human race is so new that it has no stability. The majority of species do *not* survive, and we have lived only one tenth of the span that would tilt the odds for survival in our favor. Even the species that finally survive will commonly revert several times before acquiring stability. We could revert at any time."

"Revert to what?"

"To what we were, to what we still are basically, little three-foot-high, big-headed, howling monkeys, without tools, and with only a fifth of our present life span."

"Reversions are like cosmic disasters, Minden. They take a few thousand years to happen, and by that time we'll be gone."

"No, this can happen instantly, Dismas, by a single neotic conception. And then it becomes the norm by the mechanics of mutational inhibition. The reversion will inhibit the old normal. We have already seen that inhibition at work."

The very stones crying out like demented rooks! Bushes barking like coyotes! Green-colored yowling, and laughter that sang like a bandsaw. And Ginny was in the middle of them again.

She was the howlingest kid ever pupped.

"I don't think that I will talk any more after today, Father," she said solemnly after she had cut off her other noises. "I think I'll just forget how. I'll just holler and hoot and carry on. That's more fun anyhow.

"Why aren't my servants back with my provisions? They've had almost time to get back if they did everything at breakneck speed and had good luck. They might have had to go to more than one place to get that much bread and peanut butter, though. I doubt if I'll eat it. I just want to have it if I need it, and I wanted to teach them obedience. I'll probably start to eat meadow mice and ground squirrels tomorrow.

"Here comes Mrs. Minden crying over that Krios. What's the good of that?"

There was a keening. Clarinda was running and crying, and Sally Dismas had rushed out of the house and met her.

"Clarinda, what in the world has happened?" Dr. Minden cried, rushing to his tearful wife.

"Our baby Krios has killed himself."

"I told him to," said Ginny. "I'd gotten everything I wanted from him. I'll find better ones for the other times."

"Ginny!" Her mother was horrified. "I'll whip—"

"Don't punish the child, Sally," Carinda Minden sobbed. "She's beyond good and evil. Whatever was between her and my baby Krios, it's better that I never know."

"Did I say something wrong?" Ginny asked. "The last thing I ever say, and it should be wrong? Dr. Minden, you know about things like that. What are you creatures, anyhow?"

"People, Ginny," Dr. Minden said miserably.

"Funny I never saw any of you before. I sure don't intend to get involved with people."

Raucous howling! Hound-dog hooting! Hissing of badgers, and the clattering giggle of geese! Shag-tooth shouting, and the roaring of baby bulls!

And a screaming monkey leaped and tumbled up the rocks like crazy water.

Watershed

James Blish

The mutations described in the other stories in this collection are either natural events—inexplicable accidents of the germ plasm—or else the unexpected consequences of atomic radiation. However, among James Blish's many distinguished contributions to science fiction is a group of stories dealing with what he called "pantropy"— deliberate and conscious manipulation of the genes by scientists to create mutations—and the concluding story of that series serves also to bring our present book to a close. Blish's stories, published in book form as The Seedling Stars, *depict the stages in the process of transforming man so that he might colonize the stars. In "Watershed" we see the final stage: when humanity in many guises has gone forth to take possession of space, and men of altered form look homeward toward Mother Earth.*

The murmurs of discontent—Captain Gorbel, being a military man, thought of it as "disaffection"—among the crew of the R.S.S. *Indefeasible* had reached the point where they could no longer be ignored, well before the ship had come within fifty light-years of its objective.

Sooner or later, Gorbel thought, sooner or later this idiotic seal-creature is going to notice them.

Captain Gorbel wasn't sure whether he would be sorry or glad when the Adapted Man caught on. In a way, it would make things easier. But it would be an uncomfortable moment, not only for Hoqqueah and the rest of the pantrope team, but for Gorbel himself. Maybe it would be better to keep sitting on the safety valve until Hoqqueah and the other Altarians were put off on—what was its name again? Oh yes, Earth.

But the crew plainly wasn't going to let Gorbel put it off that long.

As for Hoqqueah, he didn't appear to have a noticing center anywhere in his brain. He was as little discommoded by the emotional undertow as he was by the thin and frigid air the Rigellian crew maintained inside the battlecraft. Secure in his coat of warm blubber, his eyes brown, liquid and merry, he sat in the forward greenhouse for most of each ship's day, watching the growth of the star Sol in the black skies ahead.

And he talked. Gods of all stars, how he talked! Captain Gorbel already knew more about the ancient—the *very* ancient—history of the seeding program than he had had any desire to know, but there was still more coming. Nor was the seeding program Hoqqueah's sole subject. The Colonization Council delegate had had a vertical education, one which cut in a narrow shaft through many different fields of specialization—in contrast to Gorbel's own training, which had been spread horizontally over the whole subject of spaceflight without more than touching anything else.

Hoqqueah seemed to be making a project of enlarging the Captain's horizons, whether he wanted them enlarged or not.

"Take agriculture," he was saying at the moment. "This planet we're to seed provides an excellent argument for taking the long view of farm policy. There used to be jungles there; it was very fertile. But the people began their lives as farmers with the use of fire, and they killed themselves off in the same way."

"How?" Gorbel said automatically. Had he remained silent, Hoqqueah would have gone on anyhow; and it didn't pay to be impolite to the Colonization Council, even by proxy.

"In their own prehistory, fifteen thousand years before their official zero date, they cleared farmland by burning it off. Then they would plant a crop, harvest it, and let the jungle return. Then they burned the jungle off and went through the cycle again. At the beginning, they wiped out the greatest abundance of game animals Earth was ever to see, just by farming that way. Furthermore the method was totally destructive to the topsoil.

"But did they learn? No. Even after they achieved spaceflight, that method of farming was standard in most of the remaining jungle areas—even though the bare rock was showing through everywhere by that time."

Hoqqueah sighed. "Now, of course, there are no jungles. There are no seas, either. There's nothing but desert, naked rock, bitter cold, and thin, oxygen-poor air—or so the people would view it, if there were any of them left. Tapa farming wasn't solely responsible, but it helped."

Gorbel shot a quick glance at the hunched back of Lieutenant Averdor, his adjutant and navigator. Averdor had managed to avoid saying so much as one word to Hoqqueah or any of the other pantropists from the beginning of the trip. Of course he wasn't required to assume the diplomatic burdens involved—those were Gorbel's crosses—but the strain of dodging even normal intercourse with the seal-men was beginning to tell on him.

Sooner or later, Averdor was going to explode. He would have nobody to blame for it but himself, but that wouldn't prevent everybody on board from suffering from it.

Including Gorbel, who would lose a first-class navigator and adjutant.

Yet it was certainly beyond Gorbel's authority to order Averdor to speak to an Adapted Man. He could only suggest that Averdor run through a few mechanical courtesies, for the good of the ship. The only response had been one of the stoniest stares Gorbel had ever seen, even from Averdor, with whom the captain had been shipping for over thirty Galactic years.

And the worst of it was that Gorbel was, as a human being, wholly on Averdor's side.

"After a certain number of years, conditions change on any planet," Hoqqueah babbled solemnly, waving a flipper-like arm to include all the points of light outside the greenhouse. He was working back to his primary obsession: the seeding program. "It's only logical to insist that man be able to change with them—or, if he can't do that, he must establish himself somewhere else. Suppose he had colonized only the Earthlike planets? Not even those planets *remain* Earthlike forever, not in the biological sense."

"Why would we have limited ourselves to Earthlike planets in the first place?" Gorbel said. "Not that I know much about the place, but the specs don't make it sound like an optimum world."

"To be sure," Hoqqueah said, though as usual Gorbel didn't know which part of his own comment Hoqqueah was agreeing to. "There's no survival value in pinning one's race forever to one set of specs. It's only sensible to go on evolving with the universe, so as to stay independent of such things as the aging of worlds, or the explosions of their stars. And look at the results! Man exists now in so many forms that there's always a refuge *somewhere* for any threatened people. That's a great achievement—compared to it, what price the old arguments about sovereignty of form?"

"What, indeed?" Gorbel said, but inside his skull his other self was saying: Ah-ha, he smells the hostility after all. Once an Adapted Man, always an Adapted Man—and always fighting for equality with the basic human form. But it's no good, you seal-snouted bureaucrat. You can argue for the rest of your life, but your whiskers will always wiggle when you talk.

And obviously you'll never stop talking.

"And as a military man yourself, you'd be the first to appreciate the military advantages, Captain," Hoqqueah added earnestly. "Using pantropy, man has seized thousands of worlds that would have been inaccessible to him otherwise. It's enormously increased our chances to become masters of the galaxy, to take most of it under occupation *without* stealing anyone else's planet in the process. An occupation without dispossession—let alone without bloodshed. Yet if some race other than man should develop imperial ambitions, and try to annex *our* planets, it will find itself enormously outnumbered."

"That's true," Captain Gorbel said, interested in spite of himself. "It's probably just as well that we worked fast, way back there in the beginning. Before somebody else thought up the method, I mean. But, how come it *was* us? Seems to me that the first race to invent it should've been a race that had it—if you follow me."

"Not quite, Captain. If you will give me an example—?"

"Well, we scouted a system once where there was a race that occupied two different planets, not both at the same time, but back and forth," Gorbel said. "They had a life-cycle that had three different ent forms. In the first form they'd winter over on the outermost of the two worlds. Then they'd change to another form that could cross space, mother-naked, without ships, and spend the rest of the year on the inner planet in the third form. Then they'd change back into the second form and cross back to the colder planet.

"It's a hard thing to describe. But the point is, this wasn't anything they'd worked out; it was natural to them. They'd evolved that way." He looked at Averdor again. "The navigation was tricky around there during the swarming season."

Averdor failed to rise to the bait.

"I see; the point is well taken," Hoqqueah said, nodding with grotesque thoughtfulness. "But let me point out to you, Captain, that being already able to do a thing doesn't aid you in thinking of it as something that needs to be perfected. Oh, I've seen races like the one you describe, too—races with polymorphism, sexual alteration of generation, metamorphosis of the insect life-history type, and so on. There's a planet named Lithia, about forty light-years from here, where the dominant race undergoes complete evolutionary recapitulation *after* birth—not before it, as men do. But why should any of them think of form-changing as something extraordinary, and to be striven for? It's one of the commonplaces of their lives, after all."

A small bell chimed in the greenhouse. Hoqqueah got up at once, his movements precise and almost graceful despite his tubbiness. "Thus endeth the day," he said cheerfully. "Thank you for your courtesy, Captain."

He waddled out. He would, of course, be back tomorrow.

And the day after that.

And the next day—unless the crewmen hadn't tarred and feathered the whole bunch by then.

If only, Gorbel thought distractedly, if only the damned Adapts weren't so quick to abuse their privileges! As a delegate of the Colonization Council, Hoqqueah was a person of some importance, and could not be barred from entering the greenhouse except in an emergency. But didn't the man know that he shouldn't use the privilege each and every day, on a ship manned by basic-form human beings, most of whom could not enter the greenhouse at all without a direct order?

And the rest of the pantropists were just as bad. As passengers with the technical status of human beings, they could go almost anywhere in the ship that the crew could go—and they did, persistently and unapologetically, as though moving among equals. Legally, that was what they were—but didn't they know by this time that there was such a thing as prejudice? And that among common spacemen the prejudice against their kind—and against any Adapted Man—always hovered near the borderline of bigotry?

There was a slight hum as Averdor's power chair swung around to face the captain. Like most Rigellian men, the lieutenant's face was lean and harsh, almost like that of an ancient religious fanatic, and the starlight in the greenhouse did nothing to soften it; but to Captain Gorbel, to whom it was familiar down to its last line, it looked especially forbidding now.

"Well?" he said.

"I'd think you'd be fed to the teeth with that freak by this time," Averdor said without preamble. "Something's got to be done, Captain, before the crew gets so surly that we have to start handing out brig sentences."

"I don't like know-it-alls any better than you do," Gorbel said grimly. "Especially when they talk nonsense—and half of what this one says about space flight is nonsense, that much I'm sure of. But the man's a delegate of the Council. He's got a right to be up here if he wants to."

"You can bar anybody from the greenhouse in an emergency—even the ship's officers."

"I fail to see any emergency," Gorbel said stiffly.

"This is a hazardous part of the galaxy—potentially, anyhow. It hasn't been visited for millennia. That star up ahead has nine planets besides the one we're supposed to land on, and I don't know how many satellites of planetary size. Suppose somebody on one of them lost his head and took a crack at us as we went by?"

Gorbel frowned. "That's reaching for trouble. Besides, the area's been surveyed recently at least once—otherwise we wouldn't be here."

"A sketch job. It's still sensible to take precautions. If there should be any trouble, there's many a Board of Review that would call it risky to have unreliable second-class human types in the greenhouse when it breaks out."

"You're talking nonsense."

"Dammit, Captain, read between the lines a minute," Averdor said harshly. "I know as well as you do that there's going to be no trouble that we can't handle. And that no reviewing board would pull a complaint like that on *you* if there were. I'm just trying to give you an excuse to use on the seals."

"I'm listening."

"Good. The *Indefeasible* is the tightest ship in the Rigellian navy, her record's clean, and the crew's morale is almost a legend. We can't afford to start gigging the men for their personal prejudices—which is what it will amount to, if those seals drive them to breaking discipline. Besides, they've got a right to do their work without a lot of seal snouts poking continually over their shoulders."

"I can hear myself explaining that to Hoqqueah."

"You don't need to," Averdor said doggedly. "You can tell him, instead, that you're going to have to declare the ship on emergency status until we land. That means that the pantrope team, as passengers, will have to stick to their quarters. It's simple enough."

It was simple enough, all right. And decidedly tempting.

"I don't like it," Gorbel said. "Besides, Hoqqueah may be a know-it-all, but he's not entirely a fool. He'll see through it easily enough."

Averdor shrugged. "It's your command," he said. "But I don't see what he could do about it even if he did see through it. It'd be all on the log and according to regs. All he could report to the Council would be a suspicion—and they'd probably discount it. Everybody knows that these second-class types are quick to think they're being persecuted. It's my theory that that's why they *are* persecuted, a lot of the time at least."

"I don't follow you."

"The man I shipped under before I came on board the *Indefeasible*," Averdor said, "was one of those people who don't even trust themselves. They expect everybody they meet to slip a knife into them when their backs are turned. And there are always other people who make it almost a point of honor to knife a man like that, just because he seems to be asking for it. He didn't hold that command long."

"I see what you mean," Gorbel said. "Well, I'll think about it."

But by the next ship's day, when Hoqqueah returned to the greenhouse, Gorbel still had not made up his mind. The very fact that his own feelings were on the side of Averdor and the crew made him suspicious of Averdor's "easy" solution. The plan was tempting enough to blind a tempted man to flaws that might otherwise be obvious.

The Adapted Man settled himself comfortably and looked out through the transparent metal. "Ah," he said. "Our target is sensibly bigger now, eh, Captain? Think of it: in just a few days now, we will be—in the historical sense—home again."

And now it was riddles! "What do you mean?" Gorbel said.

"I'm sorry; I thought you knew. Earth is the home planet of the human race, Captain. There is where the basic form evolved."

Gorbel considered this unexpected bit of information cautiously. Even assuming that it was true—and it probably was, that would be the kind of thing Hoqqueah would know about a planet to which he was assigned—it didn't seem to make any special difference in the situation. But Hoqqueah had obviously brought it out for a reason. Well, he'd be trotting out the reason, too, soon enough; nobody would ever accuse the Altarian of being taciturn.

Nevertheless, he considered turning on the screen for a close look at the planet. Up to now he had felt not the slightest interest in it.

"Yes, there's where it all began," Hoqqueah said. "Of course at first it never occurred to those people that they might produce pre-adapted children. They went to all kinds of extremes to adapt their environment instead, or to carry it along with them. But they finally realized that with the planets, that won't work. You can't spend your life in a spacesuit, or under a dome, either.

"Besides, they had had form trouble in their society from their earliest days. For centuries they were absurdly touchy over minute differences in coloring and shape, and even in thinking. They had regime after regime that tried to impose its own concept of the standard citizen on everybody, and enslaved those who didn't fit the specs."

Abruptly, Hoqqueah's chatter began to make Gorbel uncomfortable. It was becoming easier and easier to sympathize with Averdor's determination to ignore the Adapted Man's existence entirely.

"It was only after they'd painfully taught themselves that such differences really don't matter that they could go on to pantropy," Hoqqueah said. "It was the logical conclusion. Of course, a certain continuity of form had to be maintained, and has been maintained to this day. You cannot totally change the form without totally changing the thought processes. If you give a man the form of a cockroach, as one ancient writer foresaw, he will wind up thinking like a cockroach, not like a human being. We recognized that. On worlds where only extreme modifications of the human form would make it suitable—for instance, a planet of the gas giant type—no seeding is attempted. The Council maintains that such worlds are the potential property of other races than the human, races whose psychotypes would not have to undergo radical change in order to survive there."

Dimly, Captain Gorbel saw where Hoqqueah was leading him, and he did not like what he saw. The seal-man, in his own maddeningly indirect way, was arguing his right to be considered an equal in fact as well as in law. He was arguing it, however, in a universe of discourse totally unfamiliar to Captain Gorbel, with facts whose validity he alone knew and whose relevance he alone could judge. He was in short, loading the dice, and the last residues of Gorbel's tolerance were evaporating rapidly.

"Of course there was resistance back there at the beginning," Hoqqueah said. "The kind of mind that had only recently been persuaded that colored men are human beings was quick to take the attitude that an Adapted Man—any Adapted Man—was the social inferior of the 'primary' or basic human type, the type that lived on Earth. But it was also a very old idea on the Earth that basic humanity inheres in the mind, not in the form.

"You see, Captain, all this might still have been prevented had it been possible to maintain the attitude that changing the form even in part makes a man less of a man than he was in the 'primary' state. But the day has come when that attitude is no longer tenable—a day that is the greatest of all moral watersheds for our race, the day that is to unite all our divergent currents of attitudes toward each other into one common reservoir of brotherhood and purpose. You and I are very fortunate to be on the scene to see it."

"Very interesting," Gorbel said coldly. "But all those things happened a long time ago, and we know very little about this part of the galaxy these days. Under the circumstances—which you'll find clearly written out in the log, together with the appropriate regulations—I'm forced to place the ship on emergency alert beginning tomorrow, and continuing until your team disembarks. I'm afraid that means that henceforth all passengers will be required to stay in quarters."

Hoqqueah turned and arose. His eyes were still warm and liquid, but there was no longer any trace of merriment in them.

"I know very well what it means," he said. "And to some extent I understand the need—though I had been hoping to see the planet of our birth first from space. But I don't think *you* quite understood *me,* Captain. The moral watershed of which I spoke is not in the past. It is now. It began the day that the Earth itself became no longer habitable for the so-called basic human type. The flowing of the streams toward the common reservoir will become bigger and bigger as word spreads through the galaxy that Earth itself has been seeded

with Adapted Men. With that news will go a shock of recognition—
the shock of realizing that the 'basic' types are now, and have been
for a long time, a very small minority, despite their pretensions."

Was Hoqqueah being absurd enough to threaten—an unarmed,
comical seal-man shaking a fist at the captain of the *Indefeasible?* Or—

"Before I go, let me ask you this one question, Captain. Down
there is your home planet, and my team and I will be going out on its
surface before long. Do you dare to follow us out of the ship?"

"And why should I?" Gorbel said.

"Why, to show the superiority of the basic type, Captain," Hoqqueah said softly. "Surely you cannot admit that a pack of seal-men
are your betters, on your own ancestral ground!"

He bowed and went to the door. Just before he reached it, he
turned and looked speculatively at Gorbel and at Lieutenant Averdor,
who was staring at him with an expression of rigid fury.

"Or can you?" he said. "It will be interesting to see how you manage to comport yourselves as a minority. I think you lack practice."

He went out. Both Gorbel and Averdor turned jerkily to the screen,
and Gorbel turned it on. The image grew, steadied, settled down.

When the next trick came on duty, both men were still staring at
the vast and tumbled desert of the Earth.